SHADES OF THE PAST

$7.95

SHADES OF THE PAST

or
INDISCREET TALES OF JAPAN

by
HAROLD S. WILLIAMS

Decorations by
JEAN WILLIAMS

CHARLES E. TUTTLE COMPANY
Rutland, Vermont & Tokyo, Japan

Representatives

Continental Europe: BOXERBOOKS, INC., *Zurich*

British Isles: PRENTICE-HALL INTERNATIONAL, INC., *London*

Australasia: BOOK WISE (AUSTRALIA) PTY. LTD.
104-108 Sussex Street, Sydney 2000

Published by the Charles E. Tuttle Company, Inc.
of Rutland, Vermont & Tokyo, Japan
with editorial offices at
Suido 1-chome, 2-6, Bunkyo-ku, Tokyo, Japan

© 1958 by Charles E. Tuttle Co., Inc.

Library of Congress Catalog Card No. 58-11102

International Standard Book No. 0-8048-1050-8

First edition, 1958
Fourth printing, 1984

PRINTED IN JAPAN

To
my Wife
who gave me much encouragement
in the writing of this book
and to
my Children
who pursued the safer course of awaiting
its reception

Opportunity may also be had to sail over to Japan where Christian men Jesuits of many countries of Christendom and perhaps some Englishmen are, at whose hands you may have great instruction and advice for our affairs in Hand.

JOHN DEE, 1580, in his letter of instruction to the Masters of the "Quinsay Haven" about to sail for China.

PREFACE

The articles in this book were compiled from notes and material gathered over three decades and originally appeared in *The Mainichi* newspaper in Japan, during 1953 to 1958, in a series entitled "Shades of the Past." Since then they have been revised and partly rewritten.

With the exception of some hearsay which enters into "The Burning of the S.S. 'America'" and "Mr. Carew's Tombstone," all are believed to be historically accurate in every detail.

Japanese names are usually written with the family name (corresponding to our surname) followed by the given name (corresponding to our Christian names). This is the order which I have maintained in most instances. In some cases, such for example as Tamaki Miura, the Japanese prima donna of prewar days, I have reversed the names and followed the order by which the person is generally known to Westerners. Even in Japanese there are exceptions to the general rule, especially in ancient and aristocratic names, artistic and professional ones, and posthumous appelations, where the subject becomes a labyrinth of complexities, as indeed do most Japanese studies.

Throughout this book Japanese words have been reproduced in the more familiar and more rational

Preface

Romanised form known as the Hepburn System, such for example as *Fuji-san* (Mount Fuji), rather than the official but eccentric form where the same word is reproduced as *Huzi-San,* which travellers are expected to recognise and pronounce as *Fuji-San,* but never do.

In a few exceptional cases, alternative or Anglicised forms have been used, for example: ricksha, rickshaw or rikishaw for *rikisha,* which is the contraction of the greater mouthful of *jinrikisha.*

Although Japanese nouns have no plural form, I have, for the convenience of non-Japanese readers and clarity of meaning, in some instances such as *Shogun* and *Tokugawa,* treated them as subject to English laws of grammar, and used the plural forms of *Shoguns* and *Tokugawas.* In doing so, I am well aware that I shall be criticised by the purists.

Grateful acknowledgments are made to my wife for the decorations, to Mr. F.D. Burrows and Mr. L.J. Nuzum for furnishing photographs, and to Mr. T. Philip Terry, the author of *Guide to Japan*—one of the most readable and comprehensive of all guide books—for permission to quote his description of the *Yoshiwara* in nighttime and in daytime.

Finally acknowledgments are made to that legion of men, commencing with Marco Polo, and including scholars, merchants, missionaries, editors, men of letters, and men of the sword, but for all of whose writings, these accounts of *"Shades of the Past"* could never have been written.

H. S. WILLIAMS

SHIOYA, JAPAN

CONTENTS

Official Secrets 17
St. George for Merrie England 28
Trading under Difficulties............................... 37
Queen Victoria's Present 51
Vortical Atoms and Crackpots 62
The Mutiny of the "Cyprus" 74
The President's Letter 80
Black-Eyed Susan 89
Murder near the *Daibutsu* 94
Some Christmas Days of Long Ago................. 99
Hara-kiri in Kobe... 106
The Sakai Massacre 113
A Forgotten Road... 123
The Loss of the U.S.S. "Oneida" 129
The Case of the "Maria Luz"......................... 140
The Burning of the S.S. "America"................ 145
Sam Patch 159
An Emperor's Grief....................................... 168
The Forgotten Medals 177
The Carew Case 184
Mr. Carew's Tombstone................................ 200
Life and Strife in the Foreign Concessions 210
The *Yoshiwara* Ladies and Pinup Girls 223
The Tourists Looked Around 229
Pilgrims Ancient and Modern........................ 238
Gold, Gold, Gold.. 247
Photograph Albums...................................... 258
Japan's National Anthem 266
A Traitor was Executed 272

11

Contents

They came to Osaka 277
Beyond the Reef 288
Antics in the Nude 294
Mesdames Chrysanthemum and Butterfly...........306
Let's Climb Fuji..312
We Buried Our Dead Here 323

About the Author..339
Chronological Table 341
Glossary 345
Index 353

ILLUSTRATIONS

(Following page 176)

PLATE I. Zempukuji in Yedo in 1859. Temple where the first U.S. Legation was located during the sojourn of Townsend Harris, first American envoy in Japan. (Courtesy of F.D. Burrows, Esq.)

PLATE II. Tozenji in Yedo in 1859. Temple where the first British Legation was located. (Courtesy of F.D. Burrows, Esq.)

PLATE III. Mansion of the Daimyo of Satsuma in Yedo, 1859—typical of the homes in which members of the families of provincial governors lived as hostages in Yedo during the Tokugawa era. (Courtesy of F.D. Burrows, Esq.)

PLATE IV. Tokaido in 1860's near the former post town of Moto-Hakone. (Courtesy of F.D. Burrows, Esq.)

PLATE V. Tokaido at Kanagawa, showing barrier gates and guardhouse about 1860. (Courtesy of F.D. Burrows, Esq.)

PLATE VI. Eleven monuments at Hojuji Temple, Sakai, of the eleven Tosa men who were executed in connection with the Sakai massacre. See chapter, "The Sakai Massacre."

13

Illustrations

PLATE VII.   Head of Mamiya Hajime on view at Yokohama after execution.   See chapter "Murder near the Daibutsu." (Courtesy of L.J. Nuzum, Esq.)

PLATE VIII.   A courtesan (generally referred to in Japanese publications as a "beauty" or "entertainer") by Utamaro.   See chapter, "The Yoshiwara Ladies and Pinup Girls."

14

SHADES OF THE PAST

OFFICIAL
SECRETS

With constabulary duties to be done, to be done,
The policeman's lot is not a happy one.

"The Pirates of Penzance"

In an article which was published recently, I commiserated with the consuls in Japan of nearly a hundred years ago, who, in addition to their regular consular duties, often had to play the parts of a judge, accountant, assessor, magistrate, arbitrator, coroner, jailer and turnkey.

Surprise having been expressed in some quarters at my statement, and doubts in others as to its accuracy, I felt sufficiently impelled to embark upon a more detailed research into those fabulous days. I soon had evidence that some consuls performed all those functions, plus a few more, for example during times of stress and emergency, and in the absence of adequate staff, even more bizarre duties such as inspector of brothels and nuisances, postmaster, and "Right Hose."

The last mentioned duty was of an extra-curricular nature, and referred to the consul's position on the local fire-cart!

The local volunteer fire brigades were important entities within the structure of the old treaty-port society. One had to be a person of some substance and respectability, quite apart from wind and muscle, to hold office in such an exclusive body as say the

Victorian Volunteer Steam Fire Engine Company of Yokohama of ninety years ago.

A new arrival had to have some "pull"—if you will pardon the pun—to gain office, even such a minor office as "Suction and Split Hose" in that particular fire brigade. After attaining that lowly position, an enthusiast could in course of time gain advancement, becoming in turn "Left Hose," "Right Hose," and finally "Foreman" if he happened to be a born fireman or was one of those persons who just cannot escape getting on in life. The coveted rank of "Foreman" was generally held by a Keswick or some such similar stalwart of one of the princely hongs, provided he had brawn and waist line, and enough wind to run a mile.

Pulling the firecart was thirsty work, and putting out fires was wet work, which perhaps explains why the annual dinners—stag of course—of the volunteer fire brigades were both strenuous and wet affairs!

"Begad, Sir, last week at the fire over at that house near Creekside, 'Suction and Split Hose' sploshed so much water over the girls that their kimono clung to their figures like chemises. Poor show! Poor show!" boomed Foreman Keswick of Jardines at one of those annual dinners.

However to return to the subject of this article, the doubts which were expressed as to whether consuls, and particularly British consuls, ever had to perform the various duties which I had ascribed to them, were a challenge which caused me to search among the papers and records which may still be found at the bottom of old oak chests, in the dusty

18

cellars of some libraries, and in the bookcases of some of those bearded and wheezy antiquarians and bibliophiles who seldom emerge outdoors—a search which extended into two continents.

In quoting verbatim as I now shall—without permission—from the despatches of Queen Victoria's Consul at Nagasaki in the years 1859–1863, I do not believe I am betraying any very important national secrets. My defence can be that none of those despatches were marked "Top Secret"—for the reason possibly that the expression had not then been invented!

Consul Morrison at Nagasaki, the second gentleman to hold that post, arrived there on 8th August, 1859, and it is interesting to note that his first four despatches to the Legation in Yedo were on routine matters, after which he promptly got down to drawing attention to *"the low rate of salary which is attached to the office I hold."* After admitting that fish and fowl were comparatively cheap and drawing attention to his own most abstemious personal habits, he came to the point:

I would take the liberty to urge that some compensation more than bare subsistence is due, in consideration of an exile to the extremity of the Earth,—of banishment from society and from the relations of Home, and exposure to discomforts and privations difficult to depict and cruel to endure. I say nothing of the climate, which is for some months in every year destructive to health and even to property, or of the water we have to use, which at this port is so bad as to be almost poisonous.

19

Neither do I dwell on the important and harassing duties with which a Consul is entrusted....

To cut a long story short it is good to be able to report that this appeal did not fall on unresponsive ears, and that in due course of time this plain speaking consul received an increase in salary which I have no doubt he well deserved.

The Consul, among his multifarious duties, was required to perform some of an accountancy nature, a task he does not seem to have always performed to the satisfaction of his superiors in Yedo, to whom on 21st September, 1859, he addressed the following tart despatch:

I have the honour to acknowledge receipt of your Despatch No. 11 returning the accounts of this Consulate....for correction. I am deprived of the facilities for this work....I shall not fail, however, to use my best endeavours to put these accounts in a proper state....Allow me to express my gratification at the confidence you entertain that under my supervision the accounts of this Consulate will in future be more satisfactorily rendered.

The Consul's negotiations with the local Governor and other officials are of course dealt with at length, and we find him echoing sentiments not unlike those which U.S. Consul-General Harris had expressed, although in more restrained tones. In Despatch No. 17 on 21st September, 1859, he informed the Legation in Yedo:

I have discovered that unhappily no reliance whatever is to be placed on the most solemn assurance of Japanese....

As was Harris, so also was Morrison exasperated at the uniform fate of his many representations to the Japanese authorities, most of which were pigeon-holed on the excuse that instructions from the central government in Yedo would have to be awaited, a slow-motion procedure which rarely reached finality.

The consuls were also required to act as judges and arbitrators in commercial disputes, but seemingly Consul Morrison, with due modesty, was unwilling to assume that he was endowed with the wisdom of Solomon, because we find him suggesting to his superior at Yedo that application should be made to the Foreign Office that he be supplied *"with such suitable law books as will assist judgement."*

Four days later the overworked Consul saw some prospects of divesting himself of the duties of a turnkey by importing from Shanghai a respectable Englishman as constable. Later, when the Legation in Yedo questioned the wages which he had agreed to pay to the constable, he had the courage to point out to his superiors, for the information of the Queen's Exchequer, that by comparison *"a breaker of stones at home is more to be envied than my constable."* He then seized the opportunity to elaborate on the high cost of living:

If considered expensive, it only exemplifies what I have elsewhere pointed out, that excepting in the simplest produce of the place, we are, here at least, in a very expensive country, the burden of which falls not less heavily on our private resources than on the public chest.

That the Consul's attention was much centred upon

21

the duties of a turnkey is evident from his despatch wherein he plans the building of a jail, and that of a few days later where he begged approval of the expenditure necessary for *"a pair of handcuffs— much needed."*

Consul Morrison's coronial duties were associated mainly with the violent deaths of sailors, whilst his magisterial duties were generally linked with the doings of sailors ashore on pleasure bound.

It is of interest to note that whilst his superior, Rutherford Alcock in Yedo, had dubbed the foreign community in Yokohama as comprising *"the scum of the earth,"* Consul Morrison had no complaints against the British community in Nagasaki. Said he on 5th January, 1861:

The existing British community at this port numbers about 25 persons, comprising merchants, smaller traders, compradores, and a butcher, and it is satisfactory to add that it is on the whole a very well ordered Community—showing no want of respect to Her Majesty's authority and giving no occasion for complaint on the part of the Japanese.

What Morrison may have thought of the non-British community in Nagasaki is not recorded!

The Consul was looking forward to the time when he would be provided with sufficient funds to engage his own staff of Japanese—or "natives" as was the expression in those days—and so enable him to dispense with the assistants and linguists already made available free by the Japanese authorities. The assistants, he considered, were government spies, and the linguists just learners of English. He was however despondent over the prospects of being able to engage suitable staff and so relieve himself of some of his multifarious duties, because of the insufficiency of funds allowed:

The total amount including the linguists does not equal the sum which I myself pay for domestic servants.

The harassed Consul, anxious to show the flag of his country, had no Department of Works official to handle his building and repair problems. On 4th November, 1859, he devoted an entire despatch to justifying certain repair expenses, which comprised the purchase of a new flagstaff and eighteen boxes of glass. The necessity for both was succinctly explained in the following words:

It is a long time since the American and Dutch flags have been suitably hoisted—which the British has hitherto flown from a pole projected from a tree top! The glass is necessary as a provision against the cold in winter—in lieu of the paper windows.

When the necessity for such moderate improvements to the Japanese temple wherein his consulate was located was questioned, he sent the acid reply:

With regard to the original character of the accommodation provided for this Consulate, I cannot but think, Sir, that you have adopted a rather erroneous impression in its favour.

It is sad to relate that the despatches of this forthright Consul do not appear to have always met with the approval of his superiors and within a few months of his appointment Her Majesty's Secretary of State

cautioned that Mr. Morrison should be *"fully alive
to the importance of moderation and patience and to
the disadvantages of vexatious or useless discussion"*
—a rebuke which the Consul did not permit to pass
without comment.

There is some reason to believe that Morrison was
more historically minded than some of the officials
in Her Majesty's Department for Foreign Affairs.
Believing that the accommodation of Her Majesty's
Consulate in a Japanese temple was a fact which
should be recorded for posterity, as also should the
appearance of Nagasaki in those early days, he had
the imagination to commission a visiting London
photographer to take a series of photographs, the
total cost of all of which work amounted to the sum
of $70 Mex. Those photographs will continue to live
long after ministers of state are forgotten.

The Legation in Yedo was however, by no means
sure that Her Majesty's Auditors would approve
such reckless expenditure. The Consul, in his own
defence, was thereupon obliged to explain that the
care which he always exercised in the expenditure
of public moneys was amply illustrated by the fact
that his country's flag, which he proudly flew from
the new flagpole, had actually cost $50 Mex. of which
only $30 Mex. was charged in his accounts.

Even the Consular boat in which the Consul visited
Her Majesty's ships, rather than flopping about on
a mat in the bottom of a Japanese sampan, or wallah-
wallah boat, had been purchased out of his own personal funds. Seemingly those were the days when
the value of the national currency was maintained

at all costs—even to the extent of the Consul in Nagasaki having to bear some portion of the expense of showing the flag.

The success of Gilbert and Sullivan's *The Pirates of Penzance* has been so overwhelming that it would require some courage at this late date to suggest that they snitched from the British Consular records of Nagasaki the idea that a policeman's lot is not a happy one.

I shall not therefore labour that theory beyond pointing out that fifteen years before *The Pirates of Penzance* was written, Consul Morrison treated his superiors in Yedo to a long despatch showing that a constable's job is *"without distinction, without profit, and without prospects"* and that *"no respectable man can be retained for any length of time in the post of constable."*

His own lot was obviously nothing to boast about, because in official correspondence he described the accommodation for himself and the consulate as *"a wretched hovel where we have struggled against the want of almost every requisite in a house."*

Apparently even the local butcher had better accommodation, because he further wrote: *"I find that the only persons in Nagasaki unprovided with comfortable habitation are the officers of H. M. Consulate."*

Seemingly that was no exaggeration because his bedroom also served as a sitting room and his dining room as a public office during the day. He had one small room as a private office, but that had to be shared with his many official visitors.

Official Secrets

The consulate was then housed in a temple, and, as millions of tourists to Japan have since discerned, it is difficult to conceive of a building that is less adaptable to a comfortable home than a Buddhist temple or an Imperial palace!

In 1861 when Morrison travelled to Yedo on official business he arrived at the British Legation just in time to be nearly murdered by Japanese *ronin* when they attacked the Legation that same night. Morrison showed conspicuous bravery in defending the Legation and his Minister's life. During the course of the fight he was wounded and narrowly missed having his head sliced off.

Consul Morrison was under no illusions as to the skill with which he had carried out his difficult duties in Nagasaki in the opening years of that port, and he considered he had earned promotion. When therefore the appointment of Secretary of Legation at Yedo was awarded to another, he had the courage to express his disappointment and to suggest that the Secretary of State had welched on a promise:

With the utmost deference to the pleasure of Her Majesty's Secretary of State on the arrangements which His Lordship pleases to make, I could but express the great disappointment which I naturally feel at the road to honourable promotion which appeared open to me under a promise, as it were conveyed in His Lordship's published despatch, upon which I relied, being thus unexpectedly and indefinitely closed.

Shortly afterwards Morrison decided there were occupations and climes where he could be more happy, and he thereupon retired from the service. And so there disappeared from the scene a consul who endears himself to us for the vigour with which he pursued his duties and the descriptions which he has left us of the early Settlement days.

Upon this note I bring to a close this first instalment of disclosures of official secrets, which offence —heinous in some countries—has been indulged in to substantiate my statement that the lot of a consul nearly a hundred years ago, like that of a policeman, could not have been a very happy one.

ST. GEORGE FOR MERRIE ENGLAND

> *St. George he was for England.*
> —Old English Ballad, 1512

April 23rd is the day when Englishmen gather together to honour their patron saint.

Every year at this time the thoughts of Englishmen in the Far East turn to the Cross of St. George: that simple design of a red cross on a white ground; that symbol of a proud Briton who lived three hundred years after Christ, and who died rather than deny his faith at the bidding of a Roman emperor; that banner which became the rallying point for the defiant war cry *For St. George and Merrie England;* that blessed flag of England.

The Cross of St. George, although rarely flown in Japan nowadays, was a familiar sight in some parts about two hundred years before the Union Jack was created. In all probability the Cross of St. George was seen in Japan for the first time after the arrival of Will Adams, the English pilot employed by the Dutch, and the first Englishman to visit Japan. That was during the reign of Elizabeth I of England.

But the first occasion on which an English vessel flying the Cross of St. George was seen by Japanese, and in all probability the first occasion (except for Will Adams) that Englishmen met Japanese, was in

1604 off Pahang in Malaya when two English ships, the "Tiger" and the "Tiger's Whelp," made a chance meeting with a junk manned by Japanese and sailing under the flag of *Hachiman*—a flag bearing the characters for *Hachiman,* the God of War. The meeting of those sea dogs of England and the Japanese pirates ended in a fight and a most bloody one that carried on until the Japanese, outnumbered and rather than surrender, died almost to the last man.

The Japanese had been pirating along the coast of China and Cambodia, which activities probably were not very different to the type of enterprise in which the "Tiger" and the "Tiger's Whelp" were engaged. The Japanese had lost their vessel by shipwreck and had seized a junk laden with rice, in which they were sailing until they could acquire something better, whilst the English were on the lookout for any prize or treasure that was worth their capturing. They met in a spirit of feigned cordiality, but each with designs upon the other. The Englishmen suspected there might be treasure concealed beneath the rice, while the Japanese had in mind capturing the English ships:

> *These Rogues being desperate in winds and fortunes, being hopelesse in that paltrie junke ever to returne to their Countrey, resolved with themselves either to gaine my shippe, or to lose their lives.*

So reads the English account.

One day the Japanese sprang a surprise attack and during a most bloody fight lasting four hours succeeded in killing the captain of the "Tiger" but were then forced back into the main cabin. There they refused to surrender and attempted to fire the ship, whereupon the English broke down the bulkhead and brought to bear upon them some of the ship's guns loaded with grape-shot.

Their legs, armes, and bodies were so torne, as it was strange to see, how the shot had massacred them. In all this conflict they never would desire their lives, though they were hopelesse to escape: such was the desperateness of these Japonians.

All the Japanese were slaughtered with the exception of one who succeeded in jumping overboard, but he was subsequently captured.

The next day....the Generall commanded his people to hang this Japonian; but he broke the Rope and fell into the Sea. I cannot tell whether he swamme to the land or not.

An officer of the "Tiger" in recounting this desperate fight concluded with the comment:

The Japanese are not suffered to land in any port in India with weapons, being accounted a people so desperate and daring that they are feared in all places where they come.

In such manner happened the first meeting between Englishmen and Japanese.

In 1606 the flags of St. George and St. Andrew were combined to form the Union Flag of Great Britain, but its use was confined by proclamation to naval vessels. English merchant ships were required to continue to fly St. George's Cross and so when the English East India Company established its trading post in Japan at Hirado in Kyushu, the Cross of St.

George became a familiar sight in those parts. There is at least one rare Dutch drawing now kept at The Hague, which shows St. George's Cross flying over what appears to be the residence of the Chief Merchant of the English factory at Hirado.

Will Adams later joined the English East India Company but on coming to Hirado he preferred to take up residence in a separate house (on which he always flew the Cross of St. George) rather than live with Capt. Saris the head of the English factory. He thereby set a wise precedent for the British mercantile community in Japan, which has been followed by thousands of young Britons ever since, namely it is better not to live with the boss.

Saris was not pleased with this display of independence and comments on Adams in his diary:

He would for two or three days repair to his colours which he had put out at an old window in a poor house, being a Cross of St. George made of coarse cloth.

In 1613 when Capt. Saris accompanied by Adams and a staff of eight Englishmen travelled to the Shogun's Court in Yedo, the Cross of St. George was carried at the head of the little cavalcade and was hung out in front of the inns at which they stayed en route. The first part of the voyage from Hirado to Osaka was made by sea and Saris describes the craft in his diary as:

A King's Gallye filled with 25 oars one aside and 40 men, which I did fit up in a very comely manner with waste clothes and ensigns (the Cross of St. George).

On arrival in Yedo, Saris presented to the Shogun a letter from King James I of England who styled himself *"by the grace of God, King for these eleven years of the three countries of Great Britain, France and Ireland"* and then in polite form and with pardonable flattery, but immense exaggeration, added that *"the greatness and the splendid fame of His Highness the Lord Shogun of Japan is notorious and well known in our country."*

Incidentally it was Saris who has recorded the first foreign complaint against Japanese servants, when he alleged that his majordomo (or house boy) had "squeezed" 10/- on the *sake* account! It may be of interest also to those foreigners who have been involved in labour disputes in Japan to know that the first such dispute occurred at the East India Company's factory at Hirado in 1617, but that the Englishmen were instructed by the Japanese Authorities not to accede to the demands.

Let not the public relations experts and the publicity agents of to-day think that they are pioneers in a new profession. In 1618 when Richard Cocks, then in charge of the English trading post, made his first official visit to Nagasaki from his headquarters in Hirado, his assistant, Will Adams, arrived there one day earlier and with the support of the Chinese merchants arranged to stage for Cocks a thunderous welcome, which Cocks described in a letter:

Langasaque (Nagasaki) *in Japan this 21st Feb., 1618. Loving Frendes,*

We arrived heare yesterday just an hower be-

32

*fore sunne seting. Capt. Adams being arrived the
day before and came out with the China Captain,
all the China junks haveing their flagges and
stremers with St. George amongst the rest and shot
affe above 40 chambers and pieces of ordinance at
my arrival.*

It is evident from this letter that Adams, although
then a naturalized Japanese, took advantage of this
opportunity to show the flag of England—the Cross
of St. George—to the people of Nagasaki and at the
same time to give his boss a royal salute of 40 guns.

After 1620, on account of the growing distrust on
the part of the Japanese officials in Christianity, the
flying of the Cross of St. George was forbidden in
Japan. A cross in any form was then a symbol to
be searched for and stamped out.

From about 1622 the persecution of Christian missionaries and converts became violent, and more than
three thousand Japanese, men, women and even
children, suffered extreme martyrdom for the Christian faith. One of the final acts in this drama was
the rebellion at Shimabara when nearly forty thous-
and Japanese, more than half of whom were women
and children, fighting under Christian banners and
crosses, were massacred.

Thereafter the Japanese authorities became so
alarmed at the effect that the spread of Christianity
might have on their own power, that they proceeded
to exterminate this new religion in Japan; churches
and monasteries were destroyed and even the Christian graveyards were uprooted, the tombstones overthrown and *"all the dead men's bones taken out of*

the ground and cast forth." Only the Dutch merchants remained enjoying a monopoly of trade, but at the cost of being cooped up on the small island of Deshima in Nagasaki harbour, and suffering various indignities.

Some years later, around 1672, some merchants in London felt that the East India Company was not sufficiently active and that opportunities for doing business with Japan and China were being lost. They thereupon began pressing for new charters to trade. Spurred by the possibility of outside competition the East India Company thereupon decided to send two ships, the "Experiment" and "Return," to the East and gave very careful consideration to the flag under which they should sail, because sailing under the Cross of St. George, or any other cross, might doom the expedition to failure. The expediency of filling in the four white corners of the cross with the arms of England, Scotland, Ireland and France and of thus rendering the cross less evident, was considered. However after arrival at Nagasaki, the "Return" flew her true colours—the Cross of St. George— which led to troublesome enquiries:

It being Sunday we put our colours with St. George's Cross; they asked why we put out our colours to-day, not having spread them before since our coming: I said this was our Sunday which came every seventh day, and it was our custom so to do....They departed not saying anything against our usual colours, having been aboard five hours and very troublesome....

About ten of the clock came aboard the inter-

*preters with two chief men and they told us that
for the future, until further orders came from Yedo
they would not advise us to wear our colours, with
the cross in them, it being so nigh the Portugal
cross....*

The result was three wearisome months of procrastination, explanations, haggling and negotiation,
after which the "Return" sailed away without having
accomplished anything.

In 1801 the Cross of St. Patrick was added to the
Union Flag to form the Union Jack which thereafter
became a familiar flag in all parts of the world, except
Japan.   The aborigines of Australia had seen the
Union Jack planted on their sunburnt continent; the
Maoris of New Zealand had fought against it; the
Hawaiians knew it when it floated over their islands;
it was unfurled over forts along the Khyber Pass and
in northern India close to the Roof of the World; it
was sniped at and ambushed; it was known from the
Falkland Islands in the south to Baffin Island in the
north and north again, and around the world to
Hongkong and beyond.   But the people of Japan
knew nothing of it.   The doors of Japan at that time
were still closed to all western countries except
Holland, and it was not until after 1854 when Japan
was forced to open her gates, that the Union Jack
was flown in Japan when Britons had occasion to
fly their flag.

As the Knights of the Garter use the Cross of St.
George, that flag was again seen in Japan in
February, 1906, when the Garter Mission under
Prince Arthur of Connaught invested Emperor Meiji

with the Order of the Garter, and conferred the Order of Merit on Field Marshals Oyama and Yamagata and Admiral Togo, victorious commanders of the Russo-Japanese War.

The Cross of St. George can still at times be seen flying in Japan on the flagships of visiting British admirals, or over Anglican churches on St. George's Day (in early times on festival days also), but otherwise the Cross of St. George is now seen only as the main emblem in the scheme of decorations on the occasion each year when Englishmen celebrate and invite others to drink with them the toast of *St. George for Merrie England.*

TRADING
UNDER
DIFFICULTIES

It was a proverb among the Dutch, that though a Dutch Man was Cunning, He could go to School to a Japanese.

CHRISTOPHER FRYKE, 1683

The Tokyo express pulls out of Nagasaki daily early in the afternoon. Five hours later when the train rumbles through the tunnel under the Straits of Shimonoseki, the floors of the carriages are littered with mandarin skins and most of the passengers are dozing. They seem to be still dozing the following morning and the litter on the floor grows deeper. But all are wide awake again when the train pulls into Tokyo station in the afternoon, making a total of twenty-six hours from Nagasaki to the capital. Allowing a full night for a geisha spree, and another for a visit to a cabaret and strip tease, an overworked government official or a busy business man from the provinces could probably complete his important tasks and be ready to leave the capital again on the third day, thereby arriving back in Nagasaki after an absence of less than a week. All this could be done, and generally is, on a single satchel of baggage.

This is fast, convenient and comparatively cheap travelling as compared with three hundred years ago when the Dutch made their periodical visits to Yedo for the purpose of paying homage to the Shogun. They took with them several hundred pieces of baggage and required about three months for the return trip. So costly were those visits that at one time the Dutch threatened, but only threatened, to close their factory and give up their trade monopoly, rather than submit to the expense.

Dr. Engelbert Kaempfer, the German physician attached to the Dutch East India Company's factory on Deshima in Nagasaki harbour, and one of the most remarkable chroniclers of all time, spent only two years in Japan, but left in five volumes a most detailed picture of Japan of those days of 263 years ago. He covered the history, geography, manners, customs, art, and religious beliefs of what was then a little-known island empire—a most remarkable achievement considering that all the Japanese with whom the Dutch came into contact were bound under oath not to disclose anything concerning the domestic affairs of the country, its religion, its politics, or its history.

The difficulties that the Dutch experienced in gaining any information about the country can well be imagined considering that about 165 years later and in a more enlightened era, Townsend Harris, the first U.S. envoy to Japan, wrote in his diary in May 1857:

I am collecting specimens of natural history, but they are meagre, as the Japanese will not bring me one, on the national principle of concealing everything.

In Kaempfer's time Nagasaki was the Paris of the

East. Consequently residents in those days did not
hanker to travel to Yedo to taste the pleasures of a
capital. The pleasures of the East were right there
in their own city, and, according to Kaempfer, numerous young and wealthy Chinese were attracted to
Nagasaki *"purely for pleasure and to spend some part
of their money with Japanese wenches which proved
beneficial to the town."* The Dutch did not at first
see much of that life. They were confined under
distressingly severe conditions on the tiny island of
Deshima, about three acres in area, and enclosed behind a high wooden palisade to cut the view.
Kaempfer described Deshima as follows:

*The place where the Dutch live is called Deshima
....It has been raised from the bottom, which is
rocky and sandy, lying bare at low water. The
foundation is of free-stone, and it rises about half
a fathom above high water mark.*

*In shape it resembles a fan without a handle....
It is joined to the town by a small stone bridge, a
few paces long, at the end of which is a guard
house, where there are soldiers constantly on duty.
On the north, or seaward side, are two strong
gates, never opened but for lading and unlading
the Dutch ships. The island is enclosed with pretty
high deal boards, covered with a small roof on the
top of which is planted a double row of pikes....
Some few paces off in the water are thirteen posts
standing at proper distances, with small wooden
tablets at the top, upon which is written in large
Japanese characters an order from the governors,
strictly forbidding all boats or vessels under severe*

*penalties to come within these posts or to approach
the island.*

The Director of the Dutch factory was required
to journey to Yedo, at first yearly and later every
two or four years, to give presents to the Shogun;
generally he was accompanied by one or two Dutch
secretaries and a physician. How complicated was
this matter of presents may be gauged from
Kaempfer's comments:

> *It is the business of the Japanese governors of
> Nagasaki to determine what might prove accept-
> able to the Court. They take out of the goods laid
> up in our warehouse what they think proper....
> Sometimes some of their own goods, they have been
> presented with by the Chinese, are put in among
> our presents, because by this means they can dis-
> pose of them to the best advantage either by oblig-
> ing us to buy them at an excessive price or by ex-
> changing them for other goods.*

To attend the three, or sometimes four, Dutchmen,
to watch their movements, to carry their baggage,
and to organize the journey, there were up to 150
Japanese; the travelling expenses, wages and gratui-
ties of this huge entourage for a period of three
months amounted to a considerable sum of money.

In addition to the multitudinous presents and
clothing, the baggage comprised a store of European
victuals and a complete assortment of kitchen utensils.
The Dutchmen preferred to eat European meals
rather than live on the countryside.

The Dutch director and the Japanese high commissioner who accompanied the party rode in palanquins

as befitted their dignity; the senior Japanese interpreter if he was old rode in a *kago* or sedan chair,
the others on horseback, and the servants on foot.

Any suggestion on the part of the Dutch that they
should stay at a different inn from former occasions,
or that any deviation should be made from the regular
routine, was met by the high commissioner referring
to his handbook of previous journeys and thus de-
monstrating that there was no precedent that would
permit of the change being made.

For the Dutch it was an irksome trip. In
Kaempfer's words they were

> *treated in a manner like prisoners, deprived of all
> liberty, except that of looking about the country
> from our horses. Nay they watch us to that degree
> that they will not leave us alone, not even for the
> most necessary reasons....It must be owned, how-
> ever, that this superabundant care and watchful-
> ness is considerably lessened upon our return, when
> we have found means to insinuate ourselves into
> their favour and by presents, and otherwise to
> procure their connivance.*

The colours and arms of the Dutch East India
Company were displayed whilst this cavalcade was
on the move, and also outside the inns where the
Dutch were accommodated

> *so that all may know and suitable precautions be
> taken....The garden is the only place in which
> we Dutchmen, being treated in all respects little
> better than prisoners, have liberty to walk.*

Beyond stepping out into the gardens at the inns
and taking a bath they were strictly confined to their

quarters, but seemingly the Dutch discovered what has been found from the beginning of time, namely that where men and wenches are concerned, chaperones are not always effective, because the good doctor noted elsewhere in his diary:

No other pleasure is allowed us, no manner of conversation with domestics, male or female, excepting what through the connivance of our inspectors, some of us found means to procure at night in private and in their own rooms.

In the matter of sowing wild oats, the regulations were somewhat more accommodating. For example no women excepting prostitutes were allowed on Deshima, but even *"they being none of the best and handsomest"* were supplied at three times the usual price.

The cavalcade set out from Nagasaki overland to the Shimonoseki straits which were reached on the sixth day, thence to Osaka through the Inland Sea, which took another six days. At Osaka, where a stop of four days was made, the Dutch found the water to be *"a little brackish, but in lieu thereof they have the best sake in the empire, which is brewed in great quantities in the neighbouring village of Tennoji."* From Osaka the journey was overland to Yedo, the entire trip from Nagasaki to Yedo occupying twenty-nine days.

On arrival at Yedo preparations were made for the audience with the Shogun. Kaempfer wrote:

When they cried out "Hollanda Capitain," he crawled on his hands and knees to a place between the presents and then kneeling he bowed his fore-

42

head quite down to the ground and so crawled backward like a crab without uttering a single word. So mean and short a thing is the audience we have of this mighty monarch....Nor are there any more ceremonies observed in the audience he gives even to the greatest and most powerful princes of the empire.

In the first trips to Yedo the proceedings terminated immediately the ceremony of kowtow at the Shogun's court was completed, but in later years the Dutchmen were conducted deeper into the palace and required to put on a show for the ladies of the court, where:

the mutual compliments being over, the succeeding part of this solemnity turned to a perfect farce. We were asked a thousand ridiculous and impertinent questions.

The doctor was required to give some free medical advice whereupon he advised a shaven priest with an ulcer on his shin not to drink so much *sake*,—"*a piece of professional stratagem which occasioned much laughter at the patient's expense.*"

The Shogun then ordered us to take off our cloaks, then to stand upright, that he might have a full view of us, again to walk, to stand still, to compliment each other, to dance, to jump, to play the drunkard, to speak broken Japanese, to read Dutch, to paint, to put our cloaks on and off, I joining to my dance a love-song in High German. In this manner, and with innumerable such other apish tricks, we must suffer ourselves to contribute to the court's diversion.

Apparently Kaempfer was determined that the laugh should not be all on one side because on being asked to translate his song, wherein he had actually extolled the physical proportions and other excellent qualities of a certain lady-love, he audaciously replied that it expressed the sincere wish that Heaven might bestow health, fortune and prosperity on the Shogun, his family and the Court—a prank that he was able to get away with because there were no Japanese interpreters at the Court who understood German.

The court ladies were of course hidden from view seated behind bamboo curtains, but the doctor noted that pieces of paper had been put between the lattices of the bamboo curtains to make the openings wider *"in order to a better and easier sight"* and counting thirty such pieces of paper the good doctor concluded that at least that number of ladies were eyeing him.

On another occasion the Dutch were required
to kiss one another like man and wife, which the ladies behind the bamboo curtains showed themselves by their laughter to be particularly well pleased with.

(Terry in his *Guide to Japan* in commenting on these happenings remarks that the natives were not as shrewd at barter then as they are now, but what the Dutchmen wrung from them in profits, the Nipponese took out of their pride. However, by the end of the seventeenth century the Court and the officials in Yedo were sufficiently acquainted with the customs and the culture of the Western world for this buffoonery to cease.)

The Dutch were also received at various high

officials' houses where the ladies especially were curious regarding the clothing, rings and tobacco pipes of the Dutchmen, some of which articles were passed behind the bamboo curtains for their inspection. Of this occasion Kaempfer records:

We could not but take notice that everything was so cordial that we made no manner of scruple of making ourselves merry and diverting the company with a song.

Prior to leaving Yedo, they were required to attend an audience at the palace to listen to the reading of the usual orders which forbade them among other things, from molesting any Chinese or ships from the Loo Choo Islands trading with Japan or to bring in any Portuguese or priests.

As a parting gift the Director was presented with *"thirty Japanese gowns (kimono) which he crept on all fours to receive."* This was followed by tea and cakes which the Dutch found as *"tough as glue,"* and then by a banquet. But the Dutch did not seem to have esteemed that dinner any more than the cakes because Kaempfer records that profiting by prior experience they were not caught napping and had already provided themselves with a *"good substantial breakfast"* before leaving their quarters. As for the meal itself they considered it *"so far from answering to the majestic magnificence of so powerful a monarch that a worse one could not have been had at any private man's house."* However according to custom what was left was taken home by the Japanese interpreter and it *"proved quite a load, especially as he was old and rheumatic."*

Trading Under Difficulties

Not only in the matter of food, but also in the matter of dress did the Dutch profit by experience gained during the course of their previous visits to Tokyo. Woodcut prints of the Nagasaki period depict the Dutch wearing long black cloaks, and although such mantles were common enough at that time in Europe, the Dutch found that by extending the length a few inches such garments were exceptionally useful on their visits to Yedo during the interminable delays in the antechambers of the palace. Etiquette demanded that they should sit on the *tatami* in Japanese style, a situation which proved so painful that they were glad to stretch out their legs on one side under cover of these long cloaks.

Kaempfer states that on the occasion he visited Yedo, 133 presents in all were received, but two were referred to as *"pretty sorry ones,"* and with the exception of those from the Shogun, which were considered to be the property of the Company, all were reckoned as the Director's perquisites.

The directors, or Hollanda Capitains, were of ambassadorial rank and were permitted to stay in Japan for such limited periods, at first for only one year, that they usually left Japan knowing little more about the country than when they first arrived. Their time was largely taken up in disposing of those "hard to get" items such as needles, fine files, spectacles and magnifying glasses, brought in among their personal baggage for purposes of private trade, and then in accumulating those goods such as silk kimono that they were permitted by custom to take back to Batavia for private trading and as presents for the

Directors in Batavia who had appointed them, because *he must not presume to return thither without valuable consideration to his benefactors, unless he intends to be excused for the future the honour of any such employment.*

The Japanese inspectors closed their eyes to a recognized amount of private trading on the part of the Directors and the other Dutchmen, but, records Kaempfer:

One of our Directors in 1686 played his cards so awkwardly that ten Japanese were beheaded for smuggling and he himself banished from the country forever.

In the matter of the Directors padding their expense accounts, Kaempfer relates that *"even those are sometimes run up to an unnecessary height"* and that while it is not his intention *"to detract from the reputation and character of probity of so many worthy gentlemen"* a directorship is worth at least thirty thousand guilders to the incumbent. Certainly it required the prospects of high reward to make the life they had to live on Deshima, behind walls and under guard, worthwhile to any but the more studious types of men.

It required more than guards and a high fence to prevent European ideas and learning from leaking out of Deshima, even if that culture had to trickle underground. The Dutch certainly helped a great deal in the making of modern Japan, but most of the credit for the influence of the Dutch interlude goes not to the Directors of the Dutch East India Company at Deshima, who were generally too busy look-

47

ing to their personal gain, but rather to a few men like Kaempfer. There were other physicians also such as Dr. Thunberg, the Swedish physician and naturalist, and much later the brilliant Dr. von Siebold.

They also made journeyings to the capital and recorded their experiences in diaries. In addition they pursued their studies into the flora and fauna of Japan and other sciences to a degree that their names live on in history as the authors of learned treatises, whilst the names of the *Hollanda Capitains* have generally been long since forgotten. With one or two exceptions the Directors contributed nothing to the world's knowledge of Japan.

Although Thunberg and von Siebold had to be represented to the Japanese inspectors as Dutch, their accents were thought by the Japanese interpreters to be so curious as to cause disbelief. However their accents were explained away as being those of *yama-Hollanda* or Dutch mountaineers. In reality Holland is one of the flattest countries in the world, but after about two hundred years residence in Japan the Dutch apparently had also learned the art of making mountains out of mole-hills!

Maps, books on mathematics, astronomy and medicine were in great demand and often smuggled in, and in addition of course the beloved schnapps of the Dutch. To cope with this demand the Dutch sea-captains favoured large and very wide silver-laced coats so designed that they could conceal upon their persons the maximum quantity of smuggled goods, and frequently came ashore so bulky and loaded

48

down with contraband that they had to be supported by a sailor on either side. In Dr. Thunberg's time a customs search was instituted and the doctor then recorded in his diary:

It was droll enough to see the astonishment which the sudden reduction in the size of our bulky captain excited in the major part of the Japanese, who before had always imagined that all our captains were actually as fat and lusty as they appeared to be.

Isaac Titsingh, who was an outstanding exception among the Directors, did contribute much to our knowledge of that time, but had so little regard for the value of his own manuscripts and collections that he left them together with a large fortune to a worthless son by an Eastern woman, who squandered the fortune and so scattered the manuscripts and collections that many were lost for all time.

Finally there was another Director, G.F. Meylan, in 1830, who contributed something to our knowledge of the customs and manners of that time. Deshima did not change much during the 200 years or so of its existence, except that in later years glass windows were brought from Batavia to replace the original paper *shoji*. The number of permanent residents however increased from about seven in Kaempfer's time to around thirteen, excluding the slaves who were brought from Batavia as servants, one to each Dutchman. In addition there were a number of Nagasaki teahouse girls who were such frequent visitors as to be regarded almost as semi-permanents. To Mr. Meylan we are indebted for the following explanation of their presence, and surely as convincing a one as the men could have hoped for:

Male Japanese servants are not allowed to remain on Deshima over night. How then could the Dutch residents otherwise manage to procure any domestic comfort in the long nights of winter—their tea-water for instance—were it not for these females.

* * * * * * * *

Let it not be imagined that the worthy Dr. Kaempfer, some of whose candid comments have been reproduced above, was given only to cynical criticism. Of the Japanese, he wrote in another part of his diary:

From this reasonable behaviour, one may judge of the civility of the whole nation in general, always excepting the officials (at Deshima) and our servants....The behaviour of the Japanese from the meanest countryman up to the greatest prince or lord is such that the whole empire might be called a school of civility and good manners.

QUEEN VICTORIA'S PRESENT

The presents from the United States government to the Japanese were landed. Among them were....and several casks of whiskey towards the latter of which they evinced a decided preference.—Journal of W. B. ALLEN (on one of Perry's Black Ships), 1854

When the Foreign Powers first sought to conclude treaties of amity and commerce with Japan, one of their greatest difficulties was to make contact with persons in authority. Generally they found themselves side-tracked in an out-port, and indulging in negotiations with minor officials, which in effect became games of patience.

When the Earl of Elgin and Kincardine, to give the noble lord his full title, set out for Japan, somebody conceived the idea of his taking along a steam yacht as a present for the Emperor. This, it was hoped, would give the British Mission a reasonable excuse for proceeding up Tokyo Bay, or Yedo Bay as it was then known, and anchoring as close to the capital as it would be possible for the British war-vessels and the yacht to go. The war-vessels selected for the mission were the "Retribution" and the "Furious," but whether they were selected because of their names or their armaments is not clear. The first port of call was to be Nagasaki, and when steaming towards that port they passed what the sailors came to refer to as the dungaree forts, which comprised long lengths of coarse calico or canvas painted to represent batteries of guns. Whether their purpose was to conceal real guns with the intention of luring ships into close range and so to destruction, or whether they were just crude shams was not discovered, because the British war-ships steamed past them without being molested. It was not until they were close to Nagasaki that they encountered the first indication that they were not welcome:

We found an obstruction represented only by one official boat, upon the deck, or rather roof, of which a gentleman was seated reading placidly and gently fanning himself. On our approaching nearer he looked up and waved us benignly back with his fan. If he was the port guardian, he was by no means a formidable janitor, for on our holding on our way, regardless of his signals, he fell to reading again, apparently satisfied that he had discharged his duty and was henceforth relieved from all farther responsibility on our account.

When the purpose of Elgin's visit became known to the authorities, a battle of wits developed and every effort was made to circumvent the English strategy. The vice-governor of Nagasaki was sent along to explain that the governor had been empowered to receive the yacht on behalf of the Emperor, whilst Elgin in turn replied that he was not authorised to deliver it anywhere but in the capital. With this impasse being reached, the Japanese officials promised to report to their superiors, and were then content to partake of a repast of *pâté de foie gras* and champagne.

After that session Elgin determined to proceed to Yedo via Shimoda after first doing some sightseeing around Nagasaki. In this the Mission's greatest difficulty was that of language. Whilst many Japanese in Nagasaki had some knowledge of Dutch, there were hardly any who knew even a few words of English.

On arrival at Shimoda they found:

> ....*the Stars and Stripes waving proudly over the premises originally occupied by some recent incarnation of Buddh (sic); and Mr. Harris, the American consul, had converted the shrine of that divinity into a four-poster.*

(As Japan had been closed for over 200 years there were no buildings set apart for the reception of foreign visitors, and no others, with the exception of temples, that could be suddenly pressed into use. A week or so later when Elgin arrived in Yedo he also was accommodated in a temple, and when Yokohama was opened a year later, the Christian missionaries who were among the first arrivals were likewise, in an act of exceptional religious tolerance, provided with quarters in Buddhist temples.)

It was said that when Elgin's ships were first sighted approaching Nagasaki Bay the news was flashed from hilltop to hilltop and reached the Shogun in Yedo before the vessels finally dropped anchor off Nagasaki town. Perhaps news of the noble lord's *pâté de foie gras* and champagne luncheons had similarly reached Shimoda, because early in the morning following Elgin's arrival at Shimoda, the

governor together with a large suite came on board
and quickly got down to the business of telling him
that he could not proceed to Yedo, and that the
yacht would be received in Shimoda. When Lord
Elgin positively refused to hand over the yacht in
Shimoda port, or in fact anywhere other than Yedo,
the governor proceeded to describe in alarming terms
the dreadful fate that would await everybody concerned, including both Elgin and himself, should the
vessels venture near the capital, but he interspersed
so many jovial chuckles into the dreadful consequences
that Elgin was reminded of Sam Weller's jovial
papa, Mr. Weller Senior of Pickwickian fame. The
negotiations soon reached the usual impasse, whereupon all sat down to appreciate a good English
luncheon. It was then that one of the Japanese
officials made a grave diplomatic blunder. He was
heard to refuse Curaçao and ask for Maraschino
instead, whereupon the astute Lord Elgin concluded
that the Japanese were not really asleep, but were
in fact much wider awake than they would have him
believe. He thereupon decided to leave the oysters
of Kakizaki to Mr. Townsend Harris, and to proceed
as soon as possible to Yedo. The latter gentleman
generously placed at Lord Elgin's disposal the services
of his Dutch interpreter, Mr. Heusken, an agreeable
and accomplished young man who was popular both
with the Japanese officials and with some of the better
looking young women of the Oyster Point teahouses.

Commodore Perry had been in Yedo Bay four years
earlier, but his ships had not gone beyond Kawasaki
Point. Elgin proceeded onwards up the bay despite

the warnings from the Japanese that the bay ahead was a dangerous anchorage. Elgin thereupon expressed anxiety for the safety of the Japanese fleet which could be plainly seen much farther up the bay, and so proceeded onwards until he anchored close by them. The usual conferences again commenced; the same ground was again covered, and the same impasses again reached, followed once more by the now famous *pâté de foie gras* and champagne luncheons.

It was at one of these meetings that the Japanese disclosed their curiosity as to the whereabouts of Kincardine. They had noted that letters delivered to them had been signed Elgin and Kincardine, but as they had thus far only met Elgin, they had assumed that Kincardine must be the senior envoy and was holding himself aloof, and that he had probably been peeping through the keyhole to make sure that Elgin was carrying out his duties in a proper manner. The mystery was soon cleared up, but that there should be no one spying on Elgin struck them as peculiar.

Among the Japanese commissioners was a *daimyo* who was losing no opportunity to study English, and who carried about on his person his vocabulary of English words written on a stock of fans, which he hid in the copious folds of his dress. For each occasion, whether it might be a *pâté de foie gras* and champagne luncheon, a cigar and liqueur tête-à-tête, or a conference, he produced from deep recesses in his costume the appropriate fan with which to fan himself, and upon which was written a vocabulary fitting for the occasion.

The Japanese authorities were required to provide
suitable accommodation on shore for the English
Mission, and this they had done in a remarkably
short space of time by furnishing a temple with exact replicas of U.S. Consul Harris' furniture, of
which they had sketches and exact measurements
among their records. Townsend Harris then began
to wonder what other details of his personal affairs
and records had been secretly compiled by the Japanese. Lord Elgin and his suite proceeded ashore to
the strains of *Rule Britannia.*

At the end of their first day in Yedo, they found
that the Shogun had thoughtfully delivered to their
place of residence a banquet in Japanese style, which
was, for some, their first introduction to a Japanese
meal. Lord Elgin's private secretary gives us a
description of it, and went on record with the following gratuitous advice to those Englishmen who might
come after him to Japan:

.... *we all plunged into the red lacker cups on the
right, or at the invitation of another, dashed recklessly at what seemed to be pickled slugs on the
left.... There was a good deal of sea-weed about it,
and we each had a capital broiled fish. With that,
and an immense bowl of rice, it was impossible to
starve; but my curiosity triumphed over my discretion, and I tasted of every pickle and condiment,
and each animal and vegetable delicacy, of every
variety of colour, consistence, and flavour; an experience from which I would recommend any future
visitor to Japan to abstain.*

Once Elgin had established himself on shore in

Yedo, he found all procrastination came to an end, and, if anything, there was a desire to speed him on to a conclusion of his task. The six Japanese commissioners quickly got down to the work of drafting the first treaty with Great Britain, and it was while this work was proceeding that a discovery of some importance was made, because it probably brought to an end the *pâté de foie gras* luncheons. To quote the private secretary once more:—

The dish that they most highly appreciate is ham. They also indulged freely in champagne.

This explains the hope that was facetiously expressed by the Daimyo of Higo, a man with a hearty appetite and a wit of most of the parties, that the first Treaty with England would not taste too much of ham and champagne!

In those days the only foreigners known to many of the inhabitants of Yedo were the Chinese, and not unnaturally Lord Elgin and his party were often mistaken for Chinese, and sometimes for Chinese hawkers. On one occasion, when contrary to the advice of the commissioners they had gone sightseeing, without a sufficiently large body of Japanese policemen to inspire awe among the populace, they were hooted, pelted, and greeted with the cry of "Chinamen! Chinamen! Have you anything to sell?" —a happening for which the commissioners never ceased to apologise.

The Englishmen had purchased *"mountains of lacker, pyramids of china,....Japanese costumes....swords....quantities of books"* and all manner of other souvenirs. Owing to the absence of any established rate of exchange, payment for these purchases was a complicated process that had to be done at a special clearing house where all the coin tendered by the Englishmen had to be weighed and balanced against the equivalent weight of Japanese coin. It is related that during the process of that complicated operation *"an amount of tea and tobacco was consumed sufficient to fumigate a seventy-four and float her afterwards."*

The treaty was finally drawn up in Dutch, Japanese and English, and required no fewer than eighty-four signatures. Some of the Japanese commissioners *"painted away at the hieroglyphics which represented their names with evident care and anxiety,"* but the jovial Daimyo of Higo *"dashed away with his brush, perfectly regardless of the opinion which people in England might form of his handwriting."*

The most important part of the day's work was yet to come, namely delivery of the yacht which was still flying the British ensign.

The commissioners arrived on board the yacht to receive delivery even before the appointed hour had arrived. According to the Elgin's secretary:

We found the commissioners had preceded us and were now strutting about the deck of the yacht in all the bravery of their most resplendent costumes.

The jovial Daimyo of Higo was donned in a striking and imposing costume *"literally covered with crabs, some of them large enough to be an honour to an English sea-port. The dress was of embroidered silk, with these crabs in raised silver, standing out in high relief."*

Lord Elgin addressed the commissioners, formally handing over to them on behalf of Her Majesty Queen Victoria the yacht as a token of friendship and goodwill. Down came the English ensign, and up went the Japanese flag. The Japanese forts fired a salute of twenty-one guns, much to the wonderment of the Japanese populace who beheld their forts conducting themselves in such an unwarlike and a totally unprecedented manner. The yacht got slowly under way, commanded by a Japanese captain, worked by Japanese engineers and manned by Japanese sailors. The occasion is now of historical interest, because it is the first recorded instance of Japan becoming the owner of a British vessel.

One final ham and champagne dinner was put on for the Japanese commissioners, and then:

At last the moment of parting arrived, and, amid many demonstrations of affection on both sides, they bade us a final farewell. . . .

Then rockets shot into the heavens and blue-lights burned at the yard-arms, and the rows of forts were illuminated in quick reply. . . .

The 26th of August, 1858, will be a date long to be remembered. . . .it will be an epoch in the history of the Japanese empire. . . .an event pregnant with important results to commerce and civilization.

* * * * * * * *

As the Shoguns in Yedo had already usurped the power of the emperors for over two hundred years, it is not surprising that the Shogun in power at the time usurped the yacht, and then in order that he might not be reminded of the fact he had the name "Emperor," which the English had given to the yacht, painted out and the new name *"Yeddo"* painted in. When the Shogun's interest in the yacht waned, he traded it for thirty thousand gold *koban* to the Daimyo of Hizen.

The Bishop of Hongkong who had previously seen the yacht in all its glory at Hongkong, before it was presented to Japan, next saw it in Nagasaki harbour after it had been in use about eighteen months. He had tea on board with the captain, and later described its condition:

The aft cabin was in a wretched state of dirt and confusion. Luggage and trunks lay scattered about. The green velvet chairs were now soiled and shabby; the glittering frames of satinwood were covered with accumulated filth; the gilt ornaments were indented and bruised; the panels of plated mirror were tarnished and dull. All looked slovenly and uncomfortable—a perfect contrast to the elegant little craft which attracted so many ad-miring visitors at Hongkong. The aft cabin was appropriated to some local official whose baggage and numerous trunks lay scattered about the un-swept and carpetless cabin floor.

* * * * * * *

The Emperor of Japan was in those days confined to his palace at Miako, as Kyoto was then known, where the largest body of water at his disposal was the fish-pond in the palace garden. It is unlikely therefore that he had any interest in yachting, or indeed had ever heard of that sport, a point which probably occurred to Lord Elgin's private secretary when he wrote at the time:

It was a cruel satire upon this unhappy potentate to present him with a yacht; one might as well request the Pope's acceptance of a wife.

VORTICAL ATOMS AND CRACKPOTS

> *His eyes were like two revolving lights in two dark caverns.*
>
> LAURENCE OLIPHANT

In 1828 an English grocer emigrated to America with his wife and a five year old son. On arrival in Utica, in New York state, he added auctioneering to his old line of groceries. His son displayed no particular aptitude for groceries or auctioneering, although in the end he did prove to be a better business man than his father, if the making of money is the criterion.

Thomas Lake Harris, for that was the boy's name, developed into a Christian mystic, a poet of sorts, an unorthodox pastor, a spiritualist, a bogus prophet, and ultimately the patriarchal leader of one of the strangest religious communities in America, a country which has produced so many crank religions.

To quote from the *Dictionary of American Biography*:

....*Meanwhile Harris himself was struggling "interiorly" to break through the natural forces of evil by rallying the "vortical atoms," and attain his spiritual "two-in-oneness," or union with his heavenly counterpart. This he finally achieved in*

1894 when he became technically immortal. The "crisis" or end of the natural world was now eagerly expected and Harris predicted its imminence repeatedly.

As we all know, Harris proved to be entirely wrong in his forecast about the end of the world, but he was not wrong, as we shall shortly see, in his faith in his own ability to make a quick dollar, or in his faith in rising land values in the United States.

According to the *Dictionary of American Biography,* Harris was, among other things, a Universalist, an Harmonic philosophist, a Swedenborgianist, and a Theosocialist. If any of my readers do not know what all that means, it only proves that Harris was right in believing that many people live in the outer darkness!

Harris became one of the minor American poets, and it is to be imagined that many major poets must have envied the unusual ease with which he turned out his verse, even if they did not admire his poetry, because according to the aforementioned authority:

About 1850 he had begun to go into trances and while in communication with the celestial world to compose long mystic poems on the theme of celestial love.

At the age of sixty-eight years he married for the third time, on this occasion his not unattractive secretary—and then spent most of the remaining fifteen years of his life writing theological works, many of which still clutter up the topmost shelves of old secondhand bookshops.

Curiously enough there is a link between this

unusual prophet and poet, and feudal Japan of nearly one hundred years ago.

As related in the previous chapter, when the Earl of Elgin headed the British Mission to Japan in 1858 it was his secretary, the same brilliant Mr. Laurence Oliphant, who said in a few words a great deal about Queen Victoria's gift of a yacht to the Emperor of Japan by remarking:

It was a cruel satire upon this unhappy potentate to present him with a yacht; one might as well request the Pope's acceptance of a wife.

Oliphant was then already very much a man of the world. He had travelled to the farthermost trouble spots in Europe and Asia, done some worthwhile espionage in Russia, attended a Nepalese durbar clad in a plaid shooting jacket and an old felt hat (and other clothing of course), served as *The Times* correspondent in the Crimea War, and as private secretary to the Governor of Canada and the British Ambassador in Washington. Indeed it was in Washington, D.C., that he experienced for the first time the sight of a young woman in bloomers, a spectacle sufficiently naughty for him to record in one of his travel books.

He saw something of the Indian Mutiny and was in the British expedition to China.

Oliphant's visit to Japan produced a pleasant book of travel and a desire on his part to see more of this unusual country which had been forced to open its doors, and then like some gaily coloured fantastic butterfly was about to emerge into the world outside. And so it was that Laurence Oliphant returned to

Japan as first secretary to the British Legation in Tokyo, or Yedo as it was known then, with the prospect of being in charge of British interests at the Court of the Tycoon during the projected visit of his chief to Europe.

Laurence Oliphant, ever the keen observer, has left us a description of Yedo of those early days, noted by him when he and his party passed along the streets on their way to the British Legation. Describing a public bathhouse, he wrote:

Bathers of both sexes regardless of the fact that they had nothing on but soap, or the Japanese equivalent of it, crowded the door to watch us pass.

In all probability he would have made a successful diplomat, and would never have met Thomas Lake Harris, had it not been that on a night in July, 1861, he was wounded, in fact almost murdered, by a party of Japanese *ronin,* armed with long swords, who attacked the British Legation. The miscreants succeeded in getting past the Japanese guards and broke into the Legation. There they fortunately became confused when one of them stepped onto the pins of an entomological collection spread on the *tatami.* In the excitement they became lost among the passageways and became split up into several groups. The five Englishmen, several of whom were armed with revolvers, succeeded in repulsing them. When the would-be assassins finally retired, the unfortunate Oliphant was lying senseless on the floor bleeding profusely from sword cuts on his arm, head, and neck.

My own theory is that the blow on the head was

much more severe than history records—an impression with which you also may agree when you have completed the reading of this article!

On account of the serious nature of the injuries received, the unfortunate Oliphant was invalided back to England, and, it is of interest to recall, on that journey he was permitted by the British Minister to act as a courier for the Japanese Government.

The port of Kobe, or rather Hyogo as it was then known, and the city of Osaka were due to be opened on 1st January, 1863, but owing to the continued opposition of a number of the clans to the entry of foreigners, as they put it, *"to the sacred soil of Japan being polluted by foreigners,"* the Authorities were seeking a postponement of the opening of Hyogo and Osaka. It was in those circumstances that the Japanese Government entrusted to Oliphant a letter from the Tycoon to be delivered to Queen Victoria in which a postponement of the opening of those ports was requested. A Japanese embassy was shortly afterwards despatched to England on board a British warship. Their mission was successful and Kobe and Osaka were therefore not opened until five years later, on 1st January, 1868.

It is also interesting to note that the Japanese Embassy left Japan with what was then the commonly accepted impression that Occidentals were barbarians. However, they were so impressed with all they saw on the British warship and abroad, that upon returning to Japan they reported *"it is not the foreigners, but we ourselves who are barbarians,"* and they declared that the Westerners who were popularly considered to be *"hairy foreigners with blue eyes like pigs, were gentlemen and not wild beasts."* Although their visit did something to correct mistaken impressions, it is but fair to remark that they mixed largely with diplomats and did not have much opportunity of meeting the masses, many of whom at that time would have resented being classified as gentlemen.

But let us rejoin Mr. Laurence Oliphant. After arrival in England he resigned from the diplomatic service, and later, on recovering from his injuries, he entered politics and was elected to parliament for a brief term. However, he displayed no particular aptitude for the political hustings, but did continue to produce witty writings. He must then have been at a loose end, because when Harris was on a lecture tour in England, both he and his mother, Lady Oliphant, fell under Harris' spell. Oliphant then deserted politics to become one of Harris' disciples. Said Oliphant, when describing Harris, *"his eyes were like revolving lights in two dark caverns."*

Having looked into those eyes, the elegant Oliphant, the one-time diplomat who had mixed with the great of many lands, began to serve a period of probation to fit himself for entry into the Brotherhood of the New Life. Whilst awaiting permission from Father Faithful, the name by which Harris was known to his disciples, Oliphant was required to devote a part of every day to sewing petticoats.

Oliphant and his mother went to America with a number of other followers whom Harris had roped in, and at the instigation of Lady Oliphant, who apparently had both money and ideas, they all chipped in to purchase 1600 acres of land at Brocton on the shores of Lake Erie, where they founded the colony of "The Brotherhood of the New Life." Harris controlled the properties of the entire group and imposed a most rigorous discipline on its members, so that each might *"attain the goal of complete self-surrender to the doctrine of Divine Use or purpose."*

On arrival at Brocton, Oliphant was separated from his mother and required to live in a shed, furnished with such things as he could make from fruit cases.

For about two years this man of fashion, who had an entree to some of the best clubs in London and some of the best homes in England, laboured as a farm hand, whilst his mother, Lady Oliphant, widow of a former Chief Justice of Ceylon, also served the Brotherhood by washing *"the gentlemen's linen"* and working in the fields with a hoe.

Although Oliphant had been nearly murdered by the Japanese and his career ruined, he did not lose his regard for their better qualities, and it was as a result of his efforts and influence that about twenty Japanese men, largely from the samurai class, came to Brocton to study Harris' gospel of the "two-in-oneness." For those who could not pay their own steamship passages Oliphant arranged for financial aid through his friends. He had a theory that the Japanese were by nature better fitted than most Occidentals to live up to the strictness of Harris' teachings.

Oliphant was not however permitted to speak to

the Japanese, nor indeed to his own mother, because of *"the danger of our states mixing and passing over to Faithful."* In a letter to a friend, Oliphant, now known in the Brotherhood as Woodbine, wrote:

I cannot speak to the Japanese, though I see them, dear souls, every day hard at work with their countenances beaming with delight.

And again:

Some more Japanese have just joined the Use. They said that their past lives in Japan had been very wicked and any punishment which Faithful saw fit to inflict they would willingly bear.

Among the Japanese who came to Brocton through the agency of Oliphant were several young samurai, who had been sent abroad to study by the Kagoshima clan. Most of them soon drifted away and later in life, when they had become famous public men in Japan, as members of the peerage and as cabinet ministers, they did their best to forget the delusions of Father Faithful. And so when it came to submitting a précis of their autobiographies for *Who's Who* they suppressed all reference to their association with *The Brotherhood of the New Life.* Their reticence is understandable enough, for the verdict of history seems to be that the Brotherhood was a community of crackpots.

However that may be Father Faithful was able to rope in so many wealthy followers that he soon had acquired over twenty thousand acres of land. The Oliphants had contributed a goodly sum to the cause.

That Oliphant threw himself into this new life with zest may be judged from a letter to a friend:

Vortical Atoms and Crackpots

...I see you began your letter to me "Mr. Oliphant"
but Mr. Oliphant has taken his departure long ago
—he disappeared almost entirely—and left only
your most affectionate and loving little Woodbine.

Such a letter from Oliphant, the brilliant writer
and conversationalist, whose company even delighted
royalty! He had actually accompanied the Prince
of Wales (later Edward VII) on several of his ex-
peditions to Paris, where Prince Edward described
him as *"sugar doodling the ladies."*

The community appears to have adopted some
unusual practices. According to *The Dictionary of
American Biography,* from which I again quote:

Their distinctive practices were "open breathing,"
a kind of respiration by which the Divine Breath
entered directly into the body: and a system of
celibate marriages whereby each person was left
free to live in spiritual union with his or her hea-
venly counter-part."

"Counter-partal marriages" were defined as the
indwelling of eternal mate with external mate.
Harris appears to have had three wives in all, but
only two eternal mates, because his third wife is
described as being his second eternal mate.

It must be all very confusing to simple married
couples, but apparently not to Oliphant or to his
Victorian wife condemned to a celibate marriage and
"martyr love." She never complained, if we are to
believe Oliphant. Her reward it seems was after
death, when as his heavenly counterpart they were
more intimate than when she was alive—at least so
said Oliphant.

As for the doings of Father Faithful he slept little and spent his nights mostly in visions with a celestial spouse. Or rather that was his story.

Eventually owing to divergences between Oliphant and Harris, the community split and Harris and a number of followers purchased a 1200 acre vineyard in California, where Harris lived in luxury much like an Oriental potentate.

Finally in 1881 the Oliphants pulled out completely and recovered most of their original investment, but only after Harris' counter move to have Oliphant certified as insane, had failed.

For some years after they had separated Oliphant continued to believe that Harris, by some form of telepathic means, could exercise control over him. In fact on Oliphant's death some years later, Harris announced with malevolent glee:

I was at the death. I watched him die and heard him talk. I did it.

And so Oliphant, one of the great English eccentrics, disappears from this particular story, although actually the remainder of his life was even more amazing than the part already told.

The Times considered him sufficiently important to devote two columns to his obituary notice.

Thomas Lake Harris, now generally recognised to have been a pious fraud more interested in the charms of his attractive secretary, known to the Brotherhood as "Dovie," than in any tenuous celestial counterpart, continued in public to pursue his vortical atoms.

Shortly before his death he assigned to five beneficiaries, one of whom was one of the original Japanese converts, the entire property then valued at $250,000—a considerable achievement for a grocer's boy and one who started out with what some commercially-minded people might consider the great handicap of being a poet.

Thomas Lake Harris then disappears from this scene, except that he maintained his interest in the Japanese as a chosen people, although according to his wife's diary he found "the sexual state of the Japanese corrupted by British influences," a statement which to me, as a Britisher, does not make much sense.

The deed which Harris had drawn up, provided that the property, which was then largely in vineyards, should eventually go to the beneficiary who lived longest and to the beneficiary's heirs. This clause later caused much confusion and litigation.

The original five beneficiaries comprised a married couple well on in years, a widow, a spinster and a Japanese. Now it would seem to a simple person such as myself, that the elderly married couple, the widow, and the husbandless old maid might have been at a distinct disadvantage in the race to win the $250,000 prize by producing an heir, unless it was that Harris had reckoned that his doctrine of celibate marriages would have put them all on a level.

A research into the newspapers of the time and into much which appeared in print on the disputes that arose, has left me more confused than ever. And so it is that I really do not know by what process the Japanese won the race. Although he did not actually live the longest, he did have an heir. It is also a fact that he was the community's expert in animal husbandry and vineyards, and so he may have known all about the birds and the bees!

However that may be he eventually got all, despite the handicap from which he may have suffered. As the son of a samurai he had been taught in his childhood that the accumulation of wealth by commerce was the lowest occupation in the land, but in the end he seems to have been the best business man of them all!

Later during the days of Prohibition he ran into difficult times, but Harris' teachings of two-in-oneness perhaps came to his aid, because whilst refusing to do any bootlegging he continued to store up large quantities of sherry which aged and became more mellow whilst he was waiting for prohibition to be repealed.

The vineyards are still flourishing, but Harris' vortical atoms, his two-in-oneness, his celibate marriages, and his celestial spouses have long since disappeared from the scene. Only his library now remains. Unlike the sherry it does not improve with age. In time the bookworms will devour it, and the *Shades of the Past* lingering within its pages will be lost.

THE
MUTINY
OF
THE
"CYPRUS"

> *Their Justice is severely executed*
> *without any partialitie upon trans-*
> *gressors of the Law.*
> WILL ADAMS, 1611

It was a far cry from the convict and bushranging
days of Australia to the feudal days of the Tokugawa
period in Japan, and an ocean separated them, but
surprisingly enough an historical incident linked the
two.

There was a time in England, and elsewhere also,
when the magistrates had the power of sentencing a
man to penal servitude for life for trifling offences
—for stealing a loaf of bread or for poaching a rabbit
on the squire's lands. Thereafter he became a
member of chain gangs and the unfortunate associate
of the dregs of the criminal world who were deserved-
ly suffering penal servitude for more heinous crimes.
At first the American Colonies were the most convenient places to which to ship such convicts. There
they were largely used on the tobacco plantations of
Virginia, although they never proved as tractable as
the Negro slaves. Finally when the American Colonies made themselves independent, the convicts had

to be kept in England, and for a while the English jails and hulks were jammed to overflowing until someone thought of the newly discovered continent of Australia.

Eleven ships, known as the First Fleet, were sent out with the first English governor, his staff, 160 marines as guards, and 757 convicts including 192 women. After a strenuous voyage of eight weary months, during which 32 of the convicts died, they arrived at Port Jackson just two days ahead of La Perouse who came hoping to claim Australia for France. Governor Phillip landed at Sydney Cove on 26th January, 1788, and hoisted the British Flag. That day is Australia Day—Australia's birthday.

Many other shiploads of convicts arrived thereafter, and they played a big part in the construction of the early ports, towns, and roads. They worked in chain gangs. Later many were released on parole as "ticket-of-leave" men, and ultimately many were pardoned and gained their freedom.

(Our English friends even nowadays do at times jokingly utter a good-natured quip at our ancestry by some allusion to the convicts, but we Australians may always reply that those early arrivals were picked out and sent out by the best judges in England!)

From time to time some of the convicts escaped and became outlaws or bushrangers as the term was in Australia. Occasionally the bushrangers captured small vessels or the convicts effected their escape by sea and embarked on a career of piracy. And it was from one such incident that developed the historical link between the convict and bushranging days of Australia and the feudal days of Japan.

In August, 1829, the brig "Cyprus" was bound from Hobart to Macquarie Harbour in New South Wales with thirty-three convicts, a crew of twelve, a guard, and eleven women and children. En route the brig anchored in Research Bay on the coast of Tasmania, then known as Van Diemen's Land, to search for an anchor and cable that had been lost there some time previously. One evening during her stay the officer of the ship's guard and several others including the coxswain of the brig—a "ticket-of-leave" man named Popjoy—set out from the brig in a longboat to do some fishing. They had not rowed far before they heard a commotion on board the brig and realised with dismay that the convicts had captured the vessel. They later learned that some of the convicts, although heavily ironed, had rushed and overcome the captain and two sentinels, and then battened down the hatchways until the remaining soldiers and crew under deck surrendered.

Those in the longboat endeavoured to get back on board but were held at bay by the mutineers who had possessed themselves of the arms of the ship. After some bargaining the convicts agreed to hand over the women and children, all of whom together with the captain, the officer of the guard, and the disarmed soldiers were then rowed ashore by the mutineers and abandoned on a small island in the bay without any means of reaching the nearest settlement far distant on the mainland. The convicts, realising that they would need the services of the coxswain, had compelled Popjoy at the point of the musket to return on board.

They thereupon raised sail and departed, but as soon as the brig was under way, Popjoy jumped overboard and swam ashore, where he rejoined those marooned on the island. Without shelter and with nothing to eat but a few shellfish gathered off the rocks, their predicament was one of great danger. Popjoy however contrived to build a rough raft on which he put to sea in the hope of intercepting another vessel and securing help. In this he was fortunately successful and eventually all the castaways were rescued. As a reward Popjoy received a full pardon and elected to return to England.

The fate of the "Cyprus" remained a mystery for some months, but in March of the following year a ship's boat landed at Canton, in China, with four men who represented themselves as being survivors of a brig "Edward" which they stated had left London Docks bound for Rio de Janeiro and on the return voyage had called at Valparaiso, and then at Sandwich Islands, as the Hawaiian Islands were then known. Afterwards they had attempted to touch at Japan for fresh water and supplies but had been fired on by a battery and heavily damaged. Leaking badly the brig was abandoned near Formosa. The four men further claimed they were the only survivors. Although their story was received with some doubt they were sent back to England as distressed British seamen on board the "Charles Grant."

A few days after their departure another boat with three men on board arrived. They also said that they were survivors from the brig "Edward," but the account which they gave differed in so many details from that of the former arrivals, that the original suspicions of the Consular Authorities were revived and the three were sent home under arrest on the ship "Killie Castle," which reached London before the "Charles Grant." When the "Charles Grant" arrived the four on board were promptly arrested. All seven were subsequently tried for piracy at the Admiralty Court and five, one of whom had been a bushranger, were hanged. The principal witness was Popjoy.

The only part of the story told by the convicts, when they arrived at Canton, which was true was their description of the reception they received in Japan. It was the year 1830, during that period of about 215 years extending from 1637 to 1853 when the Tokugawa Shogunate had decreed that Japan should seclude herself from all nations.

In 1637 Iyemitsu, the third of the Tokugawa Shoguns had ordered that all vessels of seagoing capacity should be destroyed, and that no craft should henceforth be built of sufficient size to venture beyond home waters. It was also ordered that no Japanese subject should leave Japan, or if rash enough to do so should never return.

In addition the warning was issued that:

> *So long as the sun warms the earth, let no Christian be so bold as to come to Japan, and let all know that....if even the very God of the Christians, or the great Shaka (Buddha) contravene this prohibition, they shall pay for it with their heads.*

The Mutiny of the "Cyprus"

Only the Dutch merchants were allowed to stay, cooped up on Deshima in Nagasaki harbour, and only Dutch vessels were allowed to come into the port of Nagasaki. The conditions imposed were arduous but the Dutch thought them worth while for the sake of the trade monopoly that they enjoyed.

All other vessels that came near Japan—and the brig "Cyprus" was one—were given the roughest reception that the authorities and the shore batteries considered it expedient to hand out.

While it is certain that Japan suffered an immeasurable loss by cutting herself off from the Western civilization and learning, it is equally certain that she lost nothing by driving away the "Cyprus" and her crew of desperate criminals.

THE PRESIDENT'S LETTER

The Lord Shogun of Japan is notorious and well known in our country.
KING JAMES I of England, 1613

During the time that U.S. Consul-General Townsend Harris was kicking his heels in Shimoda, making caustic entries in his diary, and having what he termed "flare-ups" with the Japanese authorities, he was reading up on Japan from all sources available to him and endeavouring to learn something of the country in which he was hidden away in an unimportant corner, living in a temple in a fishing village on the outskirts of that backwash port of Shimoda.

He read up Dr. Kaempfer's accounts of Japan written about 160 years earlier and thus learned of all that was to be seen on the great highways of the land, long before he travelled over them, only to find when he did ultimately pass along the Tokaido, it was on such a conducted tour that the sights did not resemble in the least the detailed accounts given by Kaempfer.

It will be recalled that following the treaties negotiated with the Japanese in 1854 by Commodore Perry on behalf of the United States, similar treaties were signed by Britain, Russia and Holland during the following two years. Then in August 1856, Townsend Harris was dumped by an American warship at Shimoda as the first United States Consul-General or resident envoy in Japan, and there he raised the first consular flag ever seen in Japan. He had with him a certain quantity of stores, presents, and a letter from President Pierce of the United States addressed to His Majesty the Emperor of Japan. His instructions were to conclude with the Japanese a treaty of amity and commerce. This he succeeded in doing after months of patience and perseverance, of determination and courage, and without the backing of any display of force. But over two years were to elapse before the letter could be delivered and by then Pierce had been succeeded by James Buchanan as President of the United States.

Harris on arrival at Shimoda was accompanied by a secretary and interpreter, a young Hollander, Henry C. J. Heusken, and by two Chinese servants, one a cook, the other a tailor. Because the Dutch language was the only European language of which the Japanese knew anything, the Dutch interpreter was essential. But Heusken was able to make himself better understood with some of the local wenches with whom he had many an affair, than with the official Japanese interpreters who used a mercantile patois or pidgin Dutch that had been the *lingua franca* in Nagasaki for two hundred years. This unfortunate young man was one of many Europeans who during the following years was hacked to death by the swords of assassins.

From the first day of arrival Harris was subject to what he referred to as *"the wearing down process"* which proved to be a severe strain on his nerves and on his health. Nevertheless he pursued his set course with a firm determination refusing to compromise on principles. The effect on his health was such that within six months he had lost 40 lbs in weight. The effect on his nerves and the exasperation that this lone negotiator suffered is well illustrated by various pungent entries in his diary, of which the following are samples:

> *9 Sept., 1856.*   *I am determined to take firm ground with the Japanese. I will cordially meet any real offers of amity, but words will not do. They are the greatest liars on earth.*
>
> *11 Sept., 1856.*   *Had a flare-up with the officials who told me some egregious lies.*
>
> *21 May, 1857.*   *This is a Japanese custom,— always advance the price, but never lower it.*

Christmas Day, 1856, was a lonely day. In addition he was sick and unhappy. New Year's Day was equally unhappy and was devoted to exchanging greetings with Mr. Heusken and in paying *"my Chinese servants the customary cumshaw."* On the 8th January he had a *"stormy debate"* with the governor complaining that *"not a single Japanese came near me on New Year's Day,"* demanding that the spies and guards who surrounded his consulate be withdrawn and citing various infractions of Perry's treaty and the inhospitable treatment he personally had suffered.

Half a year later he wrote in his diary:

The President's Letter

*I am now more than ten months in Japan, and have
not as yet received a single letter from the United
States. As no direct communication is allowed by
sea between Shimoda and Hakodate by Japanese
junks, my supplies might as well be at Hong-Kong
as there. I have been out of flour, bread, butter,
lard, bacon, hams, sweet oil, and in fact out of
every kind of foreign supply for more than two
months. I am living on rice, fish, and very poor
poultry.... My health is miserable. My appetite
is gone, and I am so shrunk away that I look as
though a vice-consul had been cut out of me.*

Then on 21st August, 1857, he wrote:

One year here and not a single letter from America.

His servants then comprised *"a butler, cook and his
mate, washman, two houseboys, one water-carrier,
one sweeper, one gardener, one groom—in all ten
persons, and not one that I can do without."* In addition to difficulties with his Chinese servants he also
had other housekeeping difficulties as is evidenced
by the entry:

*The wages of my two Japanese boys are at last
settled at 6 bu per month or about 2 dollars. The
Vice-Governor last December wanted me to pay
them 16 dollars per month!*

On the subject of being consistently overcharged,
Harris has much to say in his diary, but let us pass
on.

Harris was not only given to criticism. After a
visit to the Governor, his first official call, he wrote
in his diary:

Our visit lasted nearly two hours and we were

much pleased with the appearance and manners of the Japanese. I repeat they are superior to any people east of the Cape of Good Hope.

When a new Governor was appointed he made the following entry:

The new Governor was cold and rude; not even the raw brandy, which he and others drank, seemed to warm his heart or thaw him towards us.

On another occasion Harris recorded in his diary:

They were so unreasonable and so inconsistent that I could not help suspecting the champagne which I sent to them had not operated favourably.

After about ten months discussion with the Japanese commissioners who had been sent from Yedo to negotiate with him in Shimoda, an agreement was reached on all provisions for a convention with Japan, which was duly signed on 17th June, 1857.

There was still however the matter of the delivery of the President's letter to the Emperor of Japan. The Japanese wished to receive delivery in Shimoda, whereas Harris demanded and insisted upon going to Yedo and delivering it in person to the Shogun who was then believed to be the Emperor. This presented difficulties for the Japanese, because for nearly seven hundred years the *Mikado* or actual Emperor had been kept in the strictest seclusion in Kyoto, whilst the country was administered by Shoguns or powerful military dictators or families. Indeed at certain periods the common people had lost sight of the *Mikado's* existence, so much was he overshadowed by the Shogunate.

The President's Letter

So little was known or had been heard of the *Mikado* by the Western world, that the Shogun was commonly taken to be the sovereign and thus it was to him that Harris insisted upon delivering the President's letter.

No doubt with a view to reducing the deception to a minimum the Japanese endeavoured to receive delivery of the letter in Shimoda, and even produced what they represented to be an Imperial mandate claiming that the laws of the country forbade audiences with the Emperor and authorising them to receive the letter. But still Harris remained adamant. Finally in September it was agreed that he should proceed to Yedo to be received in audience by the Shogun, or the Emperor as Harris imagined, and there present the President's letter. Many negotiations then followed as to the manner in which he should travel, the procedure to be adopted at the audience, whether he should kowtow, or "knock-head" as Harris refers to it in his diary. However on all these matters Harris had definite ideas of his own, from which he never swerved.

Much preparation was necessary. Happi-coats and other clothing bearing the coat of arms of the United States of America with the motto *E pluribus unum* had to be prepared for the bearers of the palanquin and for the porters who were to carry the luggage, bedding, food, cooking utensils, and the many presents, comprising, as the temperance organizations of America must be shocked to know, a plentiful supply of champagne, sherry, cherry brandy and other liquor, cordials, decanters, books of natural history, a telescope, barometer, astral lamps and preserved fruits.

Just before departure, Harris was informed that Shogun was not the proper appelation of the ruler of Japan but that it was *Tai-kun* (Tycoon)—a matter of considerable surprise to Harris considering that for more that a year he had been talking to the Japanese negotiators and writing about the Shogun. But greater surprises were yet to come.

The procession finally got under way and started out from Shimoda on 23rd November, 1857. The whole train including the many Japanese officials and their retinue numbered over 150 persons. Harris finding riding in a palanquin far too cramped and painful, both he and Heusken rode on horseback preceded by the American flag. All packages of luggage were covered with black cotton cloth, bearing the arms of the United States.

Harris recalled Kaempfer's description of the highways of Japan and especially of the Tokaido and looked forward to seeing the bustle of life and the throng of travellers along what must then have been one of the busiest and most picturesque highways of the world. At the historic barrier, or check point, in Hakone village he refused as a diplomatic representative to submit to a search, or even to permit, as was then suggested, a token search of his empty palanquin, and he threatened to return to Shimoda if the Japanese inspectors persisted in making a search. The procession was thereupon permitted to pass.

The great Tokaido road had been cleared of all

traffic, even the surface had been swept. The travellers, priests, pilgrims, nuns, beggars, teahouse touts and mountebanks had disappeared. The houses and shops, other than teahouses and eating stalls, were closed; and the people, dressed in their best clothes, were collected in front of their houses sitting silent and motionless on the ground as he passed. The cross roads and the paths leading into the Tokaido had been closed with straw ropes. It was a conducted tour, much as the Emperor is given these days. The journey occupied seven days and Harris finally entered Yedo painfully riding in his palanquin. He had originally planned to make an entry on horseback. Harris relates that *"The vice-governor eagerly encouraged that idea. This excited my suspicion."* After much enquiry Harris discovered that only those of inferior rank entered Yedo on horseback or on foot. He thereupon changed his plans and entered Yedo painfully cramped in a palanquin.

In this manner Harris came to Yedo, the first foreigner ever to visit that city in a diplomatic capacity. A week later he became the first person ever to approach the Tycoon indoors wearing shoes. Harris always made it a pratice to put on clean new patent-leather shoes just before entering Japanese buildings; as the envoy of a great country he refused to slop about in stocking feet even when approaching Great Presences. Walking on *tatami* in shoes was thus for Harris no new experience. At long last he entered the audience chamber of the Shogun and on hearing the chamberlain announce in a loud voice *"Embassador Merican"* he advanced with due ceremony among the members of the Council who were *"prostrate on their faces"* and *"end on"* towards him. Thus at last the President's letter addressed to the Emperor of Japan was finally delivered to the Tycoon who graciously, but doubtless with tongue in cheek, received it.

During the several months that followed it gradually dawned on Harris that Yedo was not the Imperial capital, that the Shogun or Tycoon was not an Emperor, but that the sovereign of Japan was the *Mikado* who was hidden away in Kyoto, and that events were shaping in Japan which would eventually lead to the latter personage assuming again his rightful position. The great secret which the Yedo government had been attempting to hide from the Western Powers was gradually leaking out.

In short the patient and conscientious Townsend Harris after fifteen months of negotiation and effort had been hoodwinked and had delivered the President's letter to the wrong person!

BLACK-EYED SUSAN

The light that Lies in women's eyes.
THOMAS MOORE

This is an account of a bloody murder and of how prosperity and fame came to the proprietress of a roadside teahouse on the Tokaido, the main highway in Japan and the great artery in feudal days that connected the southwestern parts with Yedo, as Tokyo was then known.

The teahouse was between Kanagawa and Tokyo. It was one of many modest establishments set among the old pine trees that lined the Tokaido for much of its length. One of the many places where a traveller could rest for *ippuku*—one puff of the small pipes that were in use in those days—sip tea or rice wine and enjoy clams which were the specialty of the house. The pine trees can still be seen in some places, but alas, many were ruthlessly cut down when the overland telephone and telegraph lines were erected.

In feudal days the Tokaido was one of the most picturesque and colourful of the world's highways. Priests and pilgrims, porters and post boys, merchants and pedlars, mountebanks and minstrels, packhorses and palanquins, travellers wealthy and lowly were constantly passing along this narrow avenue overhung with curiously-shaped pine trees. In dry weather the road was dusty. In wet weather it was often a quagmire of mud. The foot travellers with their kimono tucked up to their thighs trudged along under the shade of the old trees, while the lords and ladies dozed in their palanquins hidden from the common gaze by fine bamboo blinds.

Occasionally runners came arrogantly announcing the approach of a *daimyo* (a military governor) with raucous cries of *Shita-ni-iro! Shita-ni-iro!*—"Down! Down on your knees!"—whereupon all those not of *samurai* rank (military class) were required to move to the side of the road, kneel, and when the palanquin of the lord passed to bow down until their foreheads touched the dust. The same order *Shita-ni-iro* was revived about eighty years later and became a familiar one, and one of sore trial, to Allied prisoners of war in Japanese hands.

* * * * * * *

One Sunday afternoon in September, 1862, an English lady from Hongkong and three Englishmen, two of whom were Yokohama residents and the third, Richardson by name, a business man from Shanghai on a visit to Japan before going home to retire, set out for a ride along the Tokaido. They left Yokohama by boat for Kanagawa, which was then separated from Yokohama across a small bay, and there joined the horses that had been sent on ahead. After leaving Kanagawa they were unfortunate enough to meet a large *daimyo* procession and particularly that of the Lord Shimazu, *Daimyo* of Satsuma, one of the proudest and most powerful governors of the land.

The foreigners' account of what followed differs in some details from the Japanese version which was released thirteen years later. According to the foreign account the party drew up their horses at the side of the road and then in compliance with signs that they should go back, they turned their horses towards Yokohama, when, without provocation, some of the retinue drew their swords and attacked them. All four were injured, but they managed to gallop through the ranks of their assailants. Richardson was most grievously wounded, his bowels protruding from sword cuts. Finally he fell from his horse. The other three were able to escape and eventually summoned help from the consulates in Kanagawa. The foreign military guard which then set out found the body of Richardson lying off the road dreadfully mangled with sword cuts and spear wounds and covered with matting.

It is stated in the official records of this case that Richardson must have fallen from his horse in a faint and that when he came to he was able to drag himself to the bank at the side of the road where he called for water, but that none of the spectators or those passing by dared offer him a drink. Finally his throat was cut by some of Satsuma's men, mercifully, we hope. A post-mortem examination revealed that he had suffered ten wounds any one of which could have been fatal.

The verdict of the court of inquest was:

> *that the deceased Charles Lenox Richardson was feloniously wilfully and of malice aforethought killed and murdered by certain Japanese armed with swords, lances and other arms after the fashion of their country....*

This verdict was challenged some thirteen years

later when a pamphlet written by an American was published which purported to give the Satsuma version of the incident, wherein it was alleged that the party of foreigners had given offence by disregarding the customs of the country in not dismounting while the procession passed, that Richardson had recklessly pushed his horse in and out of the groups forming the cortege, and had continued to hold the centre of the road even when the palanquin of the Lord Shimazu approached.

In this article we are interested not in apportioning the blame for a most unhappy affair, but rather in a young woman with black and lustrous eyes.

Following the murder a story circulated that when Richardson called for water a young woman who conducted a small roadside teahouse nearby brought him the drink that he so desperately needed. However, her own evidence which had been given before the British Consul, who conducted an inquiry, completely disproved the story, but that did not prevent the legend from growing. To Black-Eyed Susan—the name by which the young woman came to be familiarly known—was given the credit for mercifully tending Richardson when all others passed him by.

Thereafter her business prospered immensely and few foreigners passed along the Tokaido without stopping for refreshments at her house. The four-horse coaches, known as the "Yedo Mail," which left Yokohama in the morning for the Foreign Settlement at Tsukiji in Tokyo, and which returned to Yokohama in the evening, always stopped at Black-Eyed Susan's which had then become quite famous for its clams.

With the passing of the years the myth grew, assisted not a little by Black-Eyed Susan herself, who had grown more garrulous and would describe to her customers in vivid and imaginative detail how she had tended the stricken Richardson and quenched his thirst during his last few minutes upon this earth. Finally a time came when she was no longer seen dispensing clams in her teahouse. Presumably she had moved on to the realms to which Richardson had passed many years before.

But the name of Black-Eyed Susan had caught the imagination of the foreign community in Yokohama —the legend lived—and as the years went by that same name came to be bestowed upon numerous other young ladies in other establishments, some less reputable, all of whom came to enjoy the patronage that went to those who bore that name, and so could reap the benefit of the goodwill that accrued from the handing of a mythical cup of water to a dying man.

MURDER NEAR THE DAIBUTSU

The criminal kneeles downe on his knees and then comes the Executioner behind him and cuts off his head with a Catan.—Letter by Rev. ARTHUR HATCH, 1623

Shimizu Seiji was a brave man and a patriot of sorts. Unfortunately disappointments and frustrations had so embittered him that whatever virtues he possessed were not exercised to the benefit of his country. Tragically he opposed the policy of his country by resorting to a cold-blooded and cowardly murder and in so doing allied himself with a craven wight named Mamiya Hajime.

It happened in November, 1864. An English regiment, the 20th Foot, was then stationed in barracks on the Bluff at Yokohama as guards for the Yokohama Foreign Settlement. Two of the officers, Major Baldwin and Lieutenant Bird had gone on a sightseeing trip on horseback to Enoshima and then to Kamakura. After visiting the Daibutsu they turned into the pine avenue that runs towards the sea shore. There they were suddenly attacked by two *ronin*. Details of the murder were provided by several Japanese witnesses—the principal being a boy of twelve —and written confessions subsequently taken by the Japanese police from the murderers.

Murder Near the Daibutsu

Yokohama had been opened to foreign trade for five years. Japan was emerging from a feudal age. The structure of government and the customs of the country were rapidly changing. Shimizu Seiji, although twenty-five years of age and the son of a samurai, could find no lord who needed his services. Sadly he hid his two swords and became a labourer. He resented the opening of the country to foreigners and he resolved to kill as many as he could. He thereupon joined forces with another masterless samurai—a *ronin*—as poor and as unhappy as himself. After borrowing some money and buying new clothes, they set out together for Yokohama each wearing their two swords. Finding the Settlement too well guarded and with few opportunities for a surprise attack, they moved on to Kamakura with the intention of ambushing the first foreigners who came their way.

Whilst waiting in the pine avenue they shouted roughly at a Japanese boy loitering nearby ordering him to go away. The boy hastily scrambled over a nearby embankment and hid in the bushes, thereby becoming a witness to what followed.

Two foreign horsemen were seen approaching from the Daibutsu; Baldwin was ahead followed at a distance of about ten yards by Bird. The two *ronin* hiding behind a large pine tree, slashed at Baldwin as he came level with the tree. The unfortunate officer fell from his horse whereupon they attacked Bird. The boy then saw Baldwin, bloodstained and holding a revolver, rise and totter towards the embankment, but the precise sequence of the subsequent happenings could not be ascertained for certain and remains a mystery.

The evidence of other Japanese witnesses indicated that the two unfortunate officers had lived for some time after the attack and had spoken to each other; yet the post-mortem examination made by an English doctor showed that, in addition to terrible cuts on his arms and legs, Bird's head was almost severed from his body and that he could not have lived for a moment after receiving that wound. It was therefore supposed by some that Baldwin had died first and that Bird was later despatched by the *ronin*, or other miscreants, in order to remove him as a witness. Whether this was actually so was never ascertained and remains in doubt.

The Japanese police spared no effort in the hunt for the murderers, a sharp watch in particular being maintained in the notorious teahouses of Shinagawa. A few weeks later the landlord of one of those houses reported to the police that he suspected one of the wanted men was in his house. Shimizu Seiji was thereupon immediately arrested and under threat of torture made a full confession. The sentence that was subsequently passed by the Japanese Court read:

In consideration of the enormity of the crime of which he is guilty, Seiji is to be brought to Yokohama and after he has been led around the principal streets of the town on horseback, so that he may be seen by all, he is to be beheaded with a sword on the public execution ground.

When conducted through Yokohama on the day of his execution, Seiji sat firmly in the saddle and

showed no signs of fear. On four or five occasions
he harangued the crowd:

> ....*I am a ronin....I am to die merely because
> I cut down foreigners....These are indeed bad
> times for Japan when a samurai must die merely
> because he cut down a barbarian. This evening my
> head will fall into the pit....You will then look
> upon a face that knew not fear even in death....
> The death of a common criminal awaits me....Men
> of Yokohama, tell the patriots of Japan that the
> ronin Seiji did not tremble in the face of death.*

At the execution site he walked proudly and steadily
to where the executioner awaited him. He adjusted
the mat upon which he should kneel so that his head
might better fall into the pit. He loosened his kimono to better expose his neck for the fatal blow.
He enquired whether the executioner was well prepared and directed that the sword be wetted with hot
water that it might cut well. He made a final speech
of defiance against all foreigners, then stretching out
his neck he gave in a clear voice the final word to
the executioner that he was ready to die: *"Yoi."*

The gory head was exhibited on a pike for two
days at the entrance to Yokohama.

Not so did his craven accomplice die. Mamiya,
fortified with drink, was dragged drunk and babbling
to the execution pit. There whimpering he attempted
to run away. He had to be forced to the ground
where he was slaughtered.

* * * * * * * * *

In a shady grove in the old section of the Yokohama Foreign Cemetery there are two old lichen-

covered tombstones sacred to the memory of Major
Geo. W. Baldwin and Lieut. Robert N. Bird of H.B.M.
II Batt., XX Regt. According to the inscription these
men were:

> *Cruelly assassinated by*
> *Japanese at Kamakura*
> *Nov. 21, 1864*
> *When returning from*
> *DIEBOOTS*
> *to*
> *YOKOHAMA*

* * * * * * * *

It is a well-known fact to all who live near the pine
avenue at Kamakura that a strange murmuring can
be heard there almost any evening. To me it seems
to be the evening breeze stirring among the pine
branches, but the present-day residents who have
heard it more often, and are therefore in a better
position to form an opinion, say that it sounds like
whisperings in some foreign tongue, but beyond that
they seem to have no clear idea of what it is.

The story of the murder of Major Baldwin and
Lieutenant Bird is probably unknown to almost all
the present day residents of Kamakura. But there
was a time many years ago when some of the oldest
Japanese residents in those parts told me that on
certain evenings, if you went out alone and sat quietly
in the pine avenue, you could hear the faint whisperings and groans of the English officers, the approach
of footsteps, followed immediately by an agonized cry,
retreating footsteps, then silence.

SOME
CHRISTMAS
DAYS
OF
LONG
AGO

> *I am a man not unknown in Rat-cliffe and Limehouse.*
>
> WILL ADAMS, 1611

As each Christmas comes around it is customary for most of us to look back on past Christmases that linger in our memory, of Christmas festivities in which we personally participated or of those in other times and climes as depicted on our Christmas cards or recorded in the pages of history.

The first Christmas celebration in Japan was by the Portuguese in about the middle of the sixteenth century, and the observance of those Christmas services was described by several Jesuit priests writing from Japan around that time. During the next fifty-five years or so, until Christianity was outlawed from Japan, such Christmas services and observances were regularly and publicly held. Thereafter all such Christian services were carried out in great secrecy.

Many Christmases have passed since Will Adams, the English pilot and the first Englishman to come to Japan, ate his first Christmas dinner in Japan. That was in 1600.

Some Christmas Days of Long Ago

Will Adams died in Japan twenty years later. Some of those Christmases were spent in the company of his friends in the Dutch trading house at Hirado, some at the table of his English associates in the English House also at Hirado, some at his home in Nihonbashi, Tokyo, with his Japanese wife and child, some at his country estate near Yokosuka, and some at sea.

The Christmas dinners in Hirado comprised an abundant spread of soup, fish, shellfish, venison, "wilde-fowle, wilde-Boare, the largest and fattest that ever any of us had seene," "pickeld Herbes, Beanes, Raddishes and other Roots," chestnuts, walnuts and fruit in abundance. In addition there were conserves and other delicacies obtained from the Chinese merchants in Nagasaki. There was Japanese *sake*, and at times, but not always, brandy and Continental wines.

(As holly without berries has little appeal at Christmas, it is interesting to speculate whether the idea of wiring *nanten* (*nandina domestica*) berries onto Japanese holly branches was first thought of at those early Christmas celebrations or whether it was invented by enterprising Japanese florists two and a half centuries later.)

The first attempt by the English to trade with Japan was made by the English East India Company and was a failure. For ten years from 1613 to 1623 the Cross of St. George flew over the English House at Hirado in Kyushu and during that time Richard Cocks, the Head Merchant, made a number of business trips through the Inland Sea to Osaka or rather

"Osackay" as he quaintly spelled the name. Such journeys to Osaka were not without serious dangers; the junks frequently stranded on the shoals which at that time formed a dangerous bar across the entrance to Osaka. Cocks described one such entry:

> ....*As we passed the flattes of Osackay, we were on grownd divers tymes, yet, God be praised, we gott well offe againe, and arrived at Osackay at 3 a clock in thafter nowne; but at the same place saw one bark cast away, laden with stones for the making of the castell, but all the people saved....*

Similar journeys were made by the Dutch merchants and were likewise described in detail, especially by Engelbert Kaempfer, the German doctor at the Dutch House at Nagasaki at a somewhat later date, references being made to *Taromi, Sijwoja, Summa* and *Fiogo,* which curious spellings some readers may recognize as being for Tarumi, Shioya, Suma and Hyogo.

During one such trip in December, 1618, Cocks was hopeful of reaching Osaka on Christmas Day, but meeting with adverse winds was compelled to spend Christmas Day in Hyogo. He relates in his diary that he gave rice and fish *"to all our barkmen to dyner this day with a barso of wine in respect of Christmas Day."*

Not unlikely his own Christmas dinner was taken ashore also in Japanese style; in any case it was in all probability the first occasion on which an Englishman had partaken of Christmas dinner in Hyogo, or Kobe as we know it to-day.

Not unlikely also Cocks went for a walk that

Christmas Day under the pine trees on the fine sandy shore which then stretched from where the Hyogo wharves are to-day through what is now the Mitsubishi Dockyard, and around past Wada Point.

After the English East India Company closed their trading post in Hirado the Dutch had the field almost to themselves. Then when Japan interdicted Christianity and slammed shut her doors in the face of the world, the Dutch were cooped up in the little island of Deshima in Nagasaki harbour where for over two hundred years they ate their Christmas dinners, and celebrated Christmas as best they might without Christian observances, unless in secret. In the matter of food, drink, and such other comforts as they required, the Dutch did not do too badly. The domestic market of Nagasaki supplied their wants. There was a rich variety of food, for which they were charged especially high prices, added to which there were some opportunities for smuggling schnapps and other liquor from the Dutch trading ships, quite apart from the regular supplies which they were permitted to bring in.

There was however a thin period of four years from 1809 to 1813 when, owing to the war in Europe, the Dutch flag was largely driven from the seas and no ships whatever arrived from Batavia. To replace their shoes which wore out, they improvised shoes from Japanese straw sandals covered with undressed leather and they converted old carpets into clothing. For liquor they attempted to distil gin and corn spirit, to brew beer, and to make wine from wild grapes, but not with much success. For several Christmas dinners all they had in the way of alcoholic drinks was a gin that tasted of resinous juniper, a corn whisky that was passing good, a beer that only kept four days, and a murky fermented liquor which they all agreed was not wine.

* * * * * * * *

Townsend Harris, the first U.S. Consul-General to Japan eventually celebrated many Christmas days in Japan, but the first in 1856, before Japan had been opened to foreign trade was a lonely and unhappy one, and was spent in Shimoda. The only foreign company he had was his young Dutch interpreter. On that day he made the following entry in his diary.

Merry Christmas! How happy are those who live in lands where those joyous greetings can be exchanged! As for me, I am sick and solitary, living, as one may say, in a prison; a large one it is true but still a prison.

* * * * * * *

After the English House withdrew from Japan in 1623, which was just about the time that the Pilgrim Fathers had established themselves in America, no other Christmas Days were spent in Hyogo or in Kobe by Englishmen until the sad Christmas Day of 1867.

About six British and five American men-of-war were then gathered off Hyogo in preparation for the opening of the port to take place on New Year's Day.

An officer, Lieutenant Turnor of the British flagship H.M.S. "Rodney," had died of heart disease a few days before, and Asst. Surgeon Charles H. Page of the U.S. Navy had died of consumption on board

U.S.S. "Hartford" on the previous day. By arrangement with the Japanese authorities a plot of land near the mouth of the old Ikuta River was set apart as a cemetery and there on Christmas Day, 1867, two naval burials took place. The dead thus preceded the living in the foreign settlement of Kobe.

* * * * * * * *

Nearly 1200 years ago Kukai, a Buddhist priest, later known as Kobo Daishi, the most famous of all the Japanese Buddhist saints, twice visited the mountains behind Kobe thereby giving the name of Futatabi—signifying twice visited—to that mountain. He was searching for a suitable location on which to found a monastery, but decided against the Kobe Hills because of their restricted area. It was at Koyasan across the bay near the edge of Yamato province that he founded the great monastery. There his last years in a life of incredible toil were spent, and there he was buried, or rather—according to popular belief—it is there that he remains in a vaulted tomb awaiting the coming of Miroku, the Buddhist Messiah.

It was to those same hills behind Futatabi which Kobo Daishi twice visited, that the graves of the old foreign cemetery were recently transferred. There in the front plot of the new cemetery visitors may see the tombstones of the English naval lieutenant and the American naval surgeon, the first foreigners to be buried in Kobe—on that sad Christmas Day of ninety years ago. The inscription on the tombstone of the American surgeon can still be plainly read but the engraving on the tombstone of the English lieutenant has almost weathered away and little but the name can now be seen.

This place where once walked a Buddhist saint is a delightful spot, surrounded by wooded hills rich in historical associations. Close by is a picturesque temple in a setting of maple trees.

It is there that the new Foreign Cemetery is located. The international spirit that pervades that lovely spot, the wooded hills, the temple grounds and the inscriptions on the old gravestones seem to breathe in all truth the Christmas message of nearly two thousand years ago—PEACE ON EARTH AND GOODWILL TOWARD MEN.

HARA-KIRI
IN
KOBE

> *I saw one...who went so resolutely*
> *...that I could not but much admire,*
> *never having seen the like in Chris-*
> *tendome.*
>
> Capt. SARIS' Diary, 1613

If one stands outside the Daimaru Department Store in Kobe, it is impossible to fail to note the scurrying people and an occasional sound like gunfire, from the backfiring of a motorcycle.

Eighty-seven years ago at about that spot there was a scene of scurrying people and a sound of gunfire that echoed across the Settlement. As a consequence a very unfortunate man was ordered to die.

* * * * * * *

On 4th February, 1868, less than two months after the port of Kobe had been opened, a party of soldiers of the Lord Bizen, *Daimyo* of Okayama, landed from junks at Hyogo en route to Osaka to join the Imperialist forces which were gathering against the Tokugawa clan. It was the Tokugawa government that had made terms with the foreigners, and had opened the gates of Japan which had been closed for nearly two hundred and fifty years. The Tokugawa clan had thus permitted the foreigners to enter Japan, and as that clan was now in the process of being overthrown, these men from Bizen were looking to the time when the foreigners also would be thrown out.

The road to Osaka from Hyogo passed along Moto-machi, then along the north side of the Foreign Concession, where to-day the electric tram-line runs in front of the Daimaru Department Store. *Daimyo* processions from the southwest were under orders to bypass Kobe by travelling inland near Akashi along the newly-constructed Tokugawa Road. The Bizen party having landed at Hyogo had no option but to pass through Kobe. In any case they may not have been disposed to obey the Tokugawa edicts. As the advance party of about 150 men passed along the road the rough order *Shita ni iro! Shita ni iro!* —"Down on your knees"—was shouted as customarily at the onlookers, whereupon all not of military rank were required to kneel down and bow low until their heads touched the dust.

The few foreigners gathered on the edge of the Concession refused to bow down, whereupon an American was attacked by one of the samurai, but succeeded in escaping. The procession was as usual long strung out and did not proceed in close formation. When two French marines crossed the line of the procession the Bizen samurai were so infuriated that the order was given to cut them down. Fortunately they too escaped, although one suffered a slight wound. It was then that Taki Zenzaburo, an officer of the advance guard, gave the order to open fire. Shots echoed across the Settlement as they fired on every foreigner in sight, but their marksmanship was so bad that they only succeeded in nicking one American

107

sailor. It was said that they had just been issued with newly imported rifles, the sights of which had not been adjusted. At any rate the bullets went whistling overhead and most fell splashing into the sea.

Sir Harry Parkes, the British Minister, hurriedly turned out the Legation guard, and putting himself at the head of an armed escort galloped after the Bizen men. A substantial body of British sailors and a force of American marines were quickly landed from men-of-war in the harbour and joined in the chase, whilst a party of French marines crossed into the fields beyond Ikuta Temple, in the hope of cutting off the samurai from the hills.

The Bizen soldiers made one stand, but after firing upon the advancing foreign force they retreated in disorder towards Kumochi and Rokko, scattering their impedimenta as they ran. Several hours later the foreign soldiers and marines returned to the Concession, having expended much ammunition but without taking a single prisoner, other than an old coolie too decrepit to run fast. Many of the men however were laden down with trophies. The shooting on both sides was apparently wild, because not a single Japanese soldier appears to have been hit, nor did they succeed in hitting any of their attackers. The only casualty was an old woman who was accidentally wounded in the leg.

By the time the foreign troops got back to the Concession, they found it in a state of siege and wild excitement. Over five hundred English, French and American sailors and marines had been landed from the men-of-war in the harbour. Pickets guarded all parts of the Concession and town where foreigners resided. Earthworks had been thrown up and two twenty-four-pound howitzers guarded the main road from Hyogo. The British Consulate was protected by two Armstrong guns, and the Americans had constructed sandbag earthworks and placed guards with fieldpieces at each of the gates to the Concession. All Japanese steamers in the port of Hyogo had been seized and were being held as hostages.

Three days later word came from the *Mikado* in Kyoto that the treaty engagements entered into by the Tokugawa Shogunate with the Foreign Powers would be honoured and that foreigners would be protected. The foreign representatives thereupon released the ships, returned their forces to the men-of-war and brought the state of seige to an end.

While at this late date some portions of these happenings may have the appearance of a Gilbert and Sullivan farce, it must be remembered that Japan was then passing through a state, as she has on several other occasions, when an attempt was being made by opposition elements to govern by assassination. A Japanese Minister of State and a U.S. Legation official had been assassinated. The British Legation in Tokyo had been attacked and fired and many foreigners had been murdered. The fear was that an attack such as the Bizen men made could develop into a massacre of foreigners.

The risks of assassination did in fact continue to be very real ones for foreigners until in March, 1868, the *Mikado* issued a decree reading:

Hara-Kiri in Kobe

*...All persons in future guilty of murdering for-
eigners or of committing any acts of violence towards them will be not only acting in opposition
to Our express orders but also...Such offenders
shall be punished in proportion to the gravity of
the crime, their names if they be samurai being
erased from the roll and...*

But let us return to the happenings in Kobe. The
Japanese authorities took a serious view of the attack
on the Settlement and soon after an instruction was
issued, although perhaps reluctantly, in the name of
the *Mikado* that the officer who had given the order
to fire upon the foreigners should commit hara-kiri
in the presence of witnesses of the seven foreign
legations in Kobe. The ceremony took place at 10:30
at night in the Eifukuji Temple in Hyogo, then the
headquarters of the Imperial troops, in the presence
of the Governor of Hyogo Prefecture, other high
Japanese officials and the representatives of the foreign legations.

*I, and I alone, unwarrantably gave the order to fire
on the foreigners at Kobe, and again when they
tried to escape. For this crime, I disembowel myself, and I beg you, who are present, to do me the
honour of witnessing the act.*

Thus spoke the unfortunate Taki Zenzaburo. Then
with calm dignity and great courage he bowed to the
assemblage and allowed his garments to fall from his
shoulders, the better to expose his neck.

*Deliberately, with a steady hand, he took the dirk
that lay before him; he looked at it wistfully, almost affectionately; for a moment he seemed to*

collect his thoughts for the last time, and then stabbing himself deeply below the waist on the left-hand side, he drew the dirk slowly across to the right side, and, turning it in the wound, gave a slight cut upwards. During this sickeningly painful operation he never moved a muscle of his face. When he drew out the dirk he leaned forward and stretched out his neck; an expression of pain for the first time crossed his face, but he uttered no sound. At that moment the kaishaku, who, still crouching by his side, had been keenly watching his every movement, sprang to his feet, poised his sword for a second in the air; there was a flash, a heavy, ugly thud, a crashing fall; with one blow the head had been severed from the body.*

In those words A.B. Mitford of the British Legation described the ceremony, and in that manner died the brave but impetuous Taki Zenzaburo.

* * * * * * *

The Eifukuji Temple where this drama occurred was located in the oldest section of Hyogo. During World War II the great bronze Buddha of Hyogo and many other Buddhist statues were torn down to be turned into munitions of war, whereupon, it is said by some, that the Gods deserted Kobe, and being unprotected the city suffered terrible damage when the B-29s poured down their bombs. However that might be, it is a fact that the ancient Hyogo section suffered immense damage and many historical spots were wiped out for all time, including the Eifukuji Temple.

* *Tales of Old Japan*, by Lord Redesdale, MacMillan & Co., Ltd.

Hara-Kiri in Kobe

Two years ago we visited the site of that temple to say a prayer for the soul of brave Taki Zenzaburo. It was the anniversary day of his death. Noisome heaps of rubbish and old packing cases then littered the ground upon which once gushed the blood from his severed neck. A philopon addict was drowsing alongside his tomb.

A few days ago on re-visiting that area we had difficulty in locating the site. The land on which the Eifukuji Temple once stood had been sold. Factories had sprung up where previously we had found squalor and ruin. A high palisade had been erected by the new owners of the land, and the tomb is no longer visible from the street, but on penetrating behind the palisade we found that the tomb is being well preserved. The ground about it had been cleared and the customary offerings of flowers and greenery had been placed before it. The new owners of that land seemingly are doing everything possible to ensure that the once anguished spirit of the ill-fated Taki Zenzaburo may rest in peace.

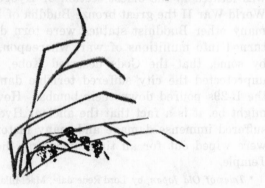

THE SAKAI MASSACRE

> *Right over against Osaca, on the
> other side of the River, lyeth another
> great Towne called Sacay, but not
> so bigge as Osaca, yet it is a Towne
> of great Trade for all the Ilands
> thereabout.*
>
> Capt. SARIS' Diary, 1613

In the previous chapter entitled "Hara-kiri in Kobe," an account was given of the attack made upon the Kobe Foreign Concession, for which the officer responsible, Taki Zenzaburo, was required to commit hara-kiri.

It will be recalled that the affair was precipitated by two French marines crossing the line of a Japanese procession—a senseless act and one probably carried out with insolence and in ignorance of the affront that was being given to persons of dignity. The attack upon the Foreign Concession that followed was treated very seriously by the foreign Ministers in Japan, who, fearing an extension of the assassinations and violence against foreigners, demanded of the Government that the officer responsible for the attack be punished. By order of the Mikado, as the Emperor was then known to the Western world, Taki Zenzaburo was required to commit hara-kiri. It needed but a hint or request from the foreign Ministers that such an extreme penalty was not required, for Taki Zenzaburo to receive some lesser punishment. Such request was not forthcoming, even though there were some who felt that something less than death would have fitted the crime.

The *Japan Times Overland Mail* of February, 1868, referred to the death of Taki Zenzaburo as "a foul deed." It charged that he had been "judicially murdered," and said:

No great harm was done by the attack on the Kobe Concession. No life was lost and the summary punishment of the two Frenchmen and a reprimand from the Government to the Bizen officer, with the offer of an apology, and a few hundred dollars as a salve for the two wounded men's hurts should have settled the question.

It then added in a prophetic vein:

But our representatives would be satisfied with nothing but blood and the creation of a vendetta between their victim's retainers and foreigners, which nothing but some European's life will satisfy.

As the *Japan Times* was known to be receiving support from the Japanese Government, its views were always under suspicion of being inspired.

Unhappily a few days later that prophecy seemed to come true, with the massacre of eleven Frenchmen at Sakai near Osaka. Whether that massacre was an act of revenge for the death of Taki Zenzaburo a few days before, or whether it was just a coincidence that Frenchmen were involved in both affairs, has never been known. Certainly different clans were responsible for each affair, which, it might be argued, indicated that a coincidence and not a vendetta existed.

It was Sunday, 8th March, 1868. The French vice-consul at Kobe and the commander of a French corvette had visited Osaka and were walking from Osaka to Sakai there to embark on a launch which had been sent by the French war vessel "Dupleix" to take them back to Kobe. They were being escorted by four Japanese, two of whom were Osaka officials.

At Sumiyoshi, which lies about half way between Osaka and Sakai, they were stopped by armed men of the Tosa clan who compelled them to return to Osaka. In the meantime the launch was waiting for them alongside the jetty at Sakai. Some of the crew were on the jetty talking with Japanese children to whom they had given some bread, others were strolling on the shore nearby. Never has it been suggested by either side that the Frenchmen did anything that might have provoked anger against them. Nevertheless they were suddenly attacked by a large body of Tosa men who fired upon them at close range. Some of the Frenchmen jumped into the sea when the attack commenced, but all, with one exception, were killed outright or fearfully wounded by the large ball bullets of those days. Those who were wounded died later. The only survivor was the engineer who had jumped overboard, and hid between the launch and other vessels nearby.

This terrible news reached the French Minister in Osaka when he was entertaining a number of Government officials. Rising from the table in intense anger he demanded the delivery of the bodies of the

murdered men within twenty-four hours, struck his
flag in Osaka, and returned to Kobe on the "Dupleix."

Two Japanese Ministers called upon the French
Minister to express their regrets, but until such time
as the bodies were returned he refused to see them.

The *Japan Weekly Mail,* fourteen years later, published translations of extracts from *"The Diary of a
Japanese Gentleman"* from which the following has
been taken:

> ....*meanwhile the fishermen of Sakai were or-
> dered to search for the bodies of the Frenchmen
> who had been killed in the sea. A reward of Yen
> 30 was offered by the local Government for each
> corpse returned. Hundreds of fishermen were soon
> engaged in the search and by 9 p.m. all bodies had
> been found.*

On Tuesday, the second day after the massacre,
the bodies were brought to Kobe by sea for delivery
to the French, but, as the result of a curious and most
unhappy blunder, the boxes containing the corpses
were delivered to the British transport "Adventur-
ous" where they were received on board and stowed
away in the mistaken belief that they contained curios
from the British Legation. It was not until late in
the afternoon that the error was discovered, after
which the coffins were conveyed to the French flagship with proper ceremony.

The funeral took place the following morning in
the old Ono-hama Cemetery of Kobe, and was attended by well-nigh all the residents of the Concession and large contingents from all foreign vessels
in the port. Although Kobe had been opened less

than three months, the desolate and wind-swept little cemetery close to the sea, and near what was then the mouth of the Ikuta River, was already dotted with many graves.

The following is a published translation of the French Minister's funeral oration:

You have been treacherously massacred without provocation and while doing your duty in your country's service.

Had your chiefs yielded to the first impulse of their affection for you, your death would have been immediately avenged by the complete destruction of a city and of thousands of its inhabitants. But they had the self-control to repress their first impulse; they recognised the fact that France should reply to such an act of barbarity as your murder by giving a proof of civilization.

But, though delayed, reparation will be more just and shall not be the less full.

I swear to you in the name of France and of the Emperor, whose noble children you are, that your death shall be avenged in such a way as to give us the hope that your comrades and your fellow-citizens shall be for the future safe from such atrocity as that of which you have been the innocent victims.

You are now near God. Pray to him to help us in our difficult task.

Following the funeral the French Minister demanded of the Japanese Government:

(a) The public execution of the guilty men, leaving the Japanese Government to determine the number, but specifying that the officer in command be included.

(b)   An apology to be made on the deck of the "Dupleix."

(c)   Payment of an indemnity of $150,000 for the benefit of the relatives of the murdered men.

(d)   Exclusion of Tosa men from all treaty ports.

The new Imperial Government was now gravely aware of the growing danger in these increasing acts of violence against foreigners, which violence had been born of their own earlier teachings that the presence of foreigners polluted the soil of Japan. Whilst the leaders of the Government had preached that doctrine a few years earlier, in their crusade of opposition to the Tokugawa Shogunate for opening Japan to the West, it was now evident to them that the situation was getting out of hand. The Imperial Government now hoped that they could reverse the doctrine of hate. All the French demands were therefore readily accepted. The French war vessels moved up the bay to Sakai, and the commander and a contingent of men proceeded ashore to the execution site nominated by the Japanese authorities, which was at the Myokokuji Temple about a mile distant from the place of the massacre.

Robert Louis Stevenson in his bizarre story, "The Suicide Club," describes the tense excitement amongst a group of men—members of the Suicide Club—when they gathered together, each waiting to learn whether Fate would decide that he should die that night.

Possibly the same emotions were being experienced by some of the twenty men whom the Japanese authorities had brought for execution. It had been left to the Japanese authorities to determine the number, and so not unnaturally an impression existed that the French might be satisfied with a lesser number than twenty. The first to be executed were the two officers. It is said that when the turn came for the men to commit hara-kiri, they contended among themselves for the privilege of being the next to follow. And it is said that each, with his last breath, prophesied woe and vengeance against the French.

The sickening ceremony proceeded, as each in turn first used his short sword against himself. When the eleventh head had been severed from the body and fell thumping onto the ground, the French commander intervened and asked that the remainder be pardoned. The Japanese officer in command replied that he could not accede to such a request without written permission from the French Minister, who at that time was on board a French warship three miles off shore. A painful delay ensued, until a written request for the suspension of the executions could be obtained from the French Minister. The nine survivors were then led away and were subsequently reprieved by the Emperor.

The *Japan Times Overland Mail* of the time saw in this act of clemency a possible termination to the blood feud which that paper professed to believe arose out of the death of Taki Zenzaburo, and so indeed it may have been because the Sakai Massacre marked the end of a long succession of such evil deeds of violence.

The Sakai Massacre

Sir Ernest Satow the veteran British diplomat in Japan was not so confident of the wisdom of such clemency. He wrote in his memoirs:

Twenty were condemned to death, and one can only regret that the French Commander judged it necessary to stop the execution when eleven had suffered, for the twenty were all equally guilty, and requiring a life for a life of the eleven Frenchmen looked more like revenge than justice.

In 1952, the Ono Foreign Cemetery, where the eleven Frenchmen were buried, was moved to Shuhogahara in the hills behind Futatabi. There in the new cemetary the old gravestones of those eleven men—the eldest was only twenty-nine years and the youngest twenty-one—may be seen. The large granite cross bears the inscription.

À LA MÉMOIRE
des
Onze Marins
du
Dupleix
MASSACRES À SAKAI
Le 8 Mars 1868
Requiescant in Pace

The Myokokuji temple in Sakai, where the eleven Japanese died with imprecations of vengeance on their lips, was mostly destroyed in the air raids of 1945, but the stone monument marking the spot where the execution was carried out is still standing among the ruins in the temple ground. Also there can still be seen an elaborate stone memorial. The central stone is carved deeply with a Buddhist prayer and is flanked with two other stones. One is to the memory of the eleven French sailors who were slaughtered—the English portion of the inscription reads *"In Memory of the French Martyrs"*—and the other stone is to the eleven Tosa men who were executed there that bleak day of ninety years ago.

A few grisly relics of the event are still preserved in one of the buildings that escaped destruction. There are two wooden trays upon which the severed heads of two of the Japanese were placed, and which are still stained with their blood. There is the hair that was cropped from the heads of all the twenty men who had been sentenced to execution and which was to remain in the temple to their memory. There are two helmets, one being that of the first officer to be executed. It is related in the booklet, which is sold at the temple, that when he committed hara-kiri he inserted his short sword into his abdomen, made a downward cut of three inches and one across of the same length, and then, before his assistant could cut off his head, he attempted to tear out his intestines and fling them at the French commander. However that may have been, it is known that the first sword stroke that was aimed at his neck, went wide of the mark and that it required a second, and yet a third blow, before the neck was hacked through.

Finally among the relics there is a torn piece of blue and white bunting, which is labelled as being a French flag captured as a trophy from the launch. It has several holes which are represented as bullet holes. The authenticity of this relic seems open to doubt, and not unlikely it was added at a much later

date. Had the Tricolor flag been taken from the
launch, the first of the demands made by the French
Minister would almost certainly have been for its
return.

The graves of the eleven Tosa men are in Hojuji,
a smaller temple which stood just at the rear of
Myokokuji. All of the temple buildings, except the
front gate, were wiped out in the air raids. A
kindergarten school now occupies the site. Fortunately the eleven graves are still there in a single row,
within a well-maintained enclosure. Perhaps not
many people these days step into the kindergarten
playground to read the inscription on those old
graves, but somebody carefully tends them, because
when I visited the place I saw a freshly-cut piece
of pine branch before each to keep alive the memory
of those Shades of the Past.

A FORGOTTEN ROAD

*Ozechya is the most famous Castle
...it is of an extraordinaire bignese.*
—Letter by Rev. ARTHUR HATCH,
1623

In several parts of the world there are roads down which men have walked and have never been seen again. Some people suggest they were fleeing from nagging wives; some think that they were escaping debts; but some believe, and some profess to know, that at a certain point along the road they just walked right out of this world.

There are roads that have neither beginning nor end. There are roads down which only the foolhardy would walk at night, and there are paths along which some country folk in some countries do not normally walk even in daytime, because it is said that the shades of the past linger in the shadows. There are roads that lead to happiness but many that lead to misery. There are roads that were carefully planned but lead to nowhere. There are even roads whose existence has been forgotten.

There is a road in Japan that has, in some measure at least, all these strange characteristics.

It is often asserted that most roads in Japan have the appearance of having been forgotten and abandoned soon after having been constructed. Actually there is a road over twenty miles in length that was constructed near Kobe under orders from the highest power in the land, but once constructed it was used on a few occasions only, then abandoned and soon forgotten. Comparatively few people now know that it ever existed, and fewer still have any idea where it started or where it ended. With the passing of eighty-six years it has been almost obliterated and little remains of it to-day. For the ordinary person there is nothing to be seen now except a narrow road, or rather a path or trail, and not even that for most of its length. But for the person who knows something of the past, a fascinating story unfolds as he wanders quietly among its shadows.

* * * * * * *

When the *Mikado* was kept cooped up in Kyoto and the Tokugawa family ruled Japan, the latter required that the feudal lords or governors should make periodical visits to Tokyo and leave their womenfolk and others behind as hostages when they departed. Such journeyings, or *daimyo* processions, involved the feudal lords in great expense and were just one of the many schemes devised by the astute Tokugawa family to compel them to spend their wealth, so that they would have less with which to finance a rebellion.

For several hundred years such processions from southwestern Japan had passed through the old city of Hyogo and then along the dusty or muddy road that ran by Sannomiya Shrine, right in front of where the Daimaru Department Store stands to-day.

Such processions sometimes comprised up to a thousand persons including porters, servants and two-sworded samurai attendants. Many of the latter were swaggering men quick to take offence and ever anxious to try their swords on an opponent.

A number of foreigners had been murdered in and around the Yokohama Settlement by two-sworded men. Consequently shortly before Kobe was opened to foreign trade, which was nine years after Yokohama, the Tokugawa Shogunate, which was then beset with increasing difficulties and opposition on all sides, was anxious to avoid becoming involved in further trouble with the Foreign Powers by reason of disturbances that might arise out of the passage of *daimyo* processions along the border of the Foreign Concession in Kobe. To that end the Shogunate ordered that a new road should be constructed which would go inland near Akashi and rejoin the Hyogo Osaka road near Sumiyoshi. In that way *daimyo* processions would be able to by-pass Kobe. The total length of the road was to be nine *ri* or a little over twenty miles and the width two *ken* or twelve feet, which would be sufficiently broad for the palanquins in the *daimyo* processions.

The work was commenced in the autumn of 1867, about three or four months before the port of Kobe was due to be opened. Two armies of coolies commenced work simultaneously from Akashi in the west and Ishiyagawa in the east, much to the surprise of the large groups of monkeys which up to that time had lived comparatively undisturbed in the deep valleys to the east of Maya-san.

Between Akashi and Maiko near the Okuradani Bridge, the road proceeded northwards along the stream toward Urushi-yama (Daisanji was on the left, and in fact excursionists who each spring and autumn travel now by tourist bus to Daisanji more often for the purpose of getting drunk than to view that delightful temple, do in spots travel over the old Tokugawa road).

The road then proceeded towards the villages of Shirakawa, Aina, and West and East Obu of Yamada. It then crossed over what is to-day the Kobe-Arima road. Then over the top of Horse Back and passing the Nagatani Pond on the left it proceeded along the base of Green Hill, commonly called Nakuto, to the twentieth crossing of the Twenty Crossings over the stream behind Futatabi. Gradually ascending eastwards until the top of Cascade Valley was reached it descended the valley southwards to Gomo passing what were then the villages of Shinohara, Yawata, and Takaha. It then followed the river bank of the Ishiyagawa and ultimately rejoined the main highway.

The road was completed in January, 1868, about a fortnight after the port of Kobe was opened. Before the contractor had received payment however, rumours reached Hyogo that the Imperialists were gathering in strength to attack Osaka Castle which was the stronghold of the Tokugawa clan in southwestern Japan. The contractor thereupon rushed to Osaka in the hope of collecting payment from the Tokugawa treasury before the Tokugawa government could be driven from power.

Such a journey was a perilous adventure. The enemies of the Tokugawa clan were gathering and beginning to move along the highways that converged on Osaka. Rivers had to be forded or crossed in flat-bottomed ferry boats. Each side would be on the watch for spies and troublemakers. However the contractor arrived safely in Osaka just when the Tokugawa officials were preparing to abandon their stronghold and make their escape. Payment was hastily made without the money bags being opened and the coins counted. The money bags were put into chests which the contractor conveyed on horseback to his home in Hyogo, where on counting the money he found to his amazement that in the excitement he had been given the wrong money bags and had been paid twenty-two thousand *ryo,* a considerable fortune in those days.

When the Imperialist troops reached Osaka on 29 January, 1868, they found that the Castle which was the stronghold of the Tokugawa forces in those parts had been abandoned. The ladies of the castle and much treasure had been sent to Yedo by sea, but so anxious were the Tokugawa samurai to escape with their lives that much was left behind. Before leaving they had blown up the magazine, and what was not destroyed in the confusion was sacked and pillaged by the Imperialists, after which they fired the castle. Thus was destroyed one of the most powerful castles in the land. The last of the Tycoons—the last of the Tokugawa Shoguns—had been overthrown. (The present-day castle, a replica of the original, was built of reinforced concrete in 1931 on the old foundation.)

The forces that had cast in their lot with the Imperialists for the purpose of re-instating the *Mi-*

kado as the sovereign power in the country, were occupying all the important cities. One corps of the Lord of Choshu had arrived in Hyogo and made its headquarters at the Shofukuji Temple at Okuhirano. News of the road contractor's good fortune soon leaked out, whereupon they made a domiciliary search of his house and discovered four chests, mostly of gold coin, all of which were confiscated.

So runs the story. But the road, out of whose construction those happenings occurred, was rarely used. The country was passing through exciting times. The military government that had ordered the construction of the road had been overthrown. The *Mikado* had been rescued from the aimless life that he and his forbears had been forced to live in Kyoto for several centuries. He would thereafter rule as Emperor from the Imperial City of Tokyo. The country was fast emerging from a feudal age. The wearing of swords was forbidden. The samurai, or professional warriors, were with pain endeavouring to find employment as civilians in occupations that they had formerly despised.

The reason for which the Tokugawa Road had been constructed no longer existed. It was rarely used. It has disintegrated and little now remains. It has neither a beginning nor an end. It leads to nowhere.

Nothing but the shades of the past now linger in its shadows.

THE
LOSS
OF
THE
U.S.S.
"ONEIDA"

> ...'tis true, 'tis pity;
> And pity 'tis, 'tis true.
> SHAKESPEARE—"*Hamlet*"

The tragic loss of the U.S.S. "Oneida" was one of the many storms that disturbed the foreign community of the Treaty Ports in the old days.

Some of those storms divided the community; some set tongues wagging in the tea party circles; some were discussed learnedly but pompously in the clubs, or with less exactitude but possibly with more tolerance in the bars and saloons; some ended up in the consular courts. But almost all in time blew themselves out like the typhoons and were forgotten. One remains engraved in granite and will last as long as the tombstones in the Yokohama Foreign Cemetery.

* * * * * * *

The U.S.S. "Oneida" was a wooden-screw steamer, 211 feet long, 1695 tons and eight guns. She had seen war service during the American Civil War when she was employed on blockade duty; then in 1867 she had been despatched to the Asiatic Squadron. Thereafter she was frequently seen in the Treaty Ports of Japan.

The Loss of the U.S.S. "Oneida"

She was stationed off Kobe shortly after the opening of that port, and a month later when Taki Zenzaburo gave the order to the Bizen soldiers to fire on the foreigners, a Japanese ricocheting bullet nicked a flesh wound in one of her marines who happened to be on shore. All the rest of the bullets went wild, and most of them fell splashing into the sea. As has been related elsewhere in this book, she was one of the vessels that then joined in the protection of the Kobe Foreign Concession. Fourteen marines were landed from her with a fieldpiece to guard one of the entrances.

About two months later the first issue of the *Hiogo News*, a weekly newspaper published in Kobe and priced at "4 boos per month," carried a notice indicating to the Kobe Foreign Concession, then only four months old, that residents could set their clocks to the correct time by watching the "Oneida," anchored off the port:

A red pointed flag will be hoistered every day at the mizzen masthead of the U.S. Steamer Oneida in a ball at 5 minutes before noon. At noon precisely the ball will break and the flag fly open.

The officers and men were popular and well-known in the foreign communities in Japan, and some had sweethearts in every port. But a time came when, after three years service in Far Eastern waters, her tour of duty was at an end and she was due to return to her home base.

It was about 6:20 P.M. on 24th January, 1870, the year that Ulysses Simpson Grant was President of the United States of America. About an hour or so earlier the "Oneida" had weighed anchor and pulled slowly out of Yokohama harbour amid farewell cheers from the men of other nations who manned the rigging of various ships of war in the harbour. Ships of all nations dipped their flags as the "Oneida" passed, homeward bound.

Later it was said that some of her officers were intoxicated, although the U.S. Minister to Japan stated that charge was "false in even its mildest form." Certain it is that she was just out of port and homeward bound, after many farewell toasts and good wishes had been pledged in wine, or something stronger.

Many of the foreign community were just arriving back in their homes after waving good-bye from the Bund and from the cliffs along the Bluff. The officers and men had been popular, and the leave-takings had been sincere and friendly. Some of the ladies of the port were tying up farewell mementos among their souvenirs. The curio shops in Main Street were restocking their shelves. Some of the saloonkeepers in Blood Town were washing the tobacco juice off their floors, whilst the less particular were just throwing down fresh sawdust to hide the stains. The girls in Dirty Village were beginning to awake from the first decent rest in a week. They were rubbing the sleep from their eyes and beginning to reckon up their takings. The ricksha-men and pimps were calling at the various houses to collect their commissions.

The ship being homeward bound after three adventuresome years in the Far East, the thoughts of

176 men on board, or at least of those awake, were of friends left behind and of those at home whom they would soon be rejoining.

The wind was freshening and the sails of the "Oneida" filled taut as she steamed down the bay. It was a fine evening, sharp and wintry, but dark. There was no local pilot on board.

At the same time the British P. & O. vessel "Bombay" was steaming up the bay, under the care of a Yokohama foreign pilot, actually a citizen of the United States, who had been taken on board at the entrance to the bay.

The two vessels sighted one another at a distance of about four miles, but from that moment the precise sequence of happenings is in doubt, because of the amazing contradictions in the evidence forthcoming from both sides, and the diametrically opposed verdicts of two different courts of inquiry. The tragic facts alone are clear, that the two vessels came into collision and within the matter of about fifteen minutes the "Oneida" sank two miles off shore with the loss of 115 members of her crew, including the captain and all but two of her commissioned officers. Two cutters managed to get away, but the captain remained on the bridge and went down with his ship.

This tragic happening soon divided the community and as passions arose each side made statements and charges against the other, many giving under oath evidence much of which could not be substantiated and some of which was manifestly untrue.

The Americans charged that immediately after the

collision the master of the "Bombay" boasted that he *"had cut the quarter off a Yankee frigate and it served her damn well right,"* and then after saying that she could beach herself had continued on his way to Yokohama and left her to look after herself. Certainly the British Court of Inquiry, whilst exonerating the "Bombay" from any blame, suspended her master's ticket for six months because:

he acted hastily and ill-advisedly, in that, instead of waiting and endeavouring to render assistance to the 'Oneida,' he, without having reason to believe that his own vessel was in a perilous position, proceeded on his voyage.

The findings and decision of that Court of Inquiry were subsequently confirmed by the Board of Trade in London.

Of the two officers of the "Oneida" who were saved, one became the principal witness for the sunken vessel. As he had been the deck officer at the time of the collision, the blame for the loss would mainly have been his, had the "Oneida" been at fault. The U.S. case was based mainly on his evidence, but as he personally had so much at stake it seems not unreasonable to assume that he would have remembered the happenings that crowded themselves into comparatively few minutes, from the most favourable angle. However that may be, the U.S. Naval Court of Inquiry found that *"no blame is to be attached to the officers or crew of the 'Oneida' for the collision."*

Some passengers of the "Bombay" were either so absorbed in their card games or were so intent upon whitewashing the master of that vessel, that they insisted they had hardly been disturbed at their game and they had no idea the "Bombay" had been in a serious collision. On the other hand the Americans alleged that their gunfire of distress signals was heard in Yokohama ten miles away.

Even on the British side the evidence seems to have been conflicting. The captain of the "Bombay" said: "The 'Oneida' must have been about one mile away from me when I first saw her light;" his second officer said "five or six miles away;" the pilot said "four or five miles." Other parts of the testimony show that all three saw the light at nearly the same instant.

In many other respects there were similar differences. The captain of the "Bombay" said the speed of the "Oneida" was fourteen knots; his chief officer said eleven or twelve; the pilot said about eight. The Americans contended it was seven. The captain of the "Bombay" said he stopped his engines for about ten minutes, whereas the logbook showed four minutes.

Tempers and passions flared to such a degree that the American Minister to Japan who attended the Court of Inquiry at one point in the proceedings pointed at the British master of the "Bombay" and thundered his intention to prosecute *"that man for whatever crime it might be shown by the evidence he was guilty of,"* a threat which indicated that His Excellency, who was a lawyer, had for the moment forgotten his law as operating in those times of consular courts. In those days a person could only be prosecuted by his own consular authorities.

The Loss of the U.S.S. "Oneida"

The pilot of the "Bombay" did not calm tempers when he declared that from the way the "Oneida" was steering he thought she was a Japanese vessel.

No matter what the facts may have been, all nationalities in the Settlement grieved over this most unhappy occurrence.

Much of what was written at the time added fuel to the bitterness because rightly or wrongly it seemed to indicate that the American warship was at fault. Not so however the U.S. Secretary of the Navy. He wrote to the Speaker of the House of Representatives confirming that, from an examination of all the evidence, *including that of the British Court of Inquiry,* his Department was of the opinion that no blame attached to the "Oneida."

A few years later, in 1876, Dr. W.E. Griffis, American missionary and historian, when referring to the loss of the "Oneida" wrote:

This is sad; but the sequel is disgraceful. Down under the fathoms the 'Oneida' has lain, thus far undisturbed, a rich and grateful Government having failed to trouble itself to raise the ship or do honour to the dead. The hulk was put up at auction and sold in 1874, with certain conditions, to a Japanese for fifteen hundred dollars.

The depth of water where the "Oneida" sank, being beyond the limit of most divers in Japan in those days, little could be done in the way of salvage. Ill luck seemed to defeat each attempt. It may well have been that the apparent ill luck that seemed to be associated with the enterprise, was the factor which finally convinced the Japanese owners of the wreck that the earlier Buddhist service to placate the spirits of the dead must have been ineffectual. At any rate in 1889, nineteen years after the disaster, they decided to hold a great Buddhist mass for the souls of the unfortunate men—a *segaki* or feast for hungry souls. The service was held at the Daishin-in Temple at Ikegami near Yokohama, and no expense was spared to enhance the gorgeousness and impressiveness of the scene. Seventy-six priests clad in full Buddhist canonicals chanted the litanies, which reverberated through the great buildings at Ikegámi, and were ultimately lost with the incense fumes among the glorious cedar groves surrounding the temple.

Attending this impressive ceremony was the Admiral of the U.S. Squadron and a contingent of sixty U.S. naval men, the U.S. Consul-General, British Embassy representatives, and over fifty foreign residents in Yokohama and Tokyo. In addition there was a vast Japanese assemblage, and most important of all the Japanese salvage men who were to actually work on the ghost-ridden wreck.

It was in all truth a remarkable and inspiring requiem service, and one in which the foreign community of the Kwanto area was glad to participate by way of marking an end of the early bitterness that had so divided the American and British sections of the community.

The foreign press and diarists of the time made much of the ceremony, but apparently they were so close to the event that they failed to understand the ghostly significance of it from the point of view of the salvors and the divers who were about to work on the wreck, around which were gathered, according to their beliefs, the distressed spirits of so many who had come to a sudden and untimely end. Foreign writers at the time described the ceremony in grateful if not somewhat extravagant terms, and closing their eyes to the fact that fifteen years had elapsed spoke of the "spontaneous sympathy" of the Japanese promoters. The latter gentlemen must no doubt have wished that this grand service had been more spontaneous, and that the fifteen years of costly failure had not already been marked up against their enterprise.

The promoters also erected a stone monument with metal lettering to commemorate the ceremony, but during the First World War, when metal prices reached high levels, some vandals stole the lettering.

During the sixty-five years that have elapsed since that service was held for the spirits of the dead, the salavage rights have changed hands several times, and much nonsense has appeared in the press, but the hulk still remains embedded in the sand, and encrusted with barnacles and seaweed.

What, however, has become more important is the legend that has grown up, or perhaps has been inspired by company promoters, that the "Oneida" was carrying a large sum in Japanese gold *koban* (currency) said to have been equivalent in value at that time to about U.S. $400,000. If such treasure exists it would, of course, be worth a great deal more to-day. The story, whether inspired or otherwise, is seemingly the incentive for various salvage enterprises that have continued over the years, some of which have ended in bankruptcy. Some deck equipment, some bones, a few cutlasses and other relics, but no treasure, have been recovered. As the salvage rights changed hands, so the new owners have generally commenced their operations with further services for the peace of the spirits of the unfortunate men who were lost.

At the moment there are in fact two rival groups, each claiming to have the rights of salvage and not a few investors, all of whom hope one day to receive dividends when the imaginary gold treasure in the "Oneida" is recovered. One group having lost faith in the efficacy of the Buddhist gods, as have many others who have deserted religion since Japan's defeat, recently conducted a Christian service after giving much advance publicity, thereby hoping that by this new approach to a difficult problem in salvage they could keep hot the enthusiasm of their financial backers.

The U.S. authorities have never admitted that there was any treasure on board. It seems unlikely they would have sold a wreck for $1,500 had they known that $400,000 of gold was on board.

* * * * * * * *

In the days and months and years that followed this tragic sinking many of the bodies, or at least the bones, of those who lost their lives were recovered —some washed ashore, others taken from the wreck, —and were interred in the Yokohama Bluff Cemetery where they have long since been marked by a fine memorial stone. The feelings aroused by that tragic happening when the British and American sections of the community were split apart, were so bitter and lived so long that even when the time came to erect the memorial the bitterness of the past could not be forgotten. In the wording that was engraved in stone there is no word of collision, but the stark accusation that the "Bombay" sank the "Oneida." And so the bitter feelings of three-quarters of a century ago, although happily now long since forgotten, will remain engraved in granite as long as the tombstones stand in the old Yokohama Foreign Cemetery.

THE
CASE
OF THE
"MARIA LUZ"

Once upon a time Japan was on the brink of war
with Peru of all countries, with Portugal hurling
threats from the sidelines, and with Britain and
America advising Japan to stand firm. The issue
was that of slavery.

The year was 1872. Queen Victoria was then the
sovereign in England, and Ulysses Simpson Grant
was president of the United States. The Abolition
of Slavery Act had been passed in England about
forty years earlier. In the United States the Civil
War had been fought and the North had won on the
issue of slavery. Alexander II, the Czar of Russia,
at the time, had come to be known as the liberator of
serfs, but possibly even before the liberation there
were fewer slaves there than now. Emperor Meiji
of Japan, then only twenty years of age, ruled a
country where, in theory at least, the only slaves were
the inmates of the licenced quarters.

The trouble with Peru all started on July 7, 1872,
when a decrepit tub, a Peruvian barque named the
"Maria Luz," although only a week or so out of
Macao, limped into Yokohama to refit, or at least
to carry out the minimum amount of repairs that
would offer her a reasonable chance of crawling back
to her home port in Peru without involving the
officers and crew in too great a risk. She had on

board, battened under deck, 232 Chinese coolies who were treated with as much, or less, consideration than so many cattle. Except that they represented so much freight, their fate was not important.

They were but one shipload of that human freight which was being shipped out of the Portuguese colony of Macao as slave labour for South American countries. The cruelty with which that coolie traffic was carried on, the fraudulent promises with which the Chinese were enticed on board or forcibly kidnapped, and the abominable conditions in the barracoons of Macao were notorious, but little could be done to interfere with the traffic, because the sailing vessels carrying the slaves, sailed from Macao direct to the ports of Peru. The trade brought a large annual revenue to Macao, and by it Peru obtained a cheap supply of forced labour for the guano diggings and the gold and silver mines.

A few evenings after the "Maria Luz" had anchored in Yokohama harbour, one of the Chinese succeeded in dropping overboard and swam two miles to the British warship "Iron Duke" where he appealed for protection. He was in turn passed on to the British Consul, who, having no jurisdiction in the matter, had to hand him on to the Japanese authorities. They returned him to the ship, where he was severely punished and had his queue cut off.

A few days later another coolie who had succeeded in getting away came alongside the H.M.S. "Iron Duke." On this occasion a collection was taken up for the refugee after which he was set at liberty, instead of being handed over to the Japanese authorities. The case was, however, reported to the British Consul, who after visiting the "Maria Luz" made representations to the Kanagawa authorities, urging on them their duty not to permit "the Government to be disgraced by affording the smallest possible countenance to the abominable traffic in which the 'Maria Luz' was engaged." At that time Peru had no treaty with Japan; consequently the "Maria Luz" had become subject to Japanese jurisdiction from the time she entered Japanese waters.

The Chinese on board thereupon claimed protection of the Japanese and asked for an investigation into the fraudulent manner in which the Portuguese had shipped them away from China. While the investigation was being conducted the Chinese had been landed. The captain of the "Maria Luz" then brought an action for indemnity, or alternatively asked that the Chinese be forced to proceed with the vessel and fulfill their contracts. The case was heard in open court where the coolies gave evidence of their kidnapping and that none desired to go to Peru. The defence on the other hand introduced into their case the form of indenture under which the girls in Japanese licenced quarters were bound, and they sought to show that it was not much different to that under which the coolies had been engaged. This manoeuvre proved most embarrassing to the Governor of Kanagawa Prefecture and other officials who were present in the court, and when Counsel for the Defence, who was well conversant with the Japanese language, began to read the form of contract entered into between prostitutes and their owners, he was stopped by the President of the Court before he had read half the document.

Some of the Powers brought pressure to bear on Japan not to interfere in the matter, but she had the strong moral support of the British and United States representatives, and resisted such pressure. Judgement was given against the master of the barque for the Chinese, who were now ordered to be released. Later they were repatriated to China by the Chinese government.

In the meantime Peru despatched her most powerful ironclad, the "Independencia," and several other vessels, and also a mission to demand an apology and an indemnity from the Japanese. When it was hinted that a British fleet would await their arrival in Japan, the Peruvian vessels were recalled, but the mission came on and subsequently agreed to the submission of the question to arbitration by the Czar of Russia. His decision given a year or so later was wholly in favour of Japan.

The verdict was hailed by abolitionists everywhere as a great victory against slavery, which of course it was. It brought about important changes in many places. It roused China to taking more effective measures to protect her nationals. Portugal under the compelling force of world opinion was roused to forbid the traffic, at least in Macao, with the result that the infamous barracoons there soon fell into decay.

In Japan it stirred the hopes of some liberals for legislation that would free from bondage the inmates of the licenced quarters, and although an edict on the subject was soon after issued, the vested money interests were so powerful that twenty-eight years elapsed before a law was passed enabling any girl to free herself by a mere declaration of that intention to the police. But even so, the power of the moneyed interests, and the demands of the internal revenue bureau for a "cut" in the profits, were so powerful that it required the untiring efforts of a section of the Japanese public over a period of another half a century before more effective legislation was passed to free those trapped within the Nightless Cities.

THE
BURNING
OF
THE
S.S. "AMERICA"

Which I wish to remark,
And my language is plain,
That for ways that are dark
And for tricks that are vain,
The heathen Chinee is peculiar.

BRET HARTE

A little over a hundred years ago it was a violation of the laws of Japan for a United States ship to enter Japanese waters. It was against the law for any but Dutch and some Chinese vessels to come to Japan. Certainly a few American ships under charter to the Dutch East India Company had slipped in. One, impudently pretending to be the annual Dutch vessel, came in, did some trade, and got out again in safety. Other vessels were not so fortunate.

There were pressing reasons to compel Japan to change her laws, to desist from turning away ships in distress, and to open her country to trade. Gold had been discovered in California, which in turn had led to a great development in Pacific trade. American investments in the whaling industry had reached large figures, and of all ships the whalers had suffered most when they put into Japanese ports in distress, or in search of water and supplies. The vessels were fired upon by shore batteries, and the crews, if captured, were thrown into prison. Railroads were beginning to stretch across America. Trade with China was increasing rapidly. The era of steam had arrived, but the voyage from San Francisco to China was inconveniently long; intermediate coaling stations in Japan were required.

Commodore Biddle, when he landed with the idea of persuading the Japanese to change their laws, was flung back into his own boat by a Japanese guard, and much "face" was lost. There were several other attempts that came to nothing. Then Commodore Perry determined he would not fail.

And so it came about that Japan changed her laws and the country was opened to foreign trade. At first one or two schooners made occasional trips from Nagasaki and Yokohama to San Francisco taking tea and bringing back general cargo. Some mail was sent by those vessels, with duplicate copies being routed via Suez. As the Suez Canal was not then completed, such mail and also passengers had to be transported overland from Suez to Alexandria. In course of time the Pacific Mail Steamship Company opened a service from China and Japan to San Francisco. The voyage from Yokohama to San Francisco took 21 days as against about 10 days to-day. From San Francisco passengers could travel by rail across the continent to New York. The first-class fare from Nagasaki right through to New York was U.S. $428.50 as compared with about U.S. $700 to-day. The railroad journey from San Francisco to New York took 6 days and 20 hours, as against about 3½ days now. In 1872 there were four regular Pacific sailings a month. Those mail steamers touched at Nagasaki and Yokohama. Kobe was not as then sufficiently important for Pacific Mail steamers to call at, but Kobe was growing fast and soon would be.

In 1872 one of the vessels on the run was the fabulous wooden paddle steamer "America." She was 4,454 tons register, 363 feet long and had cost what was then the stupendous sum of U.S. $1,600,000. She was double-planked and the largest wooden ship in the world. She arrived at Yokohama on the morning August 24, 1872. Coaling and the discharge of cargo commenced shortly after arrival. That same night fire broke out among thirty-five bundles of hay, which were intended for use on the homeward voyage, and which were stored in the after part of the steerage near the hatchway. Fire hoses were run out but little water came through them. It was suggested later on that the pressure of steam had been permitted to fall, but there were some, including the company officials, who thought the hoses may have been tampered with.

The fire spread with such fearful rapidity that there was no time to launch any lifeboats. In the panic and pandemonium that broke loose the Chinese in the 'tween decks were all so intent upon saving their belongings that none gave a thought to life-belts. Many jumped overboard with their belongings, hit the water with a splash and plummeted to the bottom of the sea. Later when their bodies were recovered it was found that their clothing was weighted down with $20 gold pieces. On one corpse U.S. $3,000 in gold coin was found. Most of those who scrambled over the side and down ropes into the sea were promptly hit on the head by the shower of chests and packages that others on the deck were throwing overboard in a frantic effort to save their possessions from the fire.

The once great wooden steamer "America," the largest wooden vessel that had ever been built, burnt to the water's edge. Four days later the remains of the hulk was still smoking. In the days that followed the bodies of three Europeans and fifty Chinese who had lost their lives were recovered. $375,000 in treasure which was on board, securely locked in the tank, was recovered later by divers.

"Relatives" quickly came forward to claim the dead. The agent of the Pacific Mail Steamship Co. in Yokohama, however, delivered the bodies, but took temporary possession of all the coin found on them to prevent it falling into the wrong hands, and until some means of ascertaining the rightful owners could be found.

The verdict of the Court of Inquiry held at Yokohama was that the cause of the fire could not be ascertained, but it was believed to have been intentionally caused by some person or persons for the purpose of plundering the Chinese passengers who were known to be carrying a huge sum of money back to China.

An astonishing feature of the case was that a bear "ring" developed on the New York Stock exchange in Pacific Mail stock a short while before the fire.

The Burning of the S.S. "America"

When, however, the disaster was announced the Company attacked the bears with such determination that the market was bulled over 20%, and, it is said, some of the "ring" were ruined. An account of the dealings in the stock appears in the New York *Times* of September 11, 1872.

The London *Times* of November 20, 1872, gave an account of the findings of the Court of Inquiry, and paid a tribute to the captain and crew for the efforts made to save the ship, but lamented the inadequacy of the means on board to cope with the conflagration.

* * * * * * *

Although Tuck Chong's descendants would deny the implication, and would probably be ready to defend the memory of their great great grandfather, even to the extent of sticking a knife into my ribs, nevertheless there may be some people who will be inclined to agree with me when I say that the burning of the "America" and the subsequent rise to wealth of Tuck Chong may not have been unrelated.

The foreigners in Yokohama of eighty years ago knew Tuck Chong as a Chinese restaurateur, and they knew also his Hang Fah Low Restaurant, named no doubt after the famed San Francisco Chinese restaurant of the same name. Actually he was a man of many parts and of wide experience. It is not possible to start at the beginning, because Tuck Chong himself never talked about his beginning. It will be sufficient for the purpose of this article if we start on August 2, 1872, at the wharf in San Francisco, where the "America" was getting ready to sail for the Orient.

The Burning of the S.S. "America"

The last few hours before sailing were bustle and confusion. Well nigh half the population of China-town must have been on board or on shore assisting in the handling of the hundreds of packages that the returning Chinese passengers were taking back to China with them. It was said that somewhere in those packages was a king's ransom in the form of silver dollars and $20 gold pieces representing the savings of half a lifetime that some of the Chinese were taking back to China on which to retire. Some were carrying their wealth in the form of bank drafts, but most had never trusted banks and pre-ferred coin. Many, who had been working in the California gold-fields, were carrying nuggets of gold too. Nobody but the owners knew what was in each package.

All of those packages were stored in the 'tween decks where the Chinese were accommodated—that is to say all except the coffins which were supposed to be stowed in the lower hold. There were over twenty coffins in all. Most of the morning they had lain forlornly on the dock alongside the ship waiting for the heavy cargo to be loaded and stowed away. For obvious reasons the coffins were always stowed where they would not be crushed by heavy cargo. There was a constant and lucrative freight business to be done in the carrying of Chinese dead back to China for burial in the land of their ancestors.

The coffins were the last items of cargo to be loaded on the "America." They were hauled up in slings and stowed on top of the cargo in the mouth of the hatch. In some way that was never explained,

the last sling load of two coffins was raised from the
dock and lowered away through the top deck hatch-
way, but as soon as the sling came level with the
'tween decks it was pulled in, the coffins removed
and the signal given to the winchman to raise the
tackle. In the matter of a few seconds the two
coffins had been whisked away into a corner of the
'tween decks where they were quickly covered with
baggage. A few well-placed bribes had no doubt
been all that was necessary to accomplish that irregularity. The hatches to the lower hold were closed,
the hatch covers put in place, and the seals attached.
A few minutes later the "America" had pulled out
from the wharf and was en route to Japan and China.

Later matting was spread over the tops of the
coffins that had thus surreptitiously been stowed in
the 'tween decks. Two of them made an excellent
couch for the party comprising Tuck Chong and his
three sons. At night two slept on that couch, and
in the daytime there was never a moment when one
or more of the party was not resting there. They
seemed to do nothing in particular. Actually they
were watching every movement that took place in
those 'tween decks. Most of all they were studying
the gambling that went on from morning to night
at fan-tan and other games in a nearby corner under
the direction of Ching Ling, who played the part of
banker. He also had three sons, but just prior to
sailing, the San Francisco police had come on board
and arrested them on some charge, the exact details
of which were not known to the rest of the ship.
Ching Ling was greatly upset at that development

and said that a terrible mistake had been made by the police. Tuck Chong may possibly have known something of that.

The presence of the coffins in the 'tween deck apparently had been gossiped about. The Chinese stewards probably heard of it and passed the information on to the officers, because on the second day out the chief officer conducted a search and reported to the captain his discovery of the coffins in the 'tween deck. The next morning when the captain made his regular tour of inspection Tuck Chong was sitting as usual with his sons on their couch seemingly looking into space at nothing, but actually he was very wide awake. He saw the captain sniff several times and then turn to the first mate.

"Don't unseal that hatch, Mr. Bower. The air in here is so foul that a few coffins couldn't make it any worse."

The gambling games continued and vast numbers of dollars changed hands, many of which passed into the hands of Ching Ling. Where they went to after that was not known. At nighttime it was customary for each family group before retiring to erect a bamboo screen around their belongings and their sleeping space. By morning all the dollars that Ching Ling had raked in had disappeared, but they began to accumulate again next day as the play of the day proceeded. Tuck Chong and his sons sat and watched, disregarding the taunts that were thrown at them for not joining in the gambling. It was the day before arrival at Yokohama that he seemingly permitted himself to be persuaded by his sons to place a small bet. He made a great show of his anxiety at the risk, and a still greater show of excitement as he scooped in his winnings. Again and again he placed his bets. The play swung backwards and forwards, but as the stakes increased so also did Tuck Chong's winnings. Finally at the end of the day he seemed to have most of the dollars that had circulated in those 'tween decks during the voyage. Many times during the day Tuck Chong's sons retired behind their bamboo screen presumably to pack away the winnings.

By evening Ching Ling had lost far more money than he said he was able to pay. After hours of wrangling and quarrelling he retired behind his bamboo curtain a very dejected man. He did not emerge as usual in the morning and when they peeked behind the curtain he was not there, nor could he be found anywhere else on board. Some thought he may have jumped overboard during the night. Some whispered other possibilities. When the whisperings came to the ears of the captain that evening he proceeded to the 'tween decks with his officers to investigate.

Tuck Chong and his sons were sitting impassive as usual on their couch. Perhaps they were thinking of the years of toil they had spent on the goldfields in California, where they had worked over the diggings that had been abandoned by others as not worth working. Perhaps they were thinking of other of their activities. At any rate their thoughts seemed to be elsewhere, and none of the captain's questions drew a worthwhile answer.

The Burning of the S.S. "America"

"Mr. Bower, call the ship's carpenter and open the lid of these coffins," ordered the captain. When the carpenter arrived Tuck Chong shifted his position to enable one of the coffins to be handled. His face as usual was inscrutable. He watched whilst the carpenter with some difficulty removed the lid of the first coffin. What they saw or what assailed their senses when the lid was raised is not recorded anywhere in the documents of this case. All that is known is that they hurriedly moved to the companionway whence a draught of fresh air was coming down from the deck above. It was then that the alarm of fire was sounded.

The captain and his officers hastened away to investigate. Panic broke out among the Chinese. What happened thereafter in the hold will never be known. All that we know for certain is that Tuck Chong and his sons escaped, and many others did not.

Tuck Chong's subsequent progress in the Yokohama Settlement can be traced in the newspapers of that time. A year after the burning of the "America" the *Japan Daily Herald* carried a short article reading:

Since the new canals have been cut and the Swamp drained, the Yokohama Foreign Concession and those sections of the native town adjoining it have made great progress and not the least has been in that section which some of our readers prefer to call Chinatown. Ten years ago there were about 200 Chinese nationals in Yokohama. To-day there are nearly 1000. Among the many new enterprises is the recently completed three-storied building

154

*housing the high-class Chinese restaurant Hang
Fah Low operated by Mr. Tuck Chong and which
has special rooms reserved for Europeans. The
speciality of this restaurant is Duck—Canton Style.*

*Mr. Tuck Chong and his sons arrived in Yoko-
hama last August on the ill-fated "America."*

*Rumour had it that Mr. Tuck Chong brought in
a fortune from gold-mining in California, but he
has informed us that he lost everything when the
'America' burnt. The enterprise of Mr. Tuck
Chong is therefore all the more praiseworthy.*

The following advertisement appeared in many
issues of the same newspaper:

Tuck Chong's High Class Chinese Restaurant
"Hang Fah Low"
Yokohama
Speciality Duck Canton Style
Special rooms for European guests

Tuck Chong's business thrived and with success
the number of his sons increased. Indeed they seemed
suddenly to spring from nowhere—and each one of
mature age. One became compradore at the Oriental
Bank, others were *shroffs* in other banks, some were
bookkeepers in foreign firms, and some assisted in
the restaurant. Little wonder, was it that Tuck
Chong's finger was always on the pulse of business
in Yokohama.

As one year followed another, the quantity of
"Duck—Canton Style" that was consumed in the
Hang Fah Low Restaurant steadily increased, but
Tuck Chong continued to sit behind the grill at the
front counter and collect the Mexican dollars that

rolled in, in ever increasing quantity. Except that
the number of his sons increased, he showed no
signs of change. He rang and squinted at every silver
dollar that passed across the counter. Those that
were cracked or chipped or faulty were dropped into
one basket, the good ones into another. Rarely did
he refuse a dollar, and only then when it was an
obvious counterfeit. He had sons who could pass
on the defective ones, and he had means of disposing
of the good ones at a premium.

The only time he left his stool was when a *taipan*
entered. Then one of his sons would slip into his
place on the stool, whilst Tuck Chong conducted the
Great One up the brass-edged grand staircase to
one of the rooms on the second floor front. Out of
consideration for the weight and shortness of breath
of some of the *taipans,* the de luxe rooms reserved
for Europeans were on the *second floor front side,*
but in recognition of the bashfulness of the juniors
of the *hongs,* who unlike the *taipans* often sought
privacy rather than limelight, there were also a
number of first class rooms on the *third floor back
side,* where a junior could treat his girl friend to a
dinner with less risk of being seen by the boss than
in one of the Settlement hotel dining rooms. For
their greater convenience, later he built an outside
staircase which spared the juniors the necessity of
walking up the brass-edged grand staircase at the
front.

Tuck Chong and his sons were students of human
nature, and in the studies which they conducted
among the foreign community of Yokohama they

found much profit. Tuck Chong, however, only encouraged eating and drinking and was not interested, except maybe in a personal way, in other weaknesses of the flesh. Those who did not find sufficient privacy behind the loose curtains at the doors of each room had to seek their entertainment in less respectable eating houses. Nor would he permit any gambling on his premises. He used to explain that he was just a simple restaurant keeper, that he never gambled himself and that good food did not mix with gambling.

As he grew older he often related his experiences when the "America" burnt. He told with great simplicity how, when he and his sons jumped in terror from the deck of the burning "America," it so happened that a sampan was tied at exactly the spot where they expected to enter the water, and so providentially they all landed one on top of the other in the bottom of the boat with much impedimenta that they happened to be carrying. According to Tuck Chong, the boatman was so shocked and frightened at the sudden intrusion that he hurriedly pushed off for shore in order to rid himself as quickly as possible of his unwelcome passengers. In this way, according to Tuck Chong, and despite any theories the Customs may have had to the contrary, he and his sons landed in Yokohama.

In course of time Tuck Chong passed out of this world, and according to his sons, his soul journeyed on to those same celestial fields to which so many of his fellow countrymen on the "America" had gone years before. His mortal remains were, however, sealed in a lead-lined coffin and transported for burial to the place of his birth in China.

Years later, in fact decades later, I was assured by a certain citizen of Chinatown, Yokohama—a person who seemed to know all the uncanny happenings of the back streets of Yokohama Settlement— that in the same coffin as his wizened shell, there were packed some marked cards, several old sets of loaded dice and some false decks of playing cards.

SAM
PATCH

*Sammy's notoriety has somewhat
spoiled his pristine modesty, and his
head, which had never been ballasted
with over two-thirds the average
quantum of wit, is occasionally
turned to the annoyance of his
master.*—Dr. W. E. GRIFFIS—*The
Mikado's Empire.*

About eighty years ago there started out from a
house in Tokyo an unusual funeral procession. The
hearse was the regular type of Japanese hearse used
by the common people—a small temple-shaped cart, a
few feet high, out of which conveyance has developed
the elaborate temple-like motor hearses of these days.
This cart had been backed up to the entrance of a
Japanese house; the sides and roof of the cart had
then been taken off and a square box, scarcely three
feet square, had been pushed on; the sides and top had
then been replaced after which the cart or hearse
was pulled away by two old men, poorly dressed,
almost in rags and tatters. The relatives of the
deceased who were gathered about the front of the
house were smiling but they were smiles of sadness
rather than of joy, in accordance with the family
precept that you must not burden others with your
sorrows for your dead. The bystanders were open-
mouthed in wonder at the strange funeral procession
that was forming.

Three double jinrikisha followed immediately behind the bier; the first carried two elderly Japanese women, the second a foreign clergyman and his wife, and in the third jinrikisha there was a Japanese convert to Christianity, a well-known Bible teacher of those days, and with him an eminent American missionary and educationalist—E. Warren Clark by name.

This unusual funeral procession—unusual because of the presence of three foreigners behind a Japanese hearse—attracted much attention as it moved down Tori, which was then the main street of Tokyo, towards Kirishitan zaka, or Christian Slope, near Shinagawa, so named from the martyrdom of a party of Christians who were burned there at the stake more than two centuries before.

(The Ginza had not been created at the time of the little funeral procession. Tori was then the main street and ran from Nihonbashi to the railway terminus at Shinagawa. The first railway in Japan, linking Yokohama to Tokyo was completed in 1872 as far as Shinagawa, whence travellers took jinrikisha or trudged the remaining two miles to the centre of the city.)

The funeral procession was bound for a Buddhist temple near Christian Slope, a distance of about two and a half miles over an abominable road that caused the hearse to rattle and shake to such a degree that Clark feared both the vehicle and the coffin might fall apart.

The procession moved along at a slow pace. Despite the impatient appeals of the foreigners to quicken the speed, the bearers of the hearse and the jinrikisha men would not hurry. It was dark when it arrived at the main gate of the cemetery. Not unlikely this had been planned by the Japanese in advance because, in accordance with ancient customs, burials were often performed at nighttime. Some people preferred the nighttime for burials, and some even after midnight at the hour of the ox when "even the grass is asleep." The lamps and lanterns used in present-day funerals are a relic of the old nighttime burial services.

The journey had taken much longer than the foreign mourners had expected. The hearse halted in the pitch darkness just inside the main gate. A heavy mist had settled over the place. Clark alighted from his jinrikisha and fumbled his way through the gravestones in search of the grave which earlier that day he had ordered to be dug. Finally he stumbled upon the square hole. (It was not until a much later date, when the population of Japan had greatly increased, that cremation was, as a matter of necessity, generally adopted throughout Japan.)

When Clark returned to the gate he found the foreign clergyman, who was in the initial stages of consumption, sheltering in a nearby hut. The clergyman was in physical distress and suffering from the cold and dampness of the place. The coffin, however, had disappeared. Clark thereupon prevailed upon the Japanese Bible teacher to escort the clergyman and his wife home, and, after bidding them good night, he set out in search of the missing coffin.

When he drew near the main temple, which he noticed was dimly illuminated within, he could hear a service being conducted inside. Out of curiosity he stepped up to the entrance and for a minute or so he stood peering into the interior. The place was dimly lighted by several candles arranged in front of the altar. Two finely robed priests were intoning the Buddhist sutras, striking every now and again the wooden gongs in front of them.

He gazed at the gilded Buddha sitting upon the golden leaves of the lotus in contemplation of all before him. He saw the incense smoke curling upwards from the great bronze brazier and he sensed that a funeral service was in progress. Finally he was able to make out among the shadows the shape of a square coffin, resting upon the top of which, he could see a wooden tablet bearing in large Japanese characters the name of the deceased. He could not read the name but suddenly a suspicion awoke within him that all was not well. He stole up alongside the priest and then he recognised the missing coffin. On the top was the same bunch of flowers that he had gathered earlier in the day.

Knowing that the corpse within the coffin was clutching in his hand a Christian Testament, Clark's first impulse was to stop the service, but then he noted that the two Japanese women kneeling on the floor were seemingly deriving comfort from the ceremony. He therefore withdrew into the shadows and waited for the service to end. He saw the priest rise and move out of the temple still chanting the prayers. He saw the two tattered old men lift up the coffin. The funeral procession to the newly-dug grave was resumed in the flickering light of several torches and a lantern. He followed the procession. He stopped when the procession moved about in circles several times in order to confuse any evilly-disposed spirits which might have been following or hovering near. He saw the coffin lowered into the grave, the last prayer said, and the onlookers depart after each had thrown into the grave a twig of the sacred *sakaki* tree, a last gift to the dead. The two tattered old men departed grumbling at the cold.

Clark scattered a handful of soil on the top of the coffin, whilst he also said a prayer:

"...*earth to earth, ashes to ashes, dust to dust*..."
He saw the gravedigger begin to strike the top of the coffin with his spade and he asked what he was doing. He learned that it was the custom to break in the head of the coffin so that the earth might fill up the inside. He told the gravedigger that he might on this occasion dispense with that custom and he waited until the grave was filled in.

Later he caused a stone cross to be erected over the grave on which were inscribed two English words —SAM PATCH.

* * * * * * * *

A hundred and more years ago the sea voyage from Osaka to Yedo sometimes took several months because the junks had to creep along the coast frequently putting into ports of refuge from storms and high seas. Often they were blown ashore or driven out into the Pacific never to return. One such junk was blown far out to sea by an off-shore gale and had then drifted helpless for fifty days before being sighted by the American brig "Auckland." The crew of

Sam Patch

seventeen rescued from the junk were carried to
San Francisco, and thereafter at least three of them
made history. In this article we are interested in
only one of the three. His name was Sentaro.

On arrival in San Francisco most of them were
transferred to a revenue cutter where they remained
for twelve months, until an opportunity arose of trans-
porting them on a U.S. sloop-of-war to China, whence
it was hoped they could be repatriated to their homeland. Later they were moved to the U.S.S. "Susquehanna." When that vessel joined Commodore Perry's
squadron in preparation for the task of forcing Japan to open her doors, all with one exception begged
to be discharged in China. They feared that if they
were returned to Japan they would be beheaded—
that or worse was often the punishment for Japanese
who left their homeland, even for castaways who
left through no fault of their own. The exception,
who was content to remain on board the "Susquehanna," was Sentaro. He had signed on as a regular
member of the crew. He was a friendly type with a
droll sense of humour. He soon became a favourite
with his shipmates. Finding his Japanese name too
awkward they nicknamed him Sam Patch, a sobriquet
which so delighted him that thenceforward he abandoned his Japanese name.

Such, according to at least one authority was the
origin of his nickname, but more than likely it was
bestowed upon him at a much earlier date, possibly
when rescued and put aboard the brig "Auckland"—
a sea-waif in clothes of threads and patches.

Upon arriving in Japan in Perry's squadron he

had prepared a letter which he wished to have forwarded to his relatives. In order that the circumstances of the letter could be explained, he was ordered to appear for presentation to the Japanese officials, whereupon on coming into their presence he prostrated himself on the deck and remained there awe-stricken, with his head bowed low. The American deck-officer sternly ordered him to rise and reminded him that as a crew member of an American man-of-war he had nothing to fear, but even so Sam Patch was still such an object of trembling servility that he was soon dismissed from their presence.

Later the Governor of Uraga requested that Sam should be allowed to remain in Japan. Sam was again called to appear and was told that he was free to leave the ship subject to the Japanese governor giving a solemn assurance that no punishment whatever would be meted out to him. Once again Sam went down on his knees before the Japanese officials and again he was ordered by the American naval officers to get up. He begged to be allowed to remain on board, so convinced was he that his life would be forfeited if he went ashore. He therefore continued in the service of the U. S. Navy.

One of the marines on board, Jonathan Goble by name, a religious type of man, had befriended him, and when the squadron subsequently returned to America, Goble left the navy and took Sam Patch to his home in New York. This was the same Goble who later returned to Japan as a missionary of the Baptist Free Missionary Society, and subsequently invented the jinrikisha. Sam was converted to the

Christian faith, and thereafter he seemed to have a simple trust in Christ which remained with him to the last.

And so it was that while young men in Japan were risking their lives, and some losing their lives, in attempts to smuggle themselves out of Japan in order to study the ways of the Western world, Sam Patch had fallen heir to all the opportunities which they were seeking. He was befriended by many, but he lacked brains and ambition to such a degree that he just drifted along, a droll and likable fellow. Eventually missionary friends sent him back to Japan, where he married and after many vicissitudes he became chief cook to E. Warren Clark, the American missionary and educationalist. Although a sore trial at times, he did in fact in that state accomplish his greatest achievement in life—the making of rice cakes for which he became locally famous.

In course of time Sam Patch became ill from beriberi a dreaded disease in Japan in those days before the principles of vitamin deficiency were known. When his end was near the lovable but timid Sam, was as timid in death as on the deck of Admiral Perry's flagship when he fell upon his knees before the Japanese governor of Uraga.

In accordance with custom his body after death was placed in a square coffin with head bowed and knees doubled up and his limbs crossed in front, as in a position of birth, thereby enabling the body to be fitted into what would appear to be an incredibly small space. It is not known whether the body of Sam Patch was fitted into the coffin whilst still supple and before rigor mortis had set in, or whether, as was more often the case, the ligaments under the big toes and knees had first to be cut. We hope not, for the common belief in those days was that the cutting of the ligaments spoiled the dreams about the Land of Bliss, dreams which we would wish were not denied to Sam Patch.

As customary the coffin lid was secured in position with nails driven in by a stone rather than a hammer, for it was the common fear then that the spirits of the dead might cling to the hammer and cause injury to those who used it afterwards.

It was Sam Patch's wife who had contrived to give him the benefits of a Buddhist funeral service, as has been told at the beginning of this article. Nevertheless before the coffin lid had been nailed down it was she also who had placed in his hands his Christian Testament, that it might accompany him into the Unknown.

AN
EMPEROR'S
GRIEF

*Their Lawes are very strict and full
of severetie, affording no other kinde
of punishment but either Death or
Banishment.*—Description of Japan
by Rev. ARTHUR HATCH, 1623

The roads in Otsu, near Lake Biwa, are wide
nowadays—wide enough to take the largest buses
and military trucks. But there was a time sixty-eight
years ago, when they were so narrow that not even a
horse-drawn carriage could pass through the town—
nothing in fact wider than a rikishaw. It was that
circumstance which made possible an incident that
caused an emperor great grief and might even have
split the world in war.

In June 1914 in Sarajevo, the capital of Bosnia, a
somewhat similar but more tragic incident occurred.
The Archduke Francis Ferdinand of Austria was
assassinated; a monstrous happening but not important enough to plunge the world in war and to
take the lives of millions of people. And yet within
little more than a month later the lamps of Europe
went out and were not lighted again for more than
four years.

In 1890 the heir-apparent of the Russian throne,
the Czarevitch or Cesarevitch as some preferred the
title, a young man of twenty-two set out on an official
tour of the Far East to acquaint himself with some

of his country's problems. This was the young man who was subsequently to become Emperor Nicholas II, that hapless Czar who in July, 1918 was shot together with his family by the Russian Communists.

From China the Czarevitch was to come to Japan where the Emperor Meiji intended to honour him as no foreign prince had ever been honoured before. The tour through Japan was to occupy a month and was intended to cement the bonds of friendship between the two countries. The Russian Minister in Tokyo had expressed in advance some anxiety for the young prince's safety, but had been assured by Emperor Meiji that every precaution would be taken, that he would be guarded and protected wherever he went, but in any event no Japanese would harm the Emperor's guest. Said the Emperor:

I take the personal responsibility of the Cesarevitch's visit. His person shall be sacred as my own. I answer for his safety with my own honour.

The Czarevitch's party, including his cousin Prince George of Greece, arrived in Japan attended by a squadron of Russian warships and after having visited Nagasaki and Kagoshima landed at Kobe, whence they proceeded to Kyoto. Before passing on towards Tokyo a visit was made to Otsu. After a trip on Lake Biwa in a steam launch, luncheon was served at the Governor's house after which the party started on the return journey to Kyoto, passing along the same narrow streets in Otsu as in the morning. The streets in Otsu were then so narrow that the journey had to be made by rikishaws, some fifty in all, each pulled by one man with another pushing behind. First came the Governor, the Chief of Police and two police inspectors, then a few paces behind them the Czarevitch, followed by Prince George of Greece, the Emperor's representative, Prince Arisugawa, the Russian Ambassador, and other Russian and Japanese dignitaries. The narrow streets were lined with police on either side, the men standing a couple of paces from one another. The procession formed an unbroken line which passed at a trot between the two rows of policemen. Every precaution had been taken for the safety of the royal visitor.

Among the police was one named Tsuda Sanzo, a middle-aged man and formerly a sergeant-major in the army. He had stood at the same spot in the morning but had given no hint of evil intent. When the Czarevitch's rikishaw drew level with him, he sprang out and drawing his sword aimed a two-handed murderous blow at the Czarevitch's head. Fortunately he had misjudged the speed of the rikishaw and the blow was deflected slightly by the prince's hat, and just when he aimed a second blow the rikishaw-man dropped the shafts and with rare coolness and courage threw himself at the feet of the policeman bringing him struggling to the ground. A second rikishaw-man thereupon snatched up the sword and dealt the fighting policeman several heavy blows. While Sanzo was being trussed up by other policemen who had rushed in from all sides, the Czarevitch, blinded with blood from a head wound, was led into an open shop where first aid was rendered. Both Japanese and Russian sources report that he pleasantly endeavoured to reassure the horrified Japanese officials that there was no need for alarm.

Do not be anxious. Ce n'est que du sang. It is nothing.

Within two hours of the news reaching Tokyo a cabinet meeting was being held, and a special train was leaving for Kyoto conveying the Emperor's representative, Prince Kitashirakawa, the Emperor's personal surgeon and other officials. A few hours later another special train left carrying a number of Cabinet Ministers, various Court officials, distinguished medical men of the capital and medical professors of Tokyo Imperial University. Early the next morning the Emperor himself, with all his staff left for Kyoto amid an outburst of national grief and indignation. In the meantime an Imperial Rescript had been issued.

It is with the most profound grief and regret that ....It is Our will that justice shall take its speedy course on the miscreant offender to the end that Our mind may be relieved, and that Our friendly and intimate relations with Our good neighbour may be secured against disturbance.

There then occured one of the most remarkable demonstrations of public sympathy that the world has witnessed. For awhile the life of the nation stood still. The theatres were closed, work stopped, shops were shut and markets abandoned as the people mourned with their Emperor. Over 20,000 persons made formal calls at the hotel in Kyoto where the Czarevitch was resting. Prefectures, cities, towns, villages, corporations, guilds and associations sent their representatives. Telegrams poured into Kyoto in such numbers that the telegraph office was barely able to cope with the traffic. All the newspapers of the Empire shared in the expressions of grief and indignation, and of sympathy for the Emperor whose honour had been so cruelly wronged. Visits were made to the shrines; incense was lighted, and the temple gongs and bells were sounded as prayers were offered to the Gods for the recovery of the Prince.

Some of the townsmen of Otsu even suggested that the name of their city had become too infamous to remain and that a new name should be selected. However, with the recovery of the Czarevitch, it was not considered necessary to carry that proposal further.

The Emperor arrived in Kyoto at 11 p.m. on the day following the attack and wished to see the Prince at once, but owing to the lateness of the hour had to postpone his call until the following morning. Later he accompanied the Czarevitch in the train to Kobe and thence to the landing-stage whence the Prince was carried on board a Russian warship. The tour of Japan had to be abandoned and four days later on learning the Czar's desire that the Czarevitch should proceed to Vladivostok, the Emperor accompanied by his suite went on board to bid him farewell. The decks, the passageways of the vessel, the cabins, and all free space were deeply encumbered by the gifts which poured in from all parts of the country. The wealthy gave of their costly possessions, the merchants and guilds sent silks and cloth, lacquers, bronzes and porcelains. Even farmers trudged for miles into Kobe to bring the traditional offerings of eggs. Rice, shoyu, dried fish, barley and beans were spontaneously brought by people who had never been able to afford many of the good things of life. Emblems of good luck and offerings of all description were piled on the deck.

Later the two rikishaw-men who had saved the life of the Czarevitch were munificently rewarded by the Russian Government with a pension of $1,000 a year for life, and with a gift of $2,500 and a Russian decoration from the Czarevitch. From their own Government they also received a pension and a medal. The two rikishaw-men on arriving on board the Russian ship to receive their awards were cheered by the Russian sailors, then seized, chaired, and toasted, and generally made so much of that they were quite bewildered at the fuss.

On the other hand the unfortunate Governor although only a few days in office was dismissed, as also was the Chief of Police.

When the Russian war vessel departed from Kobe she was escorted as far as the western entrance to the Inland Sea by a squadron of Japanese war vessels.

The world has long since forgotten this remarkable happening and forgotten too the two men who by their bravery may have saved a world from war. One of them survived all the hazards of wealth and fortune; he invested his money wisely and his family prospered. The other was made of poorer stuff; he was not strong enough to meet the good fortune that had come his way. He soon squandered his money and thereafter lived in poverty spending his pension on drink.

Following the Russian revolution in 1918 members of the Russian nobility, pseudo-princesses and others, have frequently attempted to cash in upon their avowed knowledge of Russian Court secrets by writing memoirs, in several of which the above incident, its political implications, and the assailant's motive are fancifully described. Some have even gone so far as to state that the incident so rankled in Nicholas' mind that it ultimately ushered in the disastrous Russian war with Japan.

The account given above of the actual incident is from the official Russian version as appearing in the Russian *Government Messenger* at the time, and the details of the happenings that followed it are largely taken from sources in Japan, and also from a fabulous tome of more than one thousand pages written shortly afterwards by Prince Ookhtomsky describing the Cesarevitch's travels in the Far East.

Those Russian accounts agree with the Japanese version at the time that the cause of the incident was no deeper than a psychological outburst of the disordered mind of one man. Those Russian accounts further show that the Czarevitch shared, as did the world at large, a real understanding and sympathy for the distress that the Emperor and Japan suffered as a result of this unfortunate event.

Certainly the action of the Emperor and his people stands out as a pattern of the *amende honourable* that other countries, and Japan also, might well have followed at times during the next half century. Had it been accepted by later generations as a pattern of conduct the whole course of world history might have been vastly different.

* * * * * * *

The *Review of Reviews* for June, 1896, carried an article purporting to give a translated extract from a letter said to have been written by Prince George of Greece to his father, wherein the Prince is alleged to have stated:

We passed through a narrow street decorated with flags and filled with crowds of people on both sides of the thoroughfare. I was looking towards the left when I suddenly heard something like a shriek in front of me and saw a policeman hitting Nicky a blow on the head with his sword, which he held in both hands. Nicky jumped out of the rickshaw and the policeman ran after him. Blood was flowing down Nicky's face. When I saw this I too jumped out with my stick in my hand and ran after the policeman who was about fifteen paces in front of me. Nicky ran into a shop but came out again immediately which enabled the policeman to overtake him, but I, thank God, was there in the same moment and while the policeman still had his sword high in the air I gave him a blow so hard that he had never experienced a similar one before. He now turned against me, but fainted and fell to the ground. Then two of the rickshaw pullers appeared on the scene; one got hold of his legs, while the other took up the sword which he had dropped in the falling and gave him a wound on the back of his head.

An Emperor's Grief

It was God who placed me there in that moment and who gave me the strength to deal that blow, for had I been a moment later, the policeman had perhaps cut off Nicky's head....

A writer in the *Independent* of New York referred to the spread of the story of Prince George's heroism as a modern example of myth making. It does, however, appear that Prince George did perhaps contribute in some measure to the saving of the Czarevitch although not quite in the heroic manner in which he is alleged to have described his part.

* * * * * * *

It has been said that immediately following the incident, the Emperor ordered that Tsuda should be executed without delay, but his advisers had to point out that under the constitution which he had granted his people Tsuda would have to stand trial, but that in any case he could not be executed for assault and injury and at the most he could only be given a long term of imprisonment. The Emperor was not pleased with this news; he reiterated that Tsuda would be executed.* His advisers insisted that could not be, and so he bowed, although most unwillingly, to his own laws and thus in due course of time there terminated an unfortunate incident that could have had the gravest consequences, but which in fact strengthened the love which the people of Japan had for their monarch and added to the respect of the world abroad for Emperor Meiji.

---

*Tsuda Sanzo died in prison seven years later. His death was seemingly of a suicidal nature, brought about by a refusal to eat.

PLATE I

Zempukuji in Yedo in 1859. Temple where the first U.S. Legation was located during the sojourn of Townsend Harris, first American envoy in Japan. (*Courtesy of F.D. Burrowes, Esq.*)

PLATE II

Tozenji in Yedo in 1859. Temple where the first British Legation was located. (*Courtesy of F.D. Burrows, Esq.*)

PLATE III

Mansion of the Daimyo of Satsuma in Yedo, 1859—typical of the homes in which members of the families of provincial governors lived as hostages in Yedo during the Tokugawa era. (*Courtesy of F.D. Burrows, Esq.*)

PLATE IV

Tokaido in 1860's near the former post town of Moto-Hakone. (*Courtesy of F.D. Burrows, Esq.*)

PLATE V

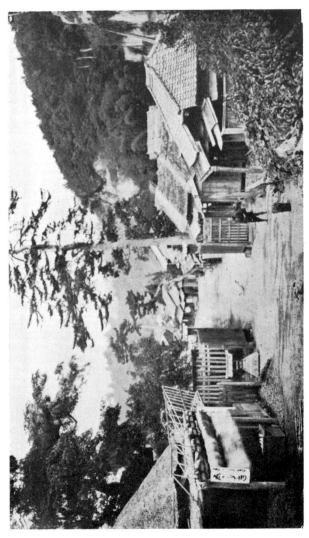

Tokaido at Kanagawa, showing barrier gates and guardhouse about 1860. (*Courtesy of F.D. Burrows, Esq.*)

PLATE VI

Eleven monuments at Hojuji Temple, Sakai, of the eleven Tosa men who were executed in connection with the Sakai massacre. See chapter, "The Sakai Massacre."

Head of Mamiya Hajime on view at Yokohama after execution. See Chapter, 'Murder near the *Daibutsu*.'
(Courtesy of L. J. Nuzum, Esq.)

PLATE VIII

A courtesan (generally referred to in Japanese publications as a "beauty" or "entertainer") by Utamaro. See chapter, "The Yoshiwara Ladies and Pinup Girls."

THE FORGOTTEN MEDALS

Honours are shadows, which from seekers fly;
But follow after those who them deny.
Richard Baxter—*"Love Breathing Thanks."*

When Lord Elgin, or the Earl of Elgin and Kincardine, to give His Lordship his full title, arrived in Japan in 1858 to conclude a treaty, he proceeded to Shimoda where he saw the Stars and Stripes flying over Townsend Harris' first U.S. Consulate at Oyster Point. The following day he entertained the Governor of Shimoda and his suite at luncheon. On hearing one of his Japanese guests refuse Curaçao and ask for Maraschino, Elgin concluded the Japanese were wider awake than they admitted and he decided to waste little time in the outer office of Shimoda but to make for the capital as soon as possible. In any case he thought so little of Oyster Point as a place for his Embassy that brushing aside all opposition he promptly sailed up the bay for Yedo where he demanded a suitable residence ashore.

A demand from any foreign envoy for a suitable residence in Yedo would have been bad enough, but coming from the Earl of Elgin and Kincardine it was doubly bad, because they had assumed that there were two personages, one Elgin and the other Kincardine. On learning something about the intricacies of English titles they were relieved to know that only one envoy had arrived, not two.

177

The Forgotten Medals

Lord Elgin quickly got down to business and a treaty was soon signed, the British using pens and the Japanese brushes, which were then exchanged as souvenirs.

The first British Minister, Sir Rutherford Alcock arrived in the following year and was provided with the commodious temple of Tozenji at Takanawa in the city of Yedo, for his residence and legation. As was not unusual on such occasions the Japanese authorities made available to the newcomers a Buddhist temple as a place of residence. Apart from official buildings, which obviously could not be handed over, there were in those days few suitable buildings other than temples available. Townsend Harris had much earlier been furnished with a Buddhist temple for his place of abode and to serve as a U.S. Consulate.

In 1859 when the port of Yokohama was opened, the British, American, French and Dutch Consuls each had their offices and residences in temples in Kanagawa. Some of the foreign missionaries likewise were accommodated in Buddhist temples, but although not at that time noted for their tolerance it is not recorded whether, as in the case of a certain Prefectural governor on taking over office in recent years, they first conducted a religious service to purify the premises after the presence of the previous incumbents.

Again in 1868 when the port of Kobe was opened some of the foreign merchants were at first given accommodation in various temples, and some in *sake* godowns.

Around a hundred years ago when the Treaty Ports in Japan were first opened there were more Japanese then than now who believed that Japan would be better off if the foreigners could be forced to leave the country, and within a few months of the first arrivals a long series of assassinations occurred. Three Russians attached to a diplomatic mission in Yokohama were murdered, soon to be followed by the killing of a Chinese servant of the French Consulate, and of a Japanese interpreter attached to the British Legation in Yedo. The French Legation was then fired and a few weeks later two Dutch merchants were cut to death in Main Street, Yokohama. Then within a year Heusken, secretary and Dutch interpreter to U.S. Consul-General Townsend Harris was murdered whilst proceeding on horseback along a street in Yedo under protection of the Tycoon's guard. (Even at a later date than this, members of the British Legation were forbidden to leave the legation compound unless accompanied by four or five Japanese guards and at least one English mounted constable.) All this lawlessness within less than two years!

Then on the night of 4th July, 1861, fourteen two-sworded men entered into a pact to attack the British Legation and kill the five British members. The Legation was guarded by 150 Japanese guards detached for that purpose by the Shogun's Government, but not all would have been on duty at the time. Despite the brave and resolute defence put up by those guards, several of whom were killed, they were unable to repel the fourteen samurai who

179

carried out their surprise attack with all the reckless valour of their class.

The assailants gained an entry into the Legation but were there met with such resistance from the Englishmen who were armed with pistols, that they withdrew leaving behind one dead. Several of the Legation members were seriously wounded with sword cuts.

Each of the assailants carried a sealed pact reading:

Although I am a person of low standing, I have not the patience to stand by, and see the sacred Empire defiled by the foreigner....If this thing that we are to do, may cause the foreigners to retire from our country....I shall take to myself the highest praise.

Although the Shogunate gave assurances that every effort would be made to apprehend and punish the offenders, several months elapsed before they dared arrest any of them. They then secretly executed three of the assailants in prison, and exposed their heads on the tops of pikes at the public execution ground. The Shogunate Government did not dare make it known that the men had really been executed for the offence of attacking the Legation. Instead the placards underneath stated that they were criminals who had been executed for breaking into a temple and stealing.

It was this incident and the sincere confession of the Japanese authorities that they were powerless to prevent such attacks that decided the British and French ministers to have their own guards and so led to the garrisoning of British and French troops in Yokohama for a period of about seven years or more, until about 1871.

In grateful recognition of the bravery of the Japanese guards, Queen Victoria had one gold and eighty-two silver medals struck off; but as the Tokugawa Government of that time refused to supply the names of the guards who had earned the decorations, which decorations would have marked the men as traitors in the eyes of most of their fellow-countrymen, the medals were packed away in a chest in the Legation, awaiting a change in public feeling when it was hoped the presentation could be made. The Tokugawa Government was strong enough to impose on its *daimyo* retainers the duty of posting guards to protect the foreign legations, but if the discharge of that duty was to include the unenviable distinction of being publicly decorated by the hated foreign powers, the guards would have been reluctant to continue their duties.

New legation buildings were constructed a few years later, but immediately they were completed they were set on fire by another band of samurai and so in course of time the British Embassy was moved to its present site in Kojimachi, facing the moat of the Imperial Palace. In one corner of the building, long since pulled down, was an enormous tower which Sir Harry Parkes insisted be built as a fitting place from which to fly the British flag. Only when the tower was completed was it discovered that any flag flown from that tower would be fluttering higher than the roofs of the Imperial Palace across the moat. A flagstaff had then to be constructed from ground level, and thereafter the tower was used to house a huge water tank, to the great alarm during earthquakes of all in the Embassy. Indeed it was somewhat irreverently whispered at that time in British diplomatic circles, mostly by junior secretaries, that the greatest hazard of the ambassadorship in Tokyo was the ever present possibility of His Excellency's enthusiasm becoming wetted at some unforeseen moment.

(Eventually the tower did come tumbling down. That was in the big earthquake of 20th June, 1894, but nobody at that late date held it against Sir Harry, because almost every other Legation in Tokyo suffered most serious damage—all in fact with the exception of the Belgian Legation, where according to Baroness d'Anethan's diary the loss was limited to a "few old empty beer bottles." The lady in question was Rider Haggard's sister and the wife of the Belgian Ambassador, and so should know.)

The circumstances of Sir Harry Parkes' flag-tower were forgotten by subsequent generations, but the outline of the story lingered on and is still told to-day with modifications and imaginary frills and with the locale being shifted from the British Embassy to one of the many tall buildings that line the Plaza in front of the Imperial Palace. Most foreigners residing in Tokyo are shown at one time or another by one of their knowledgeable friends some building which is alleged to have had the top story lopped off to prevent the occupants looking down upon the Emperor!

But let us return to the subject of this article. The

years went by. The Embassy grew in size. Ambassadors came and went. The archives of the Embassy accumulated but during those times an old chest, believed to contain old accounts was shifted from place to place. The key had long since been lost, but it was of no consequence. Then came a time in 1889 when a secretary in the chancery, imbued with what is not always deemed to be a diplomatic virtue, decided to disturb the dust of years, and in a general cleanup broke open the old chest. Then it was that the gold and silver medals and the parchment citations of bravery on the part of the Japanese guards in defending the Legation twenty-seven years before came to light. After much effort one or two of the Japanese guards for whom the medals had been struck were located. One subsequently became editor of the *Nichi Nichi Shimbun*. However, those were the days when the mercantile community still lived far apart from its consular and diplomatic representatives. The foreign press was not slow to take advantage of the discovery and added to the general amusement over the happening by offering the not very helpful suggestion that the Embassy should wait a little longer and then in a single ceremony hang the medals on the gravestones of all the recipients. In the circumstances it is not surprising that the Embassy observed a certain reticence over the matter, and so it cannot be told with absolute certainty in this article what was the ultimate fate of all those forgotten medals.

THE
CAREW
CASE

> *Though this be madness, yet there is
> method in it.*
>
> SHAKESPEARE—*"Hamlet"*

I had known for a long time that many people believed that Mrs. Carew had murdered her husband.

Edith, that is to say Mrs. Carew, was well-known
in the small foreign community of Yokohama, and
many were glad to call her a friend. She was bright,
attractive, and refined. She was a good horsewoman
and enjoyed the company of the younger and brighter
set—that is to say younger and brighter men than
her husband—no less than they enjoyed her company.
Walter, that is to say Mr. Carew, he was...well,
maybe I *am* prejudiced. His friends at the Club liked
him, and he had many friends. According to one of
their servants:

*The master had a liver, and he drank a fair bit, but
you know what clubmen are.*

He was manager of one of the gentlemen's clubs in
Japan—the Yokohama United Club. Actually I did
not know either of them. In point of fact Mr. Carew
died of arsenic poisoning before I was born.

I do confess (and so far as I know this is the only
confession in the case) Mrs. Carew had such a fascina-
tion for me that for a long while I attempted, but
without much success, to learn more about her. Eventually I forgot her, as I imagine most other people

had also, until some years ago when I was outside of
Japan and I happened to be reading a very old issue
of the London *Saturday Review*, actually of the year
1897, my attention was caught by an article on the
Carew Case. It may have been inspired by Mrs.
Carew's friends. In commenting upon the trial it
referred to the "scandalous manner" of the post-
mortem examination, the "improper admission" of
certain evidence, the "licence accorded witnesses," and
the "misdirection of the jury" which only consisted
of five men. It ended with the pungent comment:

> ...*We are certain that no English jury would have
> convicted her...One thing is at least clear, that a
> more lamentable exhibition of bemuddlement and
> imbecility on the part of all concerned in the trial
> at Yokohama has never disgraced English legisla-
> tion...*

My interest was so re-aroused that I immediately
endeavoured to locate a descriptive and detailed
account of the trial. Remembering what a stir it
had caused among foreign circles in Japan, I
imagined that would not be difficult. To my astonishment I failed to find any mention of the case in the
London Times, the *New York Times*, or the *New
York Daily Tribune* for the years 1896–1898, which
I suppose only goes to show that the news services
in those days were not as well organised as now to
gather dirt from the gutters, the boudoirs, and the
drawing rooms.

When I found that the case was not even mentioned
in such authoritative books as *Notable Trials, Famous
Poison Trials, Crimes in High Life* or *Women Blue-*

beards my interest in Mrs. Carew perceptibly waned. The search continued however and in the years that followed I must have scanned through thousands of pages of newspapers, all without success. For assistance in my long drawn out search I am indebted to patient librarians at the Oriental Library and the historical section of the Tokyo Imperial University, but most of all to courteous officials of the Ueno Public Library who permitted me to descend into the depths of the cellar storerooms and finger the dust-encrusted papers of bygone days. Then suddenly in an unexpected quarter I stumbled upon the court record. Since then I have made quite a study of the case.

Possibly the mortal remains of Mr. Carew would never have been disturbed at a post-mortem examination by a surgeon's scalpel had not two European nursemaids permitted their tongues to waggle. Of all the personalities in the case, probably the most despicable were those two European nursemaids, one English and the other Swiss. It had been the practice for the former to purloin the contents of Mrs. Carew's wastepaper basket and then to pass them on to her Swiss friend who fitted together the fragments of letters. Another little foible of the Carew nursemaid was to practice reproducing Mrs. Carew's handwriting. Her object in these activities and her relations, if any, with Mr. Carew were items of surmise. The defence sought to introduce those matters into the evidence, also to pin a case of forgery on her. Eventually counsel for the defence publicly apologised for any imputations that she had any illicit relations with Mr. Carew. He even admitted some of Mrs. Carew's

Japanese servants had perjured themselves on that
score. At least this pilfering pair of young women
gained a short period of notoriety and fame, because
it was they who furnished the prosecution with much
of the written evidence that proved so damning to
Mrs. Carew.

There were whisperings of arsenic by those two
amateur spies, and then some one slipped Dr. Wheeler,
the physician who was attending Mr. Carew, an
anonymous note reading:

Three bottles of solution of arsenic in a week.

At no time after Mr. Carew was removed to the
hospital half dead did Mrs. Carew attempt to hide
having purchased a considerable quantity of arsenic
and in addition a bottle of sugar of lead. But later
it came out at the inquest that Dr. Wheeler had himself prescribed arsenic for Mrs. Carew, who was suffering from malaria, which in part accounted for the
purchases. The last occasion on which he did so was
a couple of weeks earlier on the verandah of the
Yokohama Amateur Rowing Club. Mrs. Carew was
able to produce the prescription scrawled out on a
piece of paper torn from the regatta programme.

Mrs. Carew was also able to offer the Coroner an
explanation for the large quantity of arsenic found in
her husband's body, by explaining that for years he
has been dosing himself with arsenic for a certain
complaint and had been applying sugar of lead ex-
ternally. It was established that some years before
Mr. Carew had secretly consulted a doctor, other than
the family physician, but that he was habitually taking arsenic was not known to anyone other than Mrs.

Carew, not even to his medical advisers. It was fortunate she knew. It was also fortunate that at least one other person seemed to have had an inkling of it, if we are to believe the evidence, which of course I do! That person had already been able to soothe the nerves of the Japanese chemist who had sold the poison and was suffering from jitters at having failed to comply with all the regulations governing the sale of poisons. The Japanese chemist revealed that circumstance at the inquest, but then did not want to mention the person's name. The coroner insisted on knowing it. The Japanese chemist with much reluctance said that it was one Kobayashi Beika—a naturalised Japanese, previously known as Dr. J. E. de Becker. It so happened that Mr. Kobayashi Beika was present in the public seats in the coroners court. After the session he privately approached the British Consul, who was acting as coroner, and volunteered an explanation. He was, however, informed that he would be called as a witness and required to make his explanation under oath in open court. On doing so he related that whilst tiffining at the Yokohama United Club about a year before, the subject of medicinal poisons had cropped up and Mr. Carew had boasted:

Oh! That's nothing. I take enough poison to kill six men. I am obliged to do so.

Fortunately for Mrs. Carew other witnesses were forthcoming, later at the trial, who were prepared to swear under oath that about a year or so before his death, Mr. Carew had boasted of having taken arsenic in large quantities.

What arsenic? Why I have taken tons of it.

Furthermore it was proved that Mr. Carew had been medicating his pony with arsenic and sugar of lead. All in all, even at the inquest, it was abundantly clear to Mrs. Carew's friends, but perhaps not to the Coroner, that there could hardly have been a family more arsenic conscious than the Carew family. If all the evidence were truthful—a point on which there was some difference of opinions—there could hardly have been a house where more arsenic was "kicking about" than in the Carew home.

To my simple mind the whole matter of the poisons was thus satisfactorily accounted for, although perhaps not to the coroner or to Mr. Carew's friends.

Certainly a few loose ends remained, but they were mostly tied up by the timely entry into the case of a mysterious veiled woman in black named Annie Luke, who suddenly appeared in Yokohama twelve days before Mr. Carew's death and as mysteriously disappeared again a week after his death, without having been seen by anyone other than Mrs. Carew and her Chinese houseboy, aged twelve. When Annie knocked at the door and asked to see Mr. Carew, the houseboy actually spoke to her:

"Arimasen. No have got."

To my mind that evidence certainly proved something. There were of course some who thought it proved perjury!

During her short sojourn in Yokohama, Annie Luke had been busy writing a number of letters. There was an appealing one to Mr. Carew; a threatening one to Mrs. Carew in which Annie wrote: *"Beware!*

The Carew Case

Dare to speak one word of the truth and you shall never leave Japan alive." In addition there were letters to Mrs. Carew's counsel and to the Coroner, both of which nicely tied tight a few other loose ends. In these Mrs. Carew was dubbed *"a silly innocent"* and *"that little fool his wife."*

Those letters also hinted darkly at Annie doing away with herself and others also:

"Dead men tell no tales, no nor dead women either...."

Then most inconsiderately Annie disappeared into thin air, and with her I fear disappeared most of Mrs. Carew's chances. Despite the most diligent search, and the offer of a $500 reward, no trace was ever found of Annie Luke, alive or dead.

I might add that there was no doubt whatever in Mrs. Carew's mind that the handwriting in all those letters was that of Annie Luke, although a so-called handwriting expert did succeed in confusing the court. Some people sniffed and thought it significant that Annie Luke and Mrs. Carew both used notepaper bearing the same watermark, but not Mrs. Carew's friends, nor those who had placed bets on her innocence.

Mr. Carew, unhappily being dead, could not be called upon for any biographical details concerning Annie, but fortunately Mrs. Carew was able to supply some information of how her husband had once played fast and loose with Annie.

To my simple mind everything had been nicely explained and all the loose ends had been neatly tied, but Her Britannic Majesty's Consul-General, who, as already mentioned, was acting as coroner, obtusely refused to be convinced even of the corporeal existence of Annie and, when instructing the jury, he stated:

Gentlemen. I take upon myself the responsibility of saying that in considering your verdict, you need not complicate your minds as to the share which such a person as Annie Luke may have taken in the tragedy.

On what grounds H.B.M. Consul-General made this amazing statement I do not know, for it is well-known that Maskelyne and young Houdini were at that time causing women to disappear almost nightly!

After an inquest which lasted five days, the calling of over twenty witnesses and the asking of thousands of questions the jury returned an open verdict that Mr. Carew *"had died from the effects of arsenic, but by whom the poison was administered there is no direct evidence to show."* For this verdict they were abused by that section of the Yokohama Press which had already decided Mrs. Carew's guilt.

Mrs. Carew, not Annie Luke, was thereupon committed for trial on the charge that she

...wilfully and of malice aforethought did kill and murder one Walter Carew against the peace of Our Lady the Queen, her Crown and dignity.

The pace of drinking then slackened at the bars of all the clubs in Japan, as the members argued the case. In the stately homes on the Bluff, the rattle of teacups was stilled as the ladies gave judgement even before the court had heard the evidence; chores were forgotten in the servants quarters while the *amahs* argued with the cooks as to who had put arsenic in Mr. Carew's food.

The case became such a topic of conversation in Yokohama society and heated arguments developed to such a degree that social functions had to be curtailed. In the ensuing weeks, husbands and wives so disagreed as to the innocence or guilt of Mrs. Carew that many a wife developed homicidal tendencies and would have liked to poison her own husband.

All in all the Yokohama Foreign Concession gained so much notoriety over the case that the Kobe Foreign Concession developed a sort of inferiority complex which lasted for many years.

But let us return to Yokohama.

The age of chivalry may not be dead, for when the Court opened and the roll of jurymen was called, four had failed to answer the summons and were promptly fined fifty dollars, while five others secured exemption by presenting certificates of sickness. Finally a jury of five was sworn in.

To many of the foreign residents in Yokohama in those days, their most important purpose in life had become the matter of pleasing the boss or not offending his wife, or some other social prominence in that caste-ridden society. A jury of five therefore did not offer much of a margin of safety to an accused, especially when he or she was *persona non grata* with the *taipans'* wives. Whether the final verdict was right or wrong, Mrs. Carew was unquestionably placed in a position of great hazard. Perhaps it was that circumstance that influenced her in taking some desperate chances, as will be related hereafter.

As already remarked the case caused a tremendous stir and while the top diplomats in Tokyo may not have deserted their embassies to attend the trial, certainly a number of them sent along their ladies, some of whom commented on the case in their diaries. One of them recorded how painful the trial was. Twelve years later, when Kobayashi Beika was writing some reminiscences, he also still remembered the pain.

The time has now come to introduce an unfortunate young man, the co-respondent, as it were, in this mysterious case. Baroness d'Anethan, wife of the Belgian Ambassador, in her diary refers to him as Mr. X *"in order to spare pain."* I, being fearful of offending the great British banking institution with which he was associated, will continue in this article to hide his identity under the same title. At this stage I should make clear that the only offence established against Mr. X, apart from writing some tender and indiscreet letters to a married woman, was that his handwriting was deplorable.

The moral of this story, if such writings could possibly have a moral, is that a person whose handwriting is as illegible as mine or Mr. X's should never get mixed up with women, and certainly not in murder trials. The unfortunate Mr. X was required to read out in Court his own love letters to Mrs. Carew, because nobody else in the Court could decipher his writing! Mr. X's behaviour in court certainly gave the impression that he was less willing to protect Mrs. Carew than she was seeking to protect him, and the *Japan Mail,* it is good to record, rightly scorned him as "a renegade lover."

Annie Luke was not the only disappearance. A most indiscreet letter from Mr. X to Mrs. Carew, which was about to be entered as evidence, mysteriously disappeared from the body of the Court before the eyes of all present. It was last seen on the barristers' table, then it was no more. The Judge thereupon ordered that nobody be permitted to leave the court without permission. When Mrs. Carew left she was searched by a wardress who found that the missing letter had become stuck in the cuff of Mrs. Carew's costume. This unfortunate happening cost Mrs. Carew one of her defending counsels who immediately withdrew from the case in a huff.

As I personally came to know some of the jurymen in later years I do now assert that the contretemps of the missing love letter must have made an undue impression on their dour and unimaginative minds, much to the disadvantage of Mrs. Carew.

A mysterious red herring, one of many, was drawn across the trails that the prosecution was endeavouring to build up, when a German resident of Yokohama and a friend of Mr. Carew related that while playing billiards with him just a week before his death, Mr. Carew kept repeating:

"Le moment est arrive on il faut fair la chose."
(The moment has arrived when the thing must be done.) Whilst the defence sought to attach some special significance to this incident as indicating a determination to commit suicide, my own crude mind suggests that Mr. Carew was just drunk.

It must also be related either for or against Mr. X, according to whichever side our sympathies lie, that

Mr. X swore he saw on the day of the funeral a lady loitering near the Yokohama Club who seemed to fit the description of Annie Luke. She appeared to be greatly agitated.

Among the large number of witnesses called was Her Britannic Majesty's Envoy, Sir Ernest Satow, who was entered as a witness in respect of a letter signed A. L. Price which was sent to him protesting against the *"scandalous manner in which our Consul had conducted the inquest."* It was proved by the prosecution that Price was not in Japan at the time that letter was written. The defence was eventually forced into the admission that the letter had, in fact, been written by Mrs. Carew in a desperate effort to clear herself.

Further let me add that Mrs. Carew, or at least her counsel, set out to convince the jury that there was no motive for murder. Mrs. Carew stated that she and her husband were on good terms. He was receiving a salary as manager of the Yokohama United Club (and the perquisites that went with it) and she had an independent income of £500 per annum. Some evidence was also offered, although maybe not of a convincing nature to some of the merchant jurymen, that Mrs. Carew had almost completed arrangements to set her husband up in business as a silk merchant with a capital of £5000. Coroners and judges are never easy persons to convince, but what possible motive, I ask you, could she, in the circumstances, have had for murdering her husband?

When addressing the jury at the trial, Counsel for the defence admitted that Mrs. Carew had *"a propen-*

sity to gratify her vanity by captivating the senses of the opposite sex."—What woman hasn't?—The jury had already heard that there had been other men who were known in the Carew family by the nicknames of the *"Ferret"*, the *"Ice Cream Vendor"*, and the *"Organ Grinder"*, and finally Mr. X who was referred to as the *"Youth"*. All of those friendships, it was said, were known to Mr. Carew.

Why, asked Counsel for the defence, should Mrs. Carew wish to get rid of a husband *"who gave her every facility for amusing herself with light flirtations?"*

The majority of the foreign community believed that Mrs. Carew would secure an acquittal, as was shown by the betting odds, although the odds did shorten as the trial proceeded.

For nineteen days, dozen of witnesses were called, most of them prominent members of the Yokohama and Tokyo foreign community; thousands of questions were asked; diaries, telegrams, chit-books, and letters from Mrs. Carew's wastepaper basket and elsewhere were produced in abundance. Certainly a doubt was raised as to the authenticity of some of the letters submitted in evidence by the prosecution, the inference being that they were forgeries and the work of the perfidious nursemaid. Experts gave evidence and dissertations on the various aspects of arsenic poisoning and notorious arsenic habitues of the past. Then two days were occupied by the counsels for the defence and for the prosecution addressing the jury, followed by the learned judge summing up the case.

Finally, after twenty-one days the jury retired to

reach a verdict. Precisely twenty-five minutes later they were back again and announced GUILTY.

The judge thereupon donned the three-cornered black cap and pronounced:

The sentence of this Court upon you Edith May Hallowell Carew that you be taken from the place where you now stand to the British Consular Jail at Yokohama and there remain interned until after a convenient time when, on a subsequent day appointed by the proper authority, you shall be led out to the place of your execution within the precincts of the Consular Jail and there hanged by the neck until you are dead and your body shall then be taken down and buried within the precincts of the jail and may God have mercy upon your soul.

The verdict was argued in the clubs, in the tea-parties and in the papers. Brinkley, in the *Japan Mail,* sought to show that Mrs. Carew had never indulged in anything more serious than a mild flirtation, that she was on affectionate terms with her husband, and there was not a shred of evidence to suggest that she abhorred him as the father of her children, or that she was jealous of him—why should she have been, when he had no loves other than the Club bar! And so, argued Brinkley, love, hate and jealousy, the three mainsprings of crime, was each absent from this case. Sharp clashes on the subject took place as usual between the *Japan Mail* and the other Yokohama foreign newspapers—sure signs that, after all the excitement of a murder trial, the life of the community was slipping back into its normal sensitive grooves again.

197

It was about this time that the Empress Dowager of Japan died. An Imperial Proclamation was thereupon issued granting an amnesty to certain categories of criminals. A few days later, Sir Ernest Satow in his wisdom and discretion, thereupon decided that Mrs. Carew should not suffer a disadvantage because of having been tried in a British court, and that the same measure of grace should be extended to her as Japanese criminals were receiving. He thereupon directed that in lieu of capital punishment Mrs. Carew be imprisoned with hard labour for life.

Shortly afterwards she was transported to a jail in Hongkong and then some seven months later was sent to England to serve her sentence in the convict prison at Aylesbury. The Judicial Committee of the Privy Council refused her leave to appeal.

And so Mrs. Carew, the once popular and vivacious member of the younger set of Yokohama, disappeared from the scene.

As to whether Mrs. Carew did or did not murder her husband, I personally have never hesitated to accept the verdict of the jury of twelve good men and true; I beg your pardon, five good men and true, who were in such a hurry to discharge their duties and get back to business, that after sitting for twenty-one days listening to highly complicated, technical, prolix and perplexing evidence—and circumstantial at that—they were able in just twenty-five minutes to reach a unanimous agreement that Mrs. Carew was guilty and so should be sent to the gallows. Later it was said in extenuation of their haste that their decision had long been made up, which, in fact, only made their position worse, for it amounted to an admission that a verdict was reached before the judge had summed up the evidence. But do not mistake me. They were all honourable men. Indeed one in later years became my boss, and a man whom I look back upon with respect and affection.

Baroness d'Anethan in her book *Fourteen Years of Diplomatic Life in Japan* attempted to whitewash the jury by saying that they racked their brains for some loophole on Mrs. Carew's behalf. If that were the truth, the truth also was that the jury only permitted itself to suffer on the rack for precisely twenty-five minutes.

Whatever may be the truth, and it can never now be known, I do admit that the thought is ever fleeting through my mind that no woman would commit murder for a man, who after all did nothing much more than write illegible love letters!

MR. CAREW'S TOMBSTONE

> *As soon*
> *Seek roses in December—ice in June;*
> *Hope constancy in wind, or corn in chaff;*
> *Believe a woman or an epitaph,....*
> Lord BYRON—*"Don Juan"*

Fires and earthquakes have wiped out most of the Foreign Settlement records of the last century and most of the newspaper files also, but the patient researcher can still turn up from diaries and elsewhere forgotten pages of the past which, when pieced together, reveal scenes long since forgotten. And so it comes about that the following two scenes from Yokohama life of 1897, the year following that in which Mr. Walter Carew, manager of the Yokohama United Club, died of arsenic poisoning, can be presented.

It was a Saturday evening, in October, 1897. Trade had been falling off. The silk market had been erratic. The various strata in the social pyramid of the Yokohama foreign community had each experienced a number of storms-in-a-tea-cup. The litigation among the foreign members of the community, quite apart from a rash of cases between foreigners and Japanese, had been unusually great, and the ranks of the *taipans* had become divided by a lawsuit that had developed between two of their most exalted members. There was a temporary shortage of liquor owing to the wreck of a P. & O. vessel. It had been mail day with all the rush and bustle associated with mail in those early days. In short, tempers were frayed, and the gathering at the bar of those feeling in need of a stimulant was more numerous than usual.

Gathered around one of the many tables were six men. There was the Anglican priest who had conducted the funeral service for Mr. Carew. There was a law clerk, named Burbles, of the law firm which had defended Mrs. Carew at the murder trial. He was a rather brilliant man, generally somewhat exhilarated of an evening, but invariably moderately inebriated throughout the whole of each week end. That being Saturday evening, the week end had well started! There was Cole Watson, the *taipan* of Findlay Richardson & Co., who had been one of the jurors at the Carew murder trial. He had had a very busy day! There was the editor of the *Japan Gazette*, who had again come off second best in a clash with Capt. Brinkley of the *Japan Mail*. There was a tourist who was about to commence a three months tour of Japan—that was the thorough way in which tourists in those days toured the country. He was a visitor at the club, and had brought with him a copy of Chamberlain's *Things Japanese*, Murray's *Guide*, and Johnson's *Oriental Religions*, in the optimistic belief that, in such a citadel of European culture, by spending an hour with residents of twenty or more years standing, he would learn more in an hour about Oriental religions than in a week's reading. All three books were at his elbow with strips of paper to mark the more complicated passages on which he hoped to receive advice and instruction. The sixth man was the manager of the Hongkong & Shanghai Bank.

Cole Watson, the *taipan*, opened the conversation with the usual moan:

"What a day! What a day! The godown loaded up with Manchester cottons and still more arrived to-day. I suppose, Burbles," said he, facetiously addressing the law clerk, "business with you is dull, now that the Carew case is forgotten and done with."

"It's not done with. To-day I was ordering a tombstone. Mrs. Carew has now decided upon the inscription," replied the law clerk.

"What? Mrs. Carew erecting a tombstone! From a loving wife, I suppose."

"And why not, Watson," rejoined Burbles with some heat. "Not everybody believes the jury was right. Although most think you were in a hurry to get back to your Manchester cottons."

"That's enough, Burbles," warned the editor.

"And what a tombstone it will be," continued the irrepressible Burbles, "Don't ask me to tell you whether I chose the quotations in the epitaph:

Twilight and evening star
And one clear call for me
And may there be no moaning of the bar
When I put out to sea.

"I say," said the Anglican priest, breaking into the conversation, " that's from Tennyson's "Crossing of the Bar." I recall Mrs. Carew was often reading poetry when I called on her in the Consular Jail. I do not think she would need your help, Mr. Burbles, in selecting an epitaph."

"You have only heard half," said Burbles, "The next portion reads:

A little trust that when we die
We reap our sowing and so goodbye.

"You may not recognise that quotation, Padre. It is from du Maurier's *Trilby*."

"Sounds like a confession of guilt." said Watson, the *taipan*.

The padre turned to the tourist who had been listening attentively and whispered:

"They're talking about Mrs. Carew, who was sentenced to hard labour for life. She was declared guilty of the murder of her husband. He was manager of this club. You will not, of course, have heard of her."

"On the contrary," replied the tourist in a much louder voice, "I knew Mrs. Carew quite well. I met her last July when I was travelling from Singapore to Colombo on the P. & O. ship 'Shanghai.' Shortly after I came on board I got speaking to her. She was very attractive. That same evening we spent an hour—maybe more—together on the boat deck. I remember it was a wonderful tropical night, and the moon was rising low on the Indian Ocean. Edith was certainly a fascinating woman. She told me she had lost her husband in Yokohama. She did not mention any details, but said it was a very sad affair. It might surprise you to know she warned me against this club. She said far too many men had broken their lives on this bar counter, and more still on that of the Kobe Club. She said the reason was that the Kobe Club bar was so much longer! She was travelling with a middle-aged woman, whom I imagined to be a travelling companion. Next morning I was told by the other passengers that she was a wardress who was escorting Mrs. Carew to the convict prison at Aylesbury in England. Before I disembarked at Colombo, Edith told me a great deal. I also learned that she was very fond of poetry, but she never mentioned any of Tennyson." Then turning to the *taipan* he said severely:

"You, sir, consider the epitaph to be a confession of guilt, but I am not so sure. Have you considered the possible play on the word *bar;* and don't forget that Mrs. Carew sailed over the *seas* to England. I wonder whether it is not a bitter taunt directed at the Court by Mrs. Carew in the belief that there would have been moans of disapproval from the jury when she sailed overseas to serve life imprisonment, instead of hanging on the gallows where you, sir, had sought to place her. But, gentlemen, I do not care to pursue this topic further. So if you will excuse me, I shall depart and commence my tour of Japan." Terminating this long speech with a polite smile, he gathered up his books and departed.

"Well I'll be damned," burst out the law clerk. "Pardon my language, Padre, but what do you think of that?"

"It is all very distressing," murmured the padre, "I might add that when Mrs. Carew was in the Consular Jail awaiting to be transported overseas I frequently called on her, and I believe I enjoyed her complete confidence. Beyond that I do not care to discuss the matter further, I think I shall take my departure. Good night, gentlemen."

Mr. Carew's Tombstone

"Well there goes the second. We certainly would be learning things," continued Burbles, "if we only knew what everybody was talking about. What do you think, Cole Watson?"

"You know very well, young man, what I think. You were in court. You heard the verdict."

"I entirely agree, Watson," said the editor, "there has been far too much loose talk about this case, and I suspect my unworthy contemporary on the *Japan Mail* is behind it all. There is a telegram from London in the Shanghai papers just received. Here, I have a copy:

Important evidence in favour of Mrs. Edith Carew who poisoned her husband in Japan has been discovered and an influentially signed petition to the Queen asking for a retrial in England is preparing.
Somebody, and I suspect Brinkley, is engineering this."

"I certainly agree there has been too much loose talk." said the bank manager breaking into the conversation for the first time. "I didn't like at all the idea of Brinkley describing in his paper one of my staff as a *renegade lover*, even if Dickinson was that and worse. I have been telling my Head Office for years that this is no place for a single man. I can't be expected to watch every amorous young man, like a wife watches her husband. For the past year I have been hearing about this case from my Head Office every mail and from my wife every day. I'm tired of it. That reminds me, my wife is spending the night with friends in Tokio. I shall go home early. Goodnight."

"Now we are three! But getting back to the tombstone," said the prophetic Burbles, "the words will be engraved in granite and half a century later foreign residents in Japan may still be arguing this case, and still speculating whether Mrs. Carew really did poison her husband as our worthy jurymen did declare."

The club door-porter approached the editor.

"Your phaeton is waiting outside, sir."

"Come, Watson," said the editor "let's go. I've heard more than enough."

Burbles, left on his own, looked into his glass and mumbled: "There'll be no moaning at *this bar* when I put out to sea."

* * * * * * * *

Let us now leave the Yokohama United Club and attend one of the regular social meetings of the Women's Auxiliary of the Bluff Church held two months later in December, 1897. It followed the devotional hour at which the leader had developed the theme: *Let him who is without sin among you cast the first stone.*

As soon as the tea had been served a voice of gossip was heard above the murmur of conversation.

"I was passing through the Yokohama Cemetery this morning and saw the tombstone that has just been erected over Mr. Carew's grave. Really I do not know what to think of it. You must see it."

With the mention of the word "Carew" voices were stilled as all listened.

"Yes," said another. "So extraordinary—*may there be no moaning of the bar when I put out to sea*

and *when we die we reap our sowing.* I think that
is intended as a message from the grave, an admission by Mr. Carew that he had lived the life he chose
and had died from the consequences of the wild oats
he had sowed."

"In that case," said her friend, "we might be expected to understand that Mr. Carew is deriding the
Court for all the sadness and bitterness that had been
stirred up when he put out to sea."

"Nonsense! Certainly not!" said a fourth. "I was
speaking to Mrs. Brown-Brown yesterday evening,
and she says it is a clear admission of guilt by Mrs.
Carew. Poor Mrs. Brown-Brown, she is most distressed. There have been terrible differences of opinion
between her and her husband, whom she thinks has
been a secret admirer of Mrs. Carew. The whole
thing is most disgraceful. It is even said that Capt.
Brinkley is at the bottom of it all. More likely it is
just another of Mrs. Carew's frauds and deceptions."

"Well," said the padre's wife, "My husband claims
that there is no doubt in his mind as to the real intent of the quotations, but he just refuses to discuss
the matter with me. Really it is so maddening. But
he did mention that the quotation from Tennyson is
not quite accurate."

"Frankly," said another "I never did like Mrs.
Carew. I did not like the way she eyed my Hiram
when she met us in the street. I believe that the
whole tombstone is intended as nothing more than a
dramatic exit with which Mrs. Carew chose to leave
Yokohama—a stage on which she had played the part
of a popular, an attractive, and a so-called refined

lady."

In the corner there was sitting a very small but very old lady with silvery white hair. She had been knitting quietly with downcast eyes. When a lapse finally occurred in the conversation, which was not for quite a time, she raised her eyes and gently remarked:

"I have been in Yokohama longer than any of you. As you know I first came here on the same ship as Dr. and Mrs. J.C. Hepburn. That was back in 1859. I know more of life here perhaps than any of you, and some things in my own life I wish I could forget. Can't we all just pray and hope that the message which the tombstone sets out to convey is the truth; and let us leave those who are without sin to cast the stones."

She lowered her eyes and quietly resumed her knitting.

* * * * * * * *

The veracity of epitaphs has long been suspected. The graven word is all too frequently a device to secure immortality for one who will soon be forgotten by his best friends, and a deception to perpetuate affectionate memories that never existed. May, however, those who walk through the Yokohama Foreign Cemetery forget such human frailties when they come upon the gravestone reading:

Mr. Carew's Tombstone

WALTER RAYMOND HALLOWELL CAREW
In Loving Memory
of
My Husband
Who Died October 22nd 1896 aged 43 years

Twilight and evening star,
And one clear call for me,
And may there be no moaning of the bar
When I put out to sea.

A little trust that when we die
We reap our sowing and so goodbye.

LIFE AND STRIFE
IN THE
FOREIGN
CONCESSIONS

> *Be thou as chaste as ice, as pure as*
> *snow, thou shall not escape calumny.*
> *Get thee to a nunnery: farewell.*
> Shakespeare—*"Hamlet"*

Mud slinging has been popular right from the time millions of years ago when fishes first emerged from the river mud, wagged their tails and entered upon an amphibian life!

In most countries around a hundred years ago, and less, there was a fair amount of mud slinging, also rotten eggs and overripe tomatoes which were considered a more effective argument than reasoned words. Such times have not entirely passed. If now I rake up some of the mud that was flung around in Japan during the early days of the Foreign Settlements, it will at the most only demonstrate that there was possibly more restraint here on both sides than in many other countries.

If the editors of the early foreign newspapers did not conduct their feuds with the same vigour as did the *New York Sewer* and the *Rowdy Journal*, of Charles Dickens fame there was at least a fair amount of sniping and sufficient libel suits to enliven even those dull days.

The feuds between the *Japan Mail,* edited by Capt. F. Brinkley and some of the more independent foreign newspapers continued during his lifetime and well after his death. Brinkley, originally an English army officer, came to Japan in 1867 with a military detachment for the British Legation Guard. Later he was appointed gunnery instructor at the Japanese Naval College, but he soon forsook his military career for journalism and writing. As it was generally known that his paper, the *Japan Mail,* received some form of financial assistance from the Japanese Government, he was an easy mark for the independent papers, but nevertheless a formidable opponent.

In those times rarely a day passed without one of the papers hurling insults at the other. The chief target of the *Japan Daily Herald* was the *Tokio Times.*

> ...*the tedious verbosity and mawkish insipidity of that puny periodical...the Tokio Times, whose mission appears to be principally that of fulsome and illimitable adulations of the government.*

The *Tokio Times* was edited by Edward H. House the first American propagandist employed by the Japanese Government, and its mission, to use House's own words, was "to write Sir Harry Parkes out of Japan"—a mission incidentally in which it failed, for Sir Harry remained in Japan for several years after the *Tokio Times* passed out. Even Capt. Brinkley found himself repeatedly at variance with its editor and described the paper as a

> *pharasaical print whose weekly task it is to poison*

*as far as its feeble powers permit the minds of the
people against foreign intercourse.*

But such comment was mild compared to some of
the compliments that those editors bestowed on one
another. For example Brinkley's obituary notice of
the *Japan Herald,* when it folded up, read in part:

*It has been a disgrace to foreign journalism. Its
methods have been the methods of the thug. The
Japan Herald has been as effective and annoying
as the viperish shrillings of some side-way slut.*

The *Tokio Times* each week carried on its war with
some section of the foreign community. At one time
it attacked the German Legation to such a degree that
His German Majesty's representative in Japan asked
that "the paper be no longer sent to the Legation,"
whereupon the editor announced to his readers that
the subscription having been paid in advance he
would continue to deliver the paper, and the German
Minister could do with it what he wished. He then
added the sly quip that he had no doubt the Minister
would continue to read it as diligently as before.

In the next issue he was charging the French Minister with executing a scheme of plunder in a squab-
ble that had arisen in connection with the French
Post Office which was maintained in Yokohama in
those privileged days.

Then he lashed at the Kobe Settlement Foreign
Municipal Council, which he claimed was "pugnacious
and self-assertive":

*The election of the members of the Foreign Muni-
cipal Council is frequently attended with comparatively as much excitement as a contested election*

212

at home. Placards, political cries, canvassers, speech-making, and drink, all find a place in the Lilliputian contests. The Foreign Municipal Council has no body to be kicked and no soul to be saved. It is simply a body of individuals engaged in the unusually pleasant occupation of spending their neighbours' money and occasionally making a considerable fuss over the performance. Only that and nothing more.

By the time the memory of the *Tokio Times,* Brinkley, and other targets of the past had grown dim, some Japanese-owned English newspapers had made their debut, and the attention that had previously been bestowed on Brinkley's paper and similar enterprises was then diverted by the older established English language press, to what were described as "those near-English newspapers."

But let us go back in Japan to about the time the country was first opened and let us start high up on the Japanese social ladder, even at which exalted level there is an amusing instance of mud slinging recorded in a Japanese document, signed by various *daimyo,* answering a charge from the Japanese Government in Yedo that they had slandered the diplomatic corps.

...We never spread among our people insulting libels against foreigners. We never called Harrisoo (U.S. Consul, Townsend Harris) a fool, Arookoo (British Minister, Sir Rutherford Alcock) a..., and Berrookoroo (French Minister, Monsieur de Bellecourt) a... We never called Consooroo (Consuls) drunkards, and foreign merchants thieves."

If the daimyo did call the consuls "drunkards" and the foreign merchants "thieves"—and that probably was only half of it—they were not the only ones who had said hard things. The diplomats had called the merchants names—Sir Rutherford Alcock in particular when he dubbed the foreign mercantile community of Yokohama "the scum of the earth"—and the merchants had been even more blunt in saying what they thought of the diplomats.

Having already recorded what the *daimyo* may have thought of the consuls and merchants, I shall now avoid all charges of partiality by lifting straight out of the diary of Townsend Harris—the first American envoy to Japan—a few excerpts by way of showing what he thought of the Japanese, although in doing so it is but fair to mention that those were the days of hasty and sweeping generalizations for Townsend Harris, most of which were corrected later.

>*9th Sept., 1856*   *A greater tissue of lies was never heard.*
>
>*12th Sept., 1856*   *It was a rare scene of Japanese deceit, falsehood, flattery, and politeness.*
>
>*9th May, 1857*   *....I am satisfied that I have been constantly and systematically overcharged.*
>
>*4th July, 1857*   *My letters were very short and very guarded, as I do not doubt the Japanese open them.*

However, on 23rd August, 1856, Harris passed Japan a compliment, for he made in his diary an interesting meteorological observation:

Weather delightful. The air is like that of the United States, full of oxygen.

Let us now move on a few years to 1860 when Dr. George Smith, Bishop of Victoria (Hongkong) made a two-weeks tour of Japan. On arrival he was advised by some wags in Yokohama to leave his card on the principal of a *"young ladies boarding school"* nearby. The good bishop gladly complied and was greatly alarmed later to discover that the place was *"an infamous public institution containing two hundred female inmates dispersed over a spacious series of apartments."*

The good bishop's reputation was such that no ill effects were suffered from his innocent visit to such an establishment. However, a less reverent gentleman might not have been so fortunate, and looking around the community to-day one suspects that it would be unkind to play such a prank on some married men in these times. Nevertheless before leaving Japan the Bishop was to have a narrower escape, as is told in one of the books of that period:

In shopping in Japan the greatest care must be exercised to guard against the acquisition of indecencies which are found not only in books and pictures but on porcelains, in ivories and surreptiously conveyed in fans....I was deeply grieved to learn that even the sacred character of the Bishop of Victoria, who had neglected the precaution of a minute examination, might not have been saved. Had not an acquaintance providentially examined his porcelain cups, they would, in all probability, have been stopped and confiscated at the English

Custom House as inadmissible, even as the private property of a bishop.

On his return to Hongkong the Bishop wrote a book entitled *Ten weeks in Japan* wherein he castigated Yokohama, and not without ample reason, as a *"deplorable scene of demoralisation and profligate life"* where *"a considerable portion of the foreign community live in a state of dissoluteness exceeded in no part of the East"* and a place where *"the native officials contribute every facility for the perpetration of domestic vice and impurity"* and negotiate for young men *"the terms of payment and the selection of a partner in a dissolute mode of life."*

Among the many young men who shared his bread and bed with a Japanese girl was a studious young Englishman, who later became one of the greatest foreign scholars of the Japanese language. Then after an absence of nearly thirty years, when he returned to Japan in the highest position that an Englishman can occupy in the country, he sought out the lady and, because of the religious convictions which he had formed since his association with her, he insisted upon marrying her solely to rectify the irregularity of his earlier connections—such was the strength of the religious convictions of that remarkable man.

The commercial community was frequently divided, but not so, however, in their relations with the missionaries. Both sides stood apart and flung mud at one another fore and aft. There were so many ignorant and discreditable beings among the mercantile community, and so much intolerance among the missionaries, that even at this late date neither side can laugh off all the hard things that were said.

Dr. W.E. Griffis, the American missionary and historian, on arrival in Japan in 1870, had a poor opinion of everybody except his fellow missionaries. Wrote he:

The first foreigners were not specially noted for good morals, sensitive consciousness or sweetness of temper, and the underhand cunning and disregard of truth which seems a part of official nature in Japan were matched by the cold-blooded villainy and trickery of the unprincipled foreigners of all creeds and nationalities.

The morals of the merchants were likewise noted by his confrere, Dr. Verbeck, who went on record about the same time as saying that *"the temptations in this country are fearful....In fact very few indeed, outside of ministers and missionaries, have not fallen."* It has never been clear whether the good doctor lumped the foreign women in that indictment, or just how he knew that the missionaries resisted temptation while practically all non-missionaries fell by the wayside. Anyhow it is certain there was an element of truth in the statement and so it is satisfying to look around now and note how much we have improved!

The merchants thought equally harsh but different things about the missionaries. Fortunately as it was not customary for them to do much writing—except in ledgers—their thoughts have largely been lost to posterity.

There were almost daily tea parties at the stately houses on the Bluff in Yokohama, and later in Kitano-cho in Kobe, where Mrs. Brown-Brown and her friends loudly criticised the missionaries at one extreme and whispered about the eligible young men at the other, who had set up housekeeping on their own (more or less) in places far removed for safety from the Bluff and from Kitano-cho.

Cocktail parties had not at that time been invented, but dinner parties were held with great frequency. Considering that the community lived in a confined area of little more than half a square mile, was largely cut off from the outside world, and for some years the nearest telegraph office was at Colombo, and that most of those early arrivals knew little of Japan and cared less, it is not surprising to read in a missionary's account that the dinner parties of the merchants were characterised by *"the great number of brilliant flashes of silence and that meditations on the crockery were common."*

The criticism was probably unkind. Actually there is reason to believe that a good deal was said and drunk at those dinner parties. The Japanese authorities and the embassy and consular folk were all lumped together and dismissed without ceremony and then the conversation seems to have been mainly about the good old China days of thirty years before that period!

However it was a globe-trotter's book which dealt the foreign communities the worst blow beneath the belt. The authoress dismissed the Japanese as *"disgusting creatures"* and then wrote off the foreign community in the following terms:

It will be well understood that the life of the Eu-

ropean in Japan is after all a wretched one....
The sensual life led there has reduced many of
them to a state bordering on imbecility....The
eyes of such men are dull and they have a kind of
idiotic stare.

* * * * * * *

In 1883 the time came for Sir Harry Parkes, who
was the second British Minister to Japan, and one
of the most accomplished, to retire after eighteen
years of distinguished service in that appointment.
When he first arrived, Japan's administrative system
in many departments was in its infancy, and Sir
Harry's energy and aggressiveness did not make him
popular in government circles where most action took
place to slow-motion time. Apparently there were
some people who were not sorry when he retired, for
the valedictory notices in the Japanese Press were,
like Sir Harry's mode of speech, quite frank and to
the point. The only difference was that they were
either exaggerated or not fully accurate.

A year or so earlier in 1879 when he left Japan
on a short visit to England the *Tokio Times,* the
English language newspaper operating with Japanese
Government support, published, among other valedic-
tory messages, the following translation of the *Fuso
Shinshi* newspaper's farewell to Sir Harry:

He pursued with the eagerness of a hungry wolf,
rather than the methods or habits of a human be-
ing, his watchfulness for the promotion of British
interests....He advanced the interest of his nation
by humiliating and oppressing other states with
utter disregard for the lasting hatred and ill-will
such action caused.

Life and Strife in the Foreign Concessions

His conduct, however, has not as a rule been distinguished by high politeness; on the contrary it has been marked by most disgraceful violence and brutality. Smashing of glasses at our prime minister's table; physically assaulting at Hiogo an individual now of elevated rank; insulting the ex-minister for foreign affairs, Terashima, by the use of abusive language, and many like acts of extreme indecency....Such being the case what could be more natural than for him to find no Japanese grieving at his departure.

Despite the Press reports Sir Harry Parkes was highly respected in many Japanese circles for his outstanding talents, and remembered as being one of the most powerful supporters of the Japanese Imperial House, at a time when so many of the Foreign Powers were inclined to support the Shogunate as being the more stabilising influence in the country.

Emperor Meiji was not unmindful of the contributions which this famous envoy of Queen Victoria had made to the shaping of New Japan. Said the Emperor:

I am especially happy to acknowledge that in the early years of Meiji, your Excellency not only showed great sympathy in our reform measures but also gave us many useful suggestions regarding the material progress and advancement of our Empire. I am deeply sensible of the service you have thus rendered.

* * * * * * *

Those were the days too when the Japanese, in referring to foreigners in a derogatory sense, used the words *keto* (hairy foreigner) or *akahige* (red whiskers). It is interesting to note that while the former word is still in use, the latter has fallen into disuse, for the reason that a change of fashion has resulted in bewhiskered foreigners becoming quite a rarity. In 1898 the Tokyo *Jiji* newspaper wrote with apprehension of the growing anti-foreign spirit and criticised some school teachers for using those words when addressing their pupils. It concluded its article with the fear that the *"anti-foreign spirit is apt to endanger the existence of the Empire of Japan."*

But maybe foreigners should not feel too badly about the aforementioned expressions. When the Greeks first met the Romans they called them barbarians; when the Romans came to England they called the English barbarians; the English for a long time thought the Welsh to be....But there is no end to such mud slinging!

With the passing of years the foreign community began to extend outside the narrow confines of the Foreign Concessions, and so in course of time, as the various elements in the community were able to go their own ways without having to rub shoulders too closely with those whom they did not like, or did not choose to know, tempers improved, and feuds were to some extent forgotten. There is still a tang of the earlier days in the following extract from a letter written from Tokyo in 1894 by Professor Basil Hall Chamberlain to Lafcadio Hearn:

I care little for the Europeans here....They seem to me to be deteriorated by their surroundings. Brinkley and all that lot disgust me by their syco-

*phancy to the Japanese. Besides them there are
the diplomats, but they look down on common folk.
Then there are the teachers of the lesser sort and
the missionaries...but the atmosphere of 'an open
port'—at any rate of Yokohama and of Kobe—is
infinitely more congenial to my taste. I will grant
you that the men there know comparatively little,
...but they are men, and genuine...each man
being taken for exactly what he is worth.*

I bring this chapter to a close with an observation
by the Bishop of Homoco, the famous dialectologist—
famous at least in certain circles in Japan. His
magnum opus, *"Yokohama Dialect"* was printed by
the *Japan Gazette,* Yokohama, in 1879, and the
original edition is now a very rare book. Said the
Bishop:

*When we're rich, we ride in 'rickshaws'
But when we're poor they call us 'chickshaws'.*

---

* *Chikushō* a Japanese swear word.

THE YOSHIWARA LADIES
AND
PINUP GIRLS

*The old King brought with him
divers women to be frollicke.*
Capt. SARIS' Diary, 1613.

In the latter part of the last century when Ronald
O'Rorke stepped ashore in Kobe from a sampan at
the Meriken Hatoba—so-called by the Japanese because the United States Consular Agency was then
located right opposite on the present site of the
Nippon Yusen Kaisha—nobody would have imagined
that such a mild looking individual would shortly
be responsible for the local sales of Japanese woodblock prints slumping and then later spiralling into
a boom, or that the effect of his visit would be
written, so to speak, on the walls of many foreign
houses in Kobe for over four decades to come.

O'Rorke was not his real name but it will suffice.
The fact that he was not wearing a one-inch-thick
cork topee marked him as unorthodox, yet it was
noted that in one hand he was carrying a tin of flea
powder, so evidently he had carefully read the *Murray's Handbook for Japan* which he carried in the
other. The news soon spread around the Foreign
Settlement that he was an internationally recognized
authority on Japanese woodblock prints. Whether
or not that was actually the case is not now known;
but the vigilant committee of the Women's Club

quickly tracked him down for a lecture. That was the start of a reaction that did not stop reacting for over forty years.

He was invited to meet the committee at tea to work out preliminary details for the lecture. Long before the tea was in the tea cups, Mr. O'Rorke had launched upon a learned dissertation on the subject so near to his heart. He explained how the measure of a great Japanese artist had orginally been the ability to suggest with a few strokes of the brush something vivid or living,—a rainstorm, a toad, bamboo. Then along came unknown artists, without patrons, drawn from the common people of Yedo. who painted and drew with bold strokes and clear outline the *ukiyoe*, or pictures of the fleeting world of transient pleasures. Fortunately for posterity, they painted the Tokugawa period as it really was. The gay quarters and the primrose paths, the green rooms, the bath-rooms, the highways and the byways are recorded forever in the genius of their works.

Generally they were poor men. Their pictures were engraved on woodblocks and then printed in many colours, the final sheets being sold on the streets to the masses often for a few coppers a print. Kunisada was originally a ferryboat man, Hokusai a fish-hawker. Utamaro, among the greatest of them all, and the most dissolute, passed much of his time in the licensed quarters; but it can be said that at least some of it was spent in painting.

Genuine woodblock prints of their pictures, originally priced to meet the pockets of the working classes, are now costly rarities. It was not until the

Japanese art critics realised that many of the best of the *ukiyoe* had become concentrated in famous museums abroad, that this new medium of Japanese art came to be properly appreciated in Japan.

Females having been banned from the stage in Japan and their place taken by males—a situation that led to many other situations—and there being no cabarets in those days or professional models or mannequins, it must not be held against those *ukiyoe* artists that they went to the Yoshiwara to study the human form. That they painted life in the licensed quarters with such restraint and good taste that their pictures could be hung today on the walls of the manse, without giving offence to the parishioners, is surely some indication that their interest in the gay quarters, in part at least, was art for art's sake. If further evidence for the defence is required it might be mentioned the supremely proper Boston Museum of Art has amassed one of the most notable collections of *ukiyoe* without inciting a blue stocking riot and without any apparent deleterious effects on the morals of that great city.

Mr. O'Rorke told the ladies all these things. He explained that quite contrary to what they might read in some literature on the subject of woodblock prints "a beauty" is not the correct translation of *oiran*. And then with erudite delicacy he began to explain that while this new school of artists drew every object with clear bold lines—everything being, so to speak, above board—nevertheless the art of suggestion did enter into many pictures. An immaculately neat coiffure, the entrancing curve of the

225

back of a neck, a carelessly tied sash, a wisp of hair slightly out of place, a neat roll of paper tucked in the kimono or lying on the *tatami*—they all told a story.

Some of the ladies fidgeted. Some hastily swallowed their tea scalding hot. A few almost choked, whether from suppressed laughter or from the rockbuns is not recorded, and one, seated behind the president, distinctly giggled. Finally the ladies of the committee felt that they knew as much about certain aspects of *ukiyoe* as did Utamaro or Kiyonaga, and the meeting was hastily brought to a close.

Immediately O'Rorke had departed, Mrs. Brown-Brown, the president, rose—she always did when she had a momentous statement to utter—and announced that owing to the proximity of several typhoons, the lecture had better be postponed. *Sine die* were the exact words she used. And then, consternation dawning on her, she hastened home to examine the pictures on her wall. She was gratified to see that they were copies of masterpieces, the originals of most of her prints were in the best museums of Europe. But, oh the shame! She decided that they would all have to be removed. Before that bad resolution took shape, the vicar arrived for tea.

She hastily pressed him into a chair other than the one he usually occupied. His back was then to the worst of her pictures—in truth they were really the best! It was all very disturbing for her, because the chair that he then occupied was without an antimacassar, and the vicar did use rather much pomade. Then while attempting to concentrate upon what the good vicar was saying, she wondered whether his thoughts also might be straying to that wisp of hair. At times with a shock and a blush she realised her eyes were wandering to other parts of the prints. She blamed herself for inviting that horrible Mr. O'Rorke to lecture. If only he had been content to talk vaguely but beautifully on art, as did previous lecturers, the ladies could have gone home drunk on rhetoric, but happy.

It became plain to Mrs. Brown-Brown, as doyen of the afternoon tea party circles on the Hill, that *oiran* might be all very well on the walls of the British Museum or the Metropolitan Museum of Art in New York, but not—certainly not—on the walls of her drawing room. She disapproved of her walls becoming a picture gallery of the dubious friendships formed by gay young bloods and old roués of the eighteenth century. This she confided to her friends, but of course in more delicate phraseology.

And so there was a time during the latter part of the last century when a certain type of Japanese colour print quietly disappeared from the walls of the drawing rooms of upper Yamamoto-dori and Kitano-cho. That period coincided with the time when the local sales of such pictures went into a slump.

But the happenings at that committee meeting were not a well kept secret, and were followed shortly afterwards by a sudden blossoming forth of pictures of *oiran* on the walls of bachelor messes. That period corresponded to the time when local sales made a spurt. In fairness to the bachelors it must be emphasized that they showed real appreciation of that form of art. They concentrated only upon the best —mostly Utamaro prints, many original copies of which were then being exhibited in that most eminently respectable of all places, the Victoria & Albert Museum, London.

And so it may be said, with mild exaggeration, that it was the bachelors of Kobe who quite unknowingly over a number of years—about four decades to be exact—kept alive in certain foreign circles in Kobe a true understanding of those woodblock prints that depict the ladies of the Yoshiwara. But as one harvest of bachelors succeeded another, so the knowledge of the artful little devices introduced by the *ukiyoe* artists into their pictures of the gay ladies of the Tokugawa era became forgotten. The expert knowledge of Mr. O'Rorke was lost; and the prints became nothing more than just pictures on the wall.

This historical record would be neither complete nor accurate if I did not conclude it with the sombre statement that during the nineteen-thirties—which years marked the beginning of the era of Strip Tease —the *oiran* gradually disappeared from the bachelor establishments, their places being taken by pinup girls, abducted from the pages of *Esquire*, all of whom shivered distressingly during the cold winter months.

THE TOURISTS
LOOKED
AROUND

> *When I came on shore, the first place
> I entered into was a publick house,
> where they drunk tea, and that very
> plentifully.*
>
> CHRISTOPHER FRYKE, 1683

It has been said, somewhat maliciously I think, that just as the discovery of gold in Australia gave an impetus to immigration to that empty continent, so in a sense did the discoveries of Pierre Loti start the tourist traffic to Japan. It may be recalled that Julien Viaud was an officer on the French war vessel "Triomphante" which was laid up in Nagasaki harbour for repairs during the summer of 1885, during which time the gallant officer took a great deal of interest in some phases of Nagasaki life and recorded his discoveries in a treatise entitled *Madame Crysantheme*, using his pen name of Pierre Loti modestly to cloak his dalliance ashore. However all that may be, it is a fact that towards the end of the last century shortly after *Madame Chrysantheme* made her bow, the tourist trade began to flow into Japan, and a definite need was felt for guidebooks in English to warn new arrivals in advance of what lay in wait for them and to guide their steps after arrival here.

In saying those early guidebooks warned the tourists of what lay in wait for them, I am speaking

229

entomologically and allude to the great emphasis made
in those early books that a plentiful supply of Keat-
ing's Flea Powder should be carried. Japan was not
of course the only country in those days where the
flea population was active and prolific. Other countries had them also—both trained and untrained.
However from the frequent references to fleas in all
the early guide and travel books it is evident that
legions of the untrained variety had taken up lodgings
in the Japanese inns of those days.

To say that those guidebooks guided the tourist
after arrival to every temple and sight worth seeing
would be an over simplification. The fact is those
early books were the work of profound scholars,
mostly Britons, and contained such a mass of information that plagiarists ever since have had an almost
bottomless barrel from which to dig out material.
Those guidebooks, the first of which was published
in 1881 by Ernest Satow and Lt. Hawes, later revised
and published as *Murray's Handbook for Travellers
in Japan,* did in fact contain all the information
necessary to enable the tourist to understand all the
best things to be seen, and it was not the fault of the
authors if some saw things they should not have
seen!

Terry, an American, produced an excellent guide
in 1914, which was later revised and expanded. Unfortunately its place has since been taken by less
interesting Japanese guidebooks and it is now rarely
seen. The tourist who travelled with Terry was never
bored and always had on hand a mass of readable
material. His description, for example, of the world-

famed institution that existed in Tokyo in the district
adroitly named *Yoshiwara* (good luck moor) runs to
over six pages of material of which the following is
an example:

*Through these sometimes palatial entrances hung
with rich satin brocades, one glimpses alluring
vistas of reposeful interiors; of lotus pools and
tinkling fountains; tiny landscape gardens and
arched bridges: of cool flower-embowered, per-
fumed retreats, dimly lighted, through which bare-
footed women patter; or reclining with studied
carelessness, suggest Ionian bathing scenes or other
spectacular situations that disturb the shallow
noodle of the salaciously disposed.*

The daytime scene is described by Terry as follows:

*During the forenoon of a sunny day brilliantly
coloured sleeping garments are hung out to air
from the balconies of many of the houses, while
the capricious sultanas....are reposing in the
crepuscular shadows of the inner rooms.*

Terry was evidently a man of vision, because
although writing at a time when many women still
dragged their skirts in the dust he advocated the
wearing of silk bloomers and short skirts. He men-
tions this apropos mountain climbing, and not the
fleas which he describes as being "inordinately hungry."

In 1933 the Japan Tourist Bureau produced an
Official Guide which has since been revised twice. It
was an excellent publication modernised to meet the
needs of the modern tourist who flits at high speed
from point to point, but it lacked the interesting and

intimate facets of some of the earlier guidebooks. Being an official guide it would have its readers believe that there has never been a *Yoshiwara* in Japan, and being an official publication it could not use the common-sense and generally accepted Hepburn system of spelling Japanese words, but instead adopts the incredible official system whereby *Fuji* is written *Huzi*.

Back in 1896 the enchantingly gay light opera, *The Geisha* by Sidney Jones, was staged at Daly's Theatre, London, and ran for 760 performances with Marie Tempest as O-Mimosa San. Gilbert and Sullivan's *Mikado* had already appeared, and Puccini's *Madame Butterfly* was shortly to make her debut. All three were good advertisements for Japan and played a part in boosting the tourist trade. But all three had been staged amid scenes of such fairy-like Oriental charm, of paper houses decorated with paper lanterns and invariably set among cherry trees blossoming at all seasons, with Fujiyama in the background always snow-capped, that it is not surprising tourists ever since have been amazed to find that houses in Japan are built of something more substantial than paper and that drab shades are the prevailing colours, and even more so since the native costume has been abandoned for western dress.

Gilbert and Sullivan's *Mikado* could not be staged in Japan in prewar days, but during the Occupation days of 1946 when it was produced for the first time by the U.S. Army Services at the Ernie Pyle Theatre in Tokyo, it set a mark for historical accuracy in costumes that most likely will never be equalled again

—"the gentlemen of Japan" and some of the principal characters being dressed in costumes or outfitted with appurtenances loaned by the Imperial Household Museum at Ueno.

Tamaki Miura, as Japan's first prima donna, did something to introduce abroad correct costuming and atmosphere into the production of *Madame Butterfly,* but unfortunately she found western food so agreeable that she fast put on weight and eventually became a very stout Cho-Cho San and about twice the weight of her lover, Lieut. Pinkerton!

The Geisha, a light and charming opera, fit to be viewed by the pupils of any young ladies seminary, carried in the music the lilting strain of the *Chonkina* dance of Nagasaki teahouse days. The nature of the real *Chonkina* dance thus came to be whispered about much in the same way as the drawings on the walls of that room in the ruined city of Pompeii, which is off-limits to ladies. Many a prospective male tourist to Japan thereupon pencilled in his pocketbook the cryptic note—"See *Chonkina!*"

(After John Paris wrote his novel *Kimono* in 1921 all the secrets of the *Chonkina* were stripped bare. It must be left to the specialists to trace the transition from the *Chonkina* dance to the strip tease shows, the fan and bubble dances, and acts in ermine panties that attract tourists these days and cause pulse to flutter and eyebrows to rise.) Elsewhere in the same notebook was probably pencilled the simple address "No. 9 Yokohama." Perhaps picked up surreptitiously or maybe gleaned from a reading of Kipling's poetry where, in "MacAndrew's Hymn," are the lines:

The Tourists Looked Around

Judge not, O Lord, my steps aside at Gay Street in Hongkong....Jane Harrigan's an' Number Nine, The Reddicks an' Grant Road.

Japanese addresses are among the greatest riddles of the country, the solution of which often defies the united efforts of the local police and the oldest residents in the district, but "No. 9 Yokohama" was never in that category. Any rickshaw-man in Yokohama could have taken the tourist there at any time of the day or night—indeed the rickshaw-man would have hauled him there in any case even although he had asked to be taken to the Seamen's Mission. The pedicab drivers of to-day are often guilty of much the same trick.

Lest any wayward reader should hereafter seek to locate No. 9 I hasten to add that it burst into flame shortly after noon on 1st September, 1923, following the great earthquake that wiped out old Yokohama.

It is as true to day as it was fifty years ago that the vast majority of tourists and visitors to Japan are more interested in the scenic spots, the countryside and the temples of Japan than anything the gaily lighted night spots have to offer, although those who live in the port cities and see the highly organized efforts of the legion of touts to present the seamy side may think otherwise.

The tourists of fifty years ago were a hardy type. Armed with guidebooks and maps they did not hesitate to tramp the country roads, if there was no horsecart or rickshaw available to get them to their destination. "Pushing into the interior" was the expression used to describe some of their activities.

234

The Tourists Looked Around

They conscientiously visited all the best sights between Nikko and Miyajima taking up to two months
or more to *do* Japan as against about three days by the
modern tourist, but of course hotel prices were cheap-
er then. The ladies "Ah-ed" and "Oh-ed" in front
of each temple whilst some of their husbands furtively
ogled the Japanese lasses. They were friendly to all,
interested in everything and with the aid of their
guidebooks they came to understand most of what
they saw. Frequently on their return home they
wrote books about Japan, but as they had dipped
freely from the guidebooks the results were not always as bad as one would expect.

Armed with one of those quaint Japanese-English
conversation books that covered most social activities
such as gossiping in a public bathhouse or enquiring
after the health of a stationmaster, they had no fear
of travelling about the countryside and staying at
Japanese inns. Certainly at times they made mis-
takes and knocked at the wrong door, mistaking bath-
houses and less respectable establishments for inns,
but it was all a great adventure. If some of the
ladies may have innocently remarked that their mos-
quito nets were too large, no Japanese Lothario would
have been brash enough to take advantage of the
remark, which was an old-time invitation in Japan!

On their departure most of them of course took
souvenirs and curios according to their taste but ever
mindful of customs inspection and duties at destination. Probably the first recorded case of a misad-
venture with customs on the part of a visitor returning from Japan occurred over 300 years ago when

the English Customs in 1614 made an embarrassing discovery on examining the baggage of Capt. John Saris, commander of the "Clove," one of the ships of the English East India Company, on arrival back in England after a voyage to Japan.

Certainly the pictures and the objets d'art that were found in Capt. Saris' luggage were of such a type that the governors of the East India Company did not offer him another appointment, and in fact they burnt the collection in public. It is lamented by connoisseurs in such things that history, beyond describing them in general terms, does not record in detail the precise nature of the pictures and carvings that tickled Capt. Saris' fancy. It is therefore not possible to decide whether or not the governors of that venerable Company were just stuffy or whether the collection really was "a great scandal to the Company."

Surprisingly enough that tireless and most accomplished traveller of all times, Karl Baedeker of Leipzig, never visited Japan, which explains why there is no Baedeker's *Handbook for Travellers to Japan*. Possibly the reason was language difficulties. The fact is—and this is not generally known—that the only languages that Karl could speak were English, French, German and Italian fluently, with more than a good working knowledge of Greek, Latin, Swedish, Norwegian, Danish, Russian, Spanish and Hungarian and with a somewhat lesser knowledge of Basque, Finnish, Turkish and Arabic and a smattering of some of the languages of India!

That he never visited Japan is to us a disappointment. Knowing how keen an advocate he was of the wearing of long underwear by gents on all occasions, we might otherwise have been tempted to formulate the whimsical theory that the popularity of long underwear in Japan could be traced to Karl Baedeker of Leipzig!

PILGRIMS
ANCIENT
AND
MODERN

*On the top of a Hill was the Temple
of Quanon.*

Jesuit letter, 1585

The reason why men continued doing evil rather
than good was revealed to the Japanese as far back
as the 8th century, which is a long time ago by any
standard of comparison.

A Buddhist abbot, known as Tokudo Shonin, seemingly died, but, as his body did not grow cold, his
disciples watched over him for three days and three
nights. On awakening he described how, during his
trance, his soul had been borne to the Underworld
and there the whereabouts of the Thirty-three Holy
Places especially cared for by Kwannon, the Goddess
of Mercy, were revealed to him. As none before knew
of the existence of those places, men had continued
to fall into hell as plentifully as raindrops fall in a
thunderstorm. Anyone, however, who makes a single
pilgrimage to those Thirty-three Places would, in
addition to acquiring great merit, radiate light from
the soles of his feet and gain strength sufficient to
crush all the one hundred and thirty-six hells into
fragments. That is the legend.

About two centuries after this revelation an emperor actually set out on the pilgrimage and thus es-

tablished in the minds of the people a practice which over the centuries brought a continual stream of visitors and revenue to thirty-three temples which otherwise would have been little known—an advertising feat that has rarely been matched.

Whether or not the rewards for those who complete the pilgrimage are as great as promised is a matter of belief and experience.

Many years ago I performed the pilgrimage, but modesty precludes my drawing attention to the results! At this date I will confess to having visited the last two temples on the list by proxy, a device that is commonly resorted to by many. Certainly I entered into the deception with some misgivings, yet in my simplicity I had hoped it would pass unnoticed by the gods. That however is another story.

The only other case that I have had the opportunity of examining at close range is that of my wife, who completed the pilgrimage some sixteen years ago, without cheating. I must however in all truth admit my disappointment at the results. Merit, and especially any increase in merit, is a virtue difficult to measure at all times, except in oneself! Certainly she did not radiate any light from the soles of her feet. I can only conclude that she had failed in some technicality, possibly in chatting and joking with the priests instead of a proper attention to the special hymn that should be recited at each temple.

It might too have been decided by the Eminence who grants the reward—as has also often been done on this earthly globe—that woman's place is in the home and not gadding about on mountain tops. The

opinion of many Buddhist ecclesiastics seemingly coincided with that of some other mortals on this point,
because the presence of women in temples had long
been discouraged. Indeed their presence was deemed
so defiling that near the entrance of many temples
there was a rest house beyond which no women could
proceed. In fact there are some mountains they were
not permitted to climb at all. The times—and the
constitution—have changed, and that is now all a
thing of the past, but it can be recalled by many that
when the ban on women climbing the sacred mountain of Omine was raised not so many years ago,
some adherents of the Faith were almost as bellige-
rent as the Tibetan lamas who a year or so ago
opposed the entry of the Japanese Himalayan Expedition to Manaslu.

Although not apropos of the subject under discussion, it may be recalled here that women were not
the only joys of life that were banned from the temples. Frequently the following warning was engraved
in stone at the entrance:

*It is forbidden to carry stinking herbs and intoxi-
cating drinks through this holy gate.*

Shallots, chives, garlic, and onions were considered
as stinking herbs.

Fish was permitted in some temples but not meat.
However, some priests were willing and weak enough
to partake of wild boar, if served under the name of
yama kujira—mountain whale!

Probably in few countries in the world is the tired
—and the wayward—business man so well catered
for as in Japan. He may spend a week end in a hotel

room in Osaka, or some more romantic place, and yet, before returning to his waiting wife, purchase in the underground arcade near Osaka Station a specially wrapped and certified gift of the noted product of any prefecture in Japan, in proof of the deception that the week end was spent on business in that distant prefecture!

The still more wayward business man may spend two weeks in the same hotel room, if he so desires and if his body and his purse will stand the strain, and yet return with a collection of temple "chops" purchased in Osaka in proof of the fiction that the two weeks were devoted to a very tiring but highly meritorious pilgrimage to the Thirty-three Holy Places! Those Thirty-three Temples of Kwannon are scattered over an area that extends from Himeji to near Gifu and from Wakayama to Ama-no-hashi-date. They are all well worthy of a visit by those who are interested in the past. There are other pilgrim circuits also, but this is the best known.

The exceptionally devout and earnest pilgrims perform the pilgrimage on foot walking from one temple to the next along the valleys and over the mountains by the same route that others have trodden for many centuries, dressed in the traditional white clothes and with broad sloping straw hats, but they are comparatively few in number these days. They carry a wooden staff, the Buddhist bell, and a rosary. The route is marked by old stone direction posts, now lichen-covered and crumbling with age. The white clothes of these pilgrims, imprinted with the vermilion seals of the temples that have been visited, constitute proof of the pilgrimage and later may serve as burial shrouds. In addition the pilgrims may have the temple seals imprinted on scrolls and in books which they carry for that purpose.

Those early pilgrims made their way leisurely from one temple to the next, They performed the penances peculiar to each, in some cases of walking around the main building a hundred times, mumbling the "Hail Buddha" continuously. They kept count of the number of turns by dropping a small bamboo stick into a receptacle at the completion of each circuit, much in the some way as tally clerks tally cargo on board ships.

They spun the prayer-wheels—an invention of incalculable convenience to supplicants, and especially dumb mutes. One spin of the wheel is equivalent to reciting a whole prayer. The progenitor, as it were, of the tape-recorder. They turned the revolving libraries, a convenient device whereby the illiterate could with one twirl, and at no mental and little physical effort, do the equivalent of reading six thousand volumes of Buddhist lore.

The majority of pilgrims in this modern age perform the pilgrimage dressed in ordinary clothes and travel in small groups or as members of a large party, each wearing a distinguishing rosette, so that the various parties may not become scrambled. They squeeze the pilgrimage into the short space of time available to them between crops or other duties, travelling by modern transportation systems, fast electric tramways, funicular railways, and motor buses. While there is much to be said for the services that these companies render to the pilgrims, and to their share-holders, it is to be doubted that the modern pilgrim who performs the pilgrimage at such high speed will attain Nirvana any more quickly than the pilgrim of bygone days who trod the narrow paths through the valleys and over the mountains.

The modern pilgrim may spin the prayer-wheel, but he rarely has time to do the penances. The re-volving libraries have mostly jammed with age, so in a sense it is fair to say that the moderns have read little Buddhist literature.

It is also to be doubted whether the pilgrim of to-day travelling with excursionists on these modern conveyances is able to raise his thoughts from the mess of orange peels, the caramel cartons and empty *bento* boxes that litter the way, to an appropriate contemplation of the splendour of the Lotus, that dazzling symbol of Buddhism, that gorgeous flower that lifts its bud out of the slimy bottom of ponds, raises its unsoiled leaves and unfolds its immaculate petals without a trace of the mud from which it sprung—just as the souls of men, according to the Buddhist faith, rise from the mire of sin, advance little by little until they attain by their own efforts the blessings of Nirvana.

The pilgrims, especially during rainy weather, would rest in the *ex-voto* halls attached to the temples and gaze at the collection of temple offerings. There were the widows' mites, the hair shorn from the heads of women who had foresworn worldly things on the death of their beloved husbands, the pitiful garments of infants who had died and whose little souls had gone to the Buddhist Styx where the demons torment them and force them to pile up heaps of stones which are torn down again as fast as the children pile them up. There were paintings, carvings and pictures of all description, some designed from thousands of old coins—the *mon* or coppers, with a square hole in the centre, of a hundred years or more ago. Finally there were the flamboyant offerings of *sake* brewers and others who combined piety with commercialism.

The modern pilgrims still gaze at the same or similar types of offerings, and it can only be hoped that they note with anger how the old copper coins have largely disappeared—stolen by vandals, or removed during the war years in senseless collections of metal for machines of war, without a thought to the religious symbolism behind the coins—gifts to ease the way of wandering souls in the hereafter.

Except where towns have grown up around the temples, most are located in delightful settings of reverent quietude, in sheltered valleys, or near the mountain tops. Far too often the neighbouring slopes have been bared by the woodmen's axes, and in almost all cases the temple buildings are crumbling away with age—sad evidence of a declining income and of the numbers of Japanese who have forsaken religion in the postwar period.

The priests who in prewar days for a fee of ten sen would impress the seal of the temple on scrolls and in books, and with a writing brush would add an inscription as proof of the visit, were often master calligraphers who seemed to delight in their task.

Nowadays the fee is still trifling, but the writing generally less skilful—indeed at some temples the inscription is imprinted with an ugly rubber stamp.

At the main gates of the temples, are the huge wooden carvings, customarily set in cages, of the semi-nude and athletic-looking guardian gods, the Mio or two Deva kings of Indian mythology (Indra & Brama). They are usually painted vermilion, the conventional device adopted by the Japanese Buddhist artists to distinguish the dark-skinned Indian saints and disciples from the lighter-skinned Japanese.

For ages the believers have pelted these guardian gods with spit-balls made from chewed paper on which prayers have been written, confident that should the pellet adhere to the figure their prayer would be granted. When however the chewing-gum culture burst upon Japan, an unwholesome weapon was placed in the hands of those who would shoot at the gods for sport. Whereas the paper pellets dried out and eventually fell to the ground without much damage to the painted carvings, not so the nauseating chewing-gum. It remains as an unsightly mess firmly fixed on carvings that might even be listed as national treasures.

While it is all too evident that some postwar visitors to temples must derive some queer satisfaction in aiming a well masticated piece of chewing-gum at the Indian kings and scoring a bull's eye, nothing to me is more disturbing than to see several lumps of bubble gum stuck firmly on the eyeballs of the guardian gods, thereby giving to them the grotesque appearance of winking broadly at each visitor who passes through the temple gate.

One of the guardians is always depicted with his mouth open as if in the act of saying "Ah" and the other with lips tightly closed as if murmuring "Um." Their faces are the target for our modern young marksmen, who far too often succeed in plugging the open mouth of one and sealing the closed lips of the other with a much manducated mess of gum. It is any wonder that in these modern times we never meet anyone who has heard the one say "Ah," or the other murmur "Um?"

GOLD,
GOLD,
GOLD

> *Gold, Gold, Gold, Gold!*
> *Bright and yellow, hard and cold:*
> *Molten, graven, hammered, rolled,*
> *Hoarded, bartered, bought and sold*
> *Stolen, borrowed, squandered, doled.*
>   TOM HOOD

Following the introduction of Buddhism in the sixth century, gold was in great demand in Japan for the gilding of Buddhist images and temple ornamentations, but most of it had to be brought in from China and Korea.

In 747 when the great Buddha—the Daibutsu—at Nara was cast, a considerable quantity of gold was needed and fortunately just at that time gold was discovered in Japan as was announced by the reigning emperor in the Todaiji Temple which houses the *Daibutsu:*

> *In the land of Yamato since the beginning of Heaven and Earth, Gold, though it has been brought as an offering from other countries, was thought not to exist. But in the East of the land....Gold has been found....We will reward all those who found the gold....even down to the peasants.*

Five centuries later, around 1295, Marco Polo's account of Japan, which he had obtained second-hand from travellers and others, was the first description of Japan to reach Europe;

247

Gold, Gold, Gold

Zipangu is an Iland in the East.... the people white and faire, of gentle behaviour....They have gold in great store....and the King permits no exportation of it....the King's house is covered with gold....gilded Windows, Floores of Gold....

It was reports such as this that helped stir the minds of Columbus and others to seek a new route to the East which in turn led to the discovery of America.

In 1583, Master Fitch, a London merchant, after a voyage to the East Indies wrote:

When the Portugals goe from Macao in China to Japon they carrie much white Silke, Gold, Muske and Porcelanes; and they bring from thence nothing but Silver.

Japan had her counterpart of the Field of the Cloth of Gold when Hideyoshi in 1587 staged his famed Kitano Tea Party at Kyoto, a lavish fete that lasted ten days, followed a little later by a banquet to his more distinguished guests at which trays piled with gold and silver were given away as presents. In those early times gold was not, however, esteemed as highly in Japan as elsewhere. Except for gilding temple ornamentations and lacquer ware, and small quantities used in the weaving of brocades and in other of the arts, there was not as great a demand for it as in the world outside. The ladies did not use gold jewelery, earrings, brooches or rings, nor did the men wear gold chains, and gold was not used at banquets for plates or for drinking goblets. Those mining or holding gold as bullion could not put it to any important use, and therefore generally disposed of it eventually to the authorities at a fixed price, which was comparatively cheap in terms of the ruling price of silver in the western world.

As late as about a hundred years ago when Townsend Harris came to Japan as Consul-General for the United States, one of the things which struck him most was the great simplicity of Japanese life. There was little to remind him of the splendour and glitter of European Courts. He saw no jewels, no diamond-hilted swords or crowns of gold.

The Japanese had for centuries fixed the value of gold and silver on the basis that five parts of silver would buy one part of gold, whereas in the world outside, from which Japan had largely shut herself off for over two centuries, it required fifteen parts of silver to purchase one part of gold. When Japan was opened to foreigners about a century ago, the merchants quickly saw the possibility of profiting by bringing in silver Mexican dollars, purchasing gold and immediately shipping it abroad. Within a few years they had milked Japan of much of her gold reserves and at a tremendous profit.

Japan's hands were largely tied under the treaties wherein it was provided that for one year the currency of the merchants (mainly Mexican silver dollars) would be exchangeable weight for weight into Japanese silver *ichibu* (the yen had not at that time been invented) which meant that 311 *ichibu* were obtained for 100 Mexican dollars. Those 311 *ichibu* could then be exchanged for gold coins (*koban*) at the cheap price prevailing in Japan and upon shipment abroad the gold realized several hundred

Mexican dollars, thus returning a huge profit on the transaction, generally about 150%.

Japan's monetary system was not however geared to meet this sudden demand for silver *ichibu*, and as there was not enough coinage available to satisfy the needs of the merchants, whether to buy gold or any other commodity, there developed an unseemly scramble for what was available. The place of exchange was at the Customs House located in a row of newly erected bungalows near the old fishing village of Yokohama.

The procedure was for the foreign traders to apply for as large a quantity of *ichibu* as they had the audacity to ask for, some supplementing their applications with additional ones in fictitious names, often ribald and in bad taste.

Such was the scramble for Japanese coinage that bribery and corruption at the Customs House were rife and great indignation was felt by the reputable foreign merchants at the activities of the carpetbagger types who had flooded into Japan. Furthermore it gave rise to much of the animosity with which the Japanese regarded the early foreign arrivals.

Little wonder was it that Sir Rutherford Alcock, the British Minister, became so angered at this unseemly state of affairs that he referred to the foreign merchants in Yokohama as the "scum of the earth." The merchants in turn became angered and retaliated by barring Her Britannic Majesty's Minister and his entire staff from admission to the Yokohama Club, then deemed to be a rather exclusive affair.

It was several years before Japan could increase her coinage and to correct this scramble for currency, but in the meantime a compromise was arrived at whereby the merchants had to buy *ichibu* in the open market, while the officials, such as the ministers, consuls, the legation guard, and the naval personnel, obtained the equivalent of their salaries at the rate of 311 ichibu for $100 Mex., which if exchanged back at the open market rate of 214 netted $145 Mex., or a profit of 45%. This privilege enjoyed by the diplomatic corps and officials, and much abused by some of the minor honorary consuls who were primarily merchants, added fuel to the feud between the merchants and the diplomatic corps, and was just another of the many growing pains experienced by the foreign communities. But in course of time all was forgotten and forgiven on both sides.

It is to be noted that these traffickings in currency arose from the official rate of exchange for Japanese currency being set at a figure much below its real worth, whereas to-day it is more usual for currencies to be pegged at a figure above their real worth.

Another currency problem arose as a result of the Chinese compradores and others bringing into Japan inferior Mexican dollars, light in weight, unchopped or cracked. Everybody, including the compradores at the banks and the Japanese Customs House endeavoured to pass these inferior coins and to retain the good ones. This gave rise to a curious happening in 1863 on the occasion on which Japan was required to pay an indemnity of $440,000 Mex., representing £110,000 sterling, for the murder of

some English nationals and damage to property. The
British Legation report reads: "At early dawn of the
morning the cry of the coolies resounded through the
streets as they dragged their heavy burdens from the
treasury to the legation." All the Chinese shroffs in
Yokohama—men employed by merchants and bankers
to examine coin and see whether it was genuine—had
been mobilized at the Legation to check the delivery.
The Chinese sat on the floor of the Legation chancel-
lery testing the coins by clinking them together, and
after rejecting the bad coins, wrapped and then cased
the good ones. The procedure occupied three days.
The cases of coin were then loaded on board the
British "Euryalus" for transportation to China. A
few days later when that vessel was fired upon by
Japanese coastal batteries, some time elapsed before
she could return the fire, because, owing to the lack
of cargo space, the door of the ammunition magazine
had been obstructed by piles of these cases of dollars,
all of which had to be moved before the door could
be opened.

In addition to the inferior Mexican dollars that
were circulating in the treaty ports, a large amount
of base coinage was circulating throughout Japan.
Various gold coins that also served as bullion, and
other mintages too, were issued by the various *daimyo,* some of which coins came to be accepted in the
treaty ports as means of payment. Suddenly it was
discovered that large quantities of golden *ni-bu,* paid
by Japanese and received without suspicion by foreigners, were in fact made of a gilded base metal,
and were practically worthless. Later complaints

were made to the central government, and then in anticipation that some compensation would be paid to those holding counterfeits, a wild speculation on the part of foreign merchants and Japanese too in attempts to acquire those counterfeits at the best price possible, yet low enough to yield a profit on the hoped-for compensation.

Other coins, even including the copper coinage, were tampered with, and in order to correct this state of affairs the Japanese Government had bought up Hongkong's old minting machinery which together with other machinery imported from Europe was set up in national mints, under foreign supervision, and from 1871 the new yen coinage was issued.

In 1937 when the Japanese Army entered upon their undeclared war in China, they financed their operations with ordinary paper yen, which they forced the Chinese and others to accept for services and provisions purchased, but as such yen could not be brought back to Japan, unless smuggled in, a huge quantity accumulated in China, especially in Shanghai, and the price fell to around 8 cents U.S. per yen, whereas the official rate was set as high as 22 cents. With such a difference prevailing no amount of vigilance could prevent those cheap yen notes from being smuggled back into Japan from China.

This was the state of affairs when Serge Rubinstein was in Japan. At a later date the Japanese Army commenced using special military yen, which were not legal tender in Japan, but by then much cheap yen had been bought up in China and smuggled into Japan.

Gold, Gold, Gold

Dmitri Rubinstein was a moneylender to the Czar of Russia, and upon the outbreak of the Bolshevik revolution in 1917 he wisely decided to get out of Russia, and cut his losses—except for the jewels and securities which were sewn in the family clothing. He tried in the Balkans to rebuild the family fortunes but instead died there a bankrupt.

As Serge, the youngest son, showed unusual promise in the ways of making money, his elder brother Andre sent him to England where he graduated at Cambridge University with honours. Later in life Andre sued Serge on behalf of their mother for defamation of character because Serge, in connivance with someone in the Portuguese consular service, obtained a Portuguese passport by claiming that he was the illegitimate son of a Portuguese nobleman, and with that passport was able to gain entry into the United States.

In this article we are however only interested with his life in Japan, or at least a small part of it—and none of his Tokyo love life, which, owing to considerations of space, will be omitted entirely.

After Serge had laid the foundations to his fortune by making in France a profit of close on a million dollars in a slick deal in Chinese bonds, he turned up in London attracted by the scintillating financial deals of Mr. Martin C. Harman, a plausible British company promoter who had gained control of the Chosen Corporation Ltd., a holding company owning three gold mines in Korea. When Harman subsequently went to jail, Rubinstein stepped forward and snatched the baton, as it were, from the falling

Harman and proceeded to control the Chosen Corporation. He was then a busy man. Later an investigator for the British Board of Trade examined the books of the corporation and found a tangled mass of transactions between the Chosen Corporation, four Delaware, four New York, three Texas and four British companies, and in addition one Japanese company. Even chartered accountants became dizzy as they skidded around those tangled trails. One fact at least emerged—somewhere along the line a cool $5,-900,000 of the Chosen Corporation had disappeared.

Rubinstein, in control of the Chosen Corporation, had the authority to dispose of its valuable properties in Korea and this he proceeded to do, selling two of the mines in Tokyo to the Nippon Kogyo Co., Ltd., for thirteen million yen of which six million or £350,-000 was to be paid in sterling. It must be remembered that in prewar days these yen figures represented very large sums. The sale price was a good one, because Rubinstein had driven a hard bargain. The fact is that Japan was in great need of gold, and the military clique was willing to pay a high price to get it.

It is not a pun but a plain statement of fact that Rubinstein's assistant in this transaction was Mr. Konrad Sztykgold, which name, out of consideration for the difficulties of the foreigners and Japanese of Tokyo, was simplified to Sticgold!

When the Tokyo transaction drew to a close there were three million yen in cash and a draft for Yen 1,192,647 still in Rubinstein's control in Tokyo, but later when the Japanese Government discovered that the three million yen had disappeared they impounded the draft, thus adding another complication to a very tangled affair. It has been alleged that those three million yen were smuggled out of Japan hidden in personal baggage; another story is that the notes were hidden in the folds of *habutae* shipped out of Japan as export orders. Quite apart from the fact that such a sum of money in one hundred yen notes, then the highest denomination, would have represented a lump of nearly two cubic feet, it is difficult to imagine that a man such as Rubinstein would have risked his money or his reputation for "smart" deals in any juvenile act of smuggling. At that time there were plenty of yen to the to be picked up in Shanghai at about eight cents to the yen as against the official rate of twenty-two cents in Japan. The yen notes in Shanghai were waiting to be smuggled into Japan, while Rubinstein had yen notes in Japan that he wanted to smuggle out. Not unlikely he swapped his yen in Japan for yen in Shanghai at a favourable rate to himself. Certainly it is a fact that just about that time one of Serge's lieutenants (although he usually preferred to act as a lone wolf both in his love and business affairs) travelled from Shanghai to Honolulu and the Pacific Coast of America on a ' President" liner that touched at Japan, and he was known to have several large wardrobe trunks in his cabin. At Yokohama he was invited by the police to step ashore and view the cherry blossoms, an opportunity he had to pass up as he had confined himself to his cabin with a sick headache.

How Rubinstein actually got his three million yen

out may never be known, but it was significant that shortly afterwards yen notes were being hawked throughout Hawaii and California to Japanese residents there who reckoned that they were obtaining a bargain in buying Bank of Japan notes at 25% under the official rate. At the same time other lots were being sold over the counter in scores of banking institutions throughout the length and breadth of South America, and were even being peddled around the coffee plantations in central Brazil.

Once again Serge had found where he could sell at a satisfactory price those things that he had acquired cheaply. Serge had an uncanny instinct for finding the best markets on which to work off his crooked deals.

However, all Serge's knowledge of mathematics and the theory of probabilities did not prevent him from making a very simple miscalculation when he handed out his door key to one inamorata too many. As is well known, he was found one morning in a New York apartment in blue silk pyjamas, bound, gagged, strangled and dead.

PHOTOGRAPH
ALBUMS

Of days that used to be....
A photograph or two....
Among my souvenirs....
EDGAR LESLIE—Song Lyric

The most important book in the old-fashioned Victorian home after the family Bible and the thick tome of medical lore that was hidden away on the top shelf of the bookcase, was the family album. Unfortunately family albums suffered from the defect that the photographs were generally unlabelled, a common failure in photographic collections to-day, with the result that much historical material is lost. Nobody saw the necessity of writing Aunt Eliza's name under any of her photographs—she always made her presence felt anywhere—and how many wives would identify the photographs of their mothers-in-law so that they might not be forgotten? Nevertheless aunts and mothers-in-law do at times become famous, and the world is poorer for the failure to have labelled family albums in the past.

To meet the needs of the family photograph albums, foreign portrait photographers established themselves in Yokohama from about 1860 and in Kobe from 1868. In addition to family portraits, wedding groups, and other celebrations, many photographs of street scenes and the surrounding countryside found their way into the family albums. I have a number of such collec-

tions but more often than not the photographs of
Japan of the last century are not labelled and it is
now impossible to identify the places.

One of the treasures in my photograph album is a
photograph of folio size which my wife discovered
some fifteen years ago whilst rummaging in a second-
hand junk shop in Melbourne and which she instantly
recognized to be a photograph of Kobe taken from the
hills in the early days of the Foreign Concession. As
she showed some interest in it, the junk-man gave it
to her as a present. It shows fields where now are
Yamamoto-dori and Kitano-cho and barren hills
where now are the pine-clad Kobe hills. Around
Sannomiya Station, then located exactly where Moto-
machi Station stands to-day, can be seen a number
of foreign-styled wooden houses that were built by
the Railway Bureau as residences for the foreign
employees of the National Railways. Some of those
wooden buildings, which had always been painted
green, were still standing before the war in or near
the Hanakuma geisha quarter. All were destroyed
by fires during the air-raids of the war.

Later photographs show the foreign residences of
the *taipans* who were beginning to change their places
of residence from the Foreign Concession to stately
houses that they had commenced building in Yamamoto-dori and Kitano-cho, each house set in a large
shady garden. Several decades later, advances in
land prices and higher taxation led to the inevitable
subdivision of the land and the construction of about
five houses where only one had existed previously.

Before the beginning of the century some foreigners were beginning to move further afield to out-of-town houses extending from Suma in the west to Sumiyoshi in the east, those with something to hide often going still further afield! The most fashionable out-of-town place of residence was then Ichi-no-tani in the hills beyond Suma beach, where a number of attractive houses were built, each with a large garden and set among narrow lanes bordered with hedges rather reminiscent of the English countryside. It was in fact here that the scion of the New York Morgans spent some happy times with O-Yuki-san, his geisha friend.

By the nineteen-thirties, when Mr. E. W. James was levelling the tops of mountains and filling in valleys at Shioya, preparatory to building his remarkable Estate, the houses at Ichi-no-tani were falling into decay. To-day little remains of the Ichi-no-tani settlement except in photograph albums, but instead further west the park-like James Estate stands where once were barren and eroded hills that had lain useless for centuries.

Among the photographs in my collection are a number of groups of athletic young men of some seventy years ago, most of whom are adorned with sideboard whiskers and moustaches of varying degrees of density. They are standing in the awkward poses of that period much like so many Grecian gods.

As the conventions then decreed that even athletes should not show too much flesh, they were clad in long-sleeved singlets and short trousers, long enough to come about two inches below the knee, or to be more precise, the exact length of a decent woman's bloomers. It seems clear that those three-quarter-length trousers, or so-called "shorts" of the Victorian age, must have inspired that amazing male garment to which Japanese gentlemen of mature age and substance were addicted. I refer of course to *han-zubon* of the walking-out variety which may still be seen occasionally in the skittish springtime.

Bermuda shorts would have been considered immodest, if not downright immoral, in those early days and only suitable for the Parisienne stage. Perhaps it is this feature of modesty and morality that accounts for our American male friends taking about thirty years to catch up with us Britishers in the wearing of above-the-knee shorts! By the same token it might be imagined that in Japan in about one decade hence the one-time fashionable *han-zubon* for walkers will have crept upwards and the original half-way-to-the-heels variety will then be as great a rarity in Japan as is to-day that one-time essential appendage of a well-dressed Japanese in his native costume —the bowler hat, about fifty-four different varieties of which appear in my photographic collection.

* * * * * * *

Included in one album in my possession, compiled by some student of the past, are a number of early photographs in the Yumoto district beyond Nikko, of small shrines adorned with emblems in stone clearly illustrating the original naturalistic worship that so quickly vanished in most places after the country was opened to western ideas nearly a century ago. To the student of anthropology, or just to the observant person, there are still examples in a camouflaged form to be seen in some shrines and in some old gardens.

Recently in a prewar millionaire's garden in which a great deal of money had been expended on very old stone lanterns and other such ornamentations, I detected hidden among the trees several such old stone objects showing clear traces of such early worship.

"Isn't it lovely?" enquired my foreign hostess as she conducted me around the garden of which she had become the proud tenant.

"It is indeed beautiful and it is twice as interesting as it is beautiful," I replied.

"What do you mean?" she enquired.

I found myself mumbling something about the origins of some aspects of Shintoism and wishing I could remember the exact number of the volume of the *Transactions of the Asiatic Society of Japan* to which I might refer her for more information, and so escape the embarrassment in which I had placed myself. Others before me had found themselves in a similar predicament and one was no less a person than that great authority on Japan, Basil Hall Chamberlain, but he had wit enough to extricate himself. The incident probably occurred at some embassy reception in Tokyo, for that great scholar usually moved only in exalted circles.

In a letter written to Lafcadio Hearn in 1894 he described the incident, how one day in mixed company a young lady suddenly enquired of him: "Oh! Mr. Chamberlain, you know everything. Do tell me what phallic means." Hoping to escape he professed complete ignorance.

"But," retorted the young lady "it is in your book. You must know it."

"Ah," flashed Chamberlain "You see I'm only responsible for half of *Murrays' Handbook for Japan.* It must be in the other half which Mr. Mason wrote."

* * * * * * * *

If we accept the angry words of the first British Minister to Japan, the foreign mercantile community then comprised "the scum of the earth," but his Excellency spoke in anger and was exaggerating. Included in the first arrivals were undoubtedly some of the dregs from the China ports, but they were in the minority. Many of the oldest and most respected foreign firms in the Far East such as Jardine Matheson & Co., had come in with the first arrivals. The latter firm has in fact been trading in Japan since the Treaty Ports were first opened and in early years was interested in a greater variety of activities than in later years.

Indeed, in the year 1890 outside their Kobe Office there were hanging three brass balls—the sign of a pawnbroker's establishment—and an announcement that loans were granted on any reasonable security. To make the meaning clearer, a battered bowler hat and an old pair of trousers were on display.

In case the management of that esteemed company may consider my statement libellous, I do declare that I have truthfully described an authentic photograph in my possession. It has taken me some time to discover the story behind it. It now appears that the Trust & Loan Agency Co., a bank of a special type established to make advances against property, was represented in Kobe by Jardine Matheson & Co. One morning soon after the agency opened, it was found that some youthful wags of the foreign community, considering that the name Trust & Loan Agency Co., rather suggested a pawnbroker's business, had during the night time erected over the door the three brass balls and the announcement regarding the granting of loans, and had hung out the old clothing. In those days the foreign community had to find its own amusement and such pranks were not unusual.

It had been hoped that the Trust & Loan Agency Co. would develop into a banking institution, but it never counted among the banks of Kobe.

* * * * * * *

Among the most interesting photographic collections that I have there is one—and it is my own—that is meticulously labelled with names, places and dates, the kind of record which in other circumstances divorce court lawyers dream of but seldom meet. It is now open before me. As I turn its pages and look again at some of our present-day worthy but rather stuffy pillars of the foreign community as they appeared twenty-five years ago, with one arm clutching a tankard of beer and the other supporting the waist of Skinny Lizzie or some other notable young lady of the period, I do imagine that some of them were more human then than now. Certainly they were more trim amidships.

There comes a time in men's lives—it generally occurs a few days, weeks or months before their wedding day—when they have a grand spring cleaning, and the skeletons in their cupboards are taken out and hurled into the dust bin. I went through the same period but after a mental struggle between what I deemed to be a course of safety and an historian's urge to preserve records of the past, my photograph album remained intact. Years later this circumstance used to worry some of my friends a great deal especially perhaps on the occasion of a visit to my home with their wives, because it was known that my children, who were much younger then, gained some amusement from turning the pages of this amazing album, and might at anytime pop a question such as:

"Daddy, where is the Cozy Corner Cafe? And did Uncle know Skinny Lizzie too?"

JAPAN'S
NATIONAL
ANTHEM

> ....and making musique after the
> Countrey fashion, although harsh
> to our hearings.
>
> Capt. SARIS' Diary, 1613

Arising out of the desire in some quarters of recent years that the *Kimigayo*—the national anthem of Japan—be outlawed because of the manner in which the ultra-nationalists exploited it in prewar days, there have of late been a number of references to it in the English language newspapers in Japan. Most of the articles have been sketchy and some entirely inaccurate. In some, credit for composing the *Kimigayo* has been given to a Japanese musician, in some to an English bandmaster, in others to a German.

The fact is that the *Kimigayo* is not the creation of any one man. While many contributed in effort towards a national anthem, the main credit for the *Kimigayo* in its present dignified form must go to a German, Franz Eckert, a musical director of considerable accomplishments.

While it would be an obvious over-estimation of Franz Eckert's achievements to place him in the leading ranks of that illustrious band of scholars and specialists who during the latter part of the last century interpreted little-known Japan to the Western world, nevertheless he earned a place in that company of men. To those foreigners, along with so many of the great Japanese statesmen and the liberals of the Meiji era, must go much of the credit for Japan having been able so quickly to take a place among the nations of the world.

As early as the 16th century the Jesuits and other Catholic missionaries sent home long letters interpreting Japan from their points of view, but the world had to await the arrival in Japan in 1690 of Engelbert Kaempfer, the remarkable German doctor attached to the Dutch East India Company, for the first fairly accurate account of the history, geography, resources, manners and customs of the country which he recorded in several celebrated books, written after a brief stay of only twenty-six months.

However, as late as one hundred years ago when Japan was striving to emerge from seclusion and to take her place among the nations of the world, it was still a country regarding which relatively little was known abroad. It was the brilliant European scholars and the enthusiastic and industrious specialists of the following decades who interpreted Japan to the West. Every phase of life and culture in Japan and all the arts and sciences were studied by those scholars and recorded in learned treatises and publications.

Franz Eckert contributed his share in the field of music.

* * * * * * *

In 1860 when the first Japanese embassy visited the United States, the lack of a national anthem presented a difficulty on the occasion of the arrival of the Japanese party at a grand ball given in their honour at the Metropolitan Hotel in New York. The band, presumably under an Irish bandmaster, did their best by striking up the tuneful melody "Kathleen Mavourneen."

Eight years later in 1868 the Mikado, the term by which the Japanese sovereign was then known, passed along the Tokaido near Hodogaya to make his first entry into Tokyo, which thereafter was to be his imperial capital. On that occasion the English regimental band from Yokohama, under Bandmaster John William Fenton, in the absence of a national anthem, saluted him en route with the lively tune of *The British Grenadiers*.

Upon Tokyo becoming the Imperial city and the Emperor ceasing to be a personage cooped up in a palace, hidden from and unknown to his subjects, the needs of a national anthem soon became felt. Bandmaster Fenton thereupon composed the music for a national anthem, but the authorities did not feel that his composition was entirely suitable and a select committee was set up to consider the whole matter. A poem from an ancient anthology in the form of a Japanese musical composition by Hiromori Hayashi, a Court musician, was selected and harmonised by Franz Eckert, at that time director of the Marine Band of Japan. In an early issue of the *Transactions of the Asiatic Society of Japan,* Herr Eckert's own modest statement can be found, of which the following is a translation:

Sometime ago I was asked by the Ministry of Marine to compose a national anthem, as one did not exist at that time. Having asked for them, I received several Japanese melodies from which I selected the following. I harmonized it and arranged it for European instruments....The poem is from the famous Kokinshu and is about a thousand years old.

The *Kimigayo* was played at Court in the presence of Emperor Meiji on the occasion of his birthday in 1881.

Although Eckert is not entitled to be called the composer of the national anthem, he accomplished his task with distinction and presented in final form a national hymn permeated with the calm and dignity of a bygone age. Many translations of the anthem have been made, but the following free translation by Basil Hall Chamberlain is probably the best:

A thousand years of happy reign be thine.
Rule on, my lord, till what are pebbles now,
By age united to mighty rocks shall grow,
Whose venerable sides the moss doth line.

It has a distinct characteristic of its own which places it among the most dignified national anthems in the world, but unfortunately it is so often played in Japan from old and scratched gramophone records that it frequently sounds more like the groans of some barbaric funeral dirge. In 1955 when the N.B.C. Symphony of the Air played the Japanese National Anthem most people who heard it had a new concept of the *Kimigayo*.

It is of passing interest to note that in *Scribners Magazine* of July, 1891, there was an article on the strides being made in Japan in modernising a nation, in which brief reference was made to her having acquired this national anthem.

* * * * * * *

Franz Eckert, born in Silesia in 1852, studied at several schools of music in Germany. On coming to Japan he was appointed director of the Marine Band of Japan from 1879-98. He founded the Toyama Military Band in Tokyo, and also the military band of the Imperial Guards. After eighteen years service his connection with the Ministry of Marine terminated in 1900 and he returned to Germany where he directed a Prussian military band in Berlin. In 1901 he came back to the East and became director of the Imperial Band in the Kingdom of Korea, and there composed the national anthem of Korea, thus achieving the distinction, and probably a unique one, of being responsible for the national anthems of two countries. Following the annexation of Korea by Japan in 1910, the Korean anthem was suppressed and the *Kimigayo* was then substituted for it.

In addition Eckert harmonized a great number of Japanese airs, which works were popular in Japan and were generally played without acknowledgement even during his lifetime and long after his death. Eckert died in Seoul in 1916.

* * * * * * *

Should it become the will of the Japanese people to outlaw the *Kimigayo*, a hazardous gamble would then have to be taken of discarding a sonorous national hymn of great dignity that verily breathes the spirit of Old Japan in favour of something new —possibly something modern but not great. For-

Japan's National Anthem

tunately the danger that once existed now seems to
have passed.

The preceding article first appeared in *The Mainichi* on
18th July, 1954, at a time when some Japanese were expres-
sing the view that the national anthem, having been dis-
credited by the warmongers, should be discarded in favour
of a new and modern anthem.

A TRAITOR
WAS
EXECUTED

I remember, I remember
The fir-trees dark and high.

THOMAS HOOD

In December, 1940, a young man was drowsing fitfully on a cot in Pentonville Prison in England. Within the short space of a few hours his life, which had commenced in the Kansai district in Japan, would come to a close.

During those final hours of his last night upon this earth his thoughts jumped from person to person, from place to place, but always wandered back to the years of childhood and youth which had been spent in the suburb of Sumiyoshi and in the cities of Osaka and Kobe.

He recalled his European father who had met with business reverses in Osaka and had subsequently died a broken and disappointed man. He recalled his Japanese mother. He remembered more clearly the following years of his early youth spent among kind friends and he remembered well his playmates at the foreign school in Kobe.

He remembered vividly his frequent wanderings through the Kobe Hills which he generally approached through Hunter's Gap, or up the Ice Road at Sumiyoshi, a path so named by the early foreigners in Kobe Settlement because it was down that path were brought the first supplies of ice cut from the ponds

272

on Rokko-san. The ponds froze to a greater depth then than they do now. He remembered clambering along Castle Ridge, swimming in the deeper pools around Twenty Crossings and paddling in the rippling waters of Cascade Valley. He remembered netting cicadas and dragon flies in the summer time, and in the autumn hunting for fallen chestnuts along the cool Mill Road to Futatabi.

He remembered how he attempted to ring the bell at the Futatabi Temple on every occasion that he visited it, which became easier as he grew taller.

He remembered the two grand old pine trees—Gog and Magog—which stood astride the narrow path to Futatabi, before there was any motor road. All that remains to-day of those giants is a portion of the trunk of one, gaunt and decaying.

He remembered camping on the sandy waste which surrounded the reedy pond on Shiogahara behind Futatabi, a spot then so bleak that it was known to foreigners as Aden, the same place that has since been transformed by Kobe City into a picturesque lake and play ground bordered with fine maple trees and red pines.

He recalled with a grin the day when he and his playmates caught two salamanders in the pond at Aden and wandered along Panoramic Ridge, over Kettle Hill and clambered down to the Arima Road by Goblin Rock. Then while resting at the Nikenchaya tea-house, and discovering the salamanders had died, they quickly dropped them into the teakettle while the *obasan* was not looking.

He remembered climbing to the top of Inscription

Rock in Karasuwara Valley around the source of
some of Kobe City's water supply, and wondering
what might be the meaning of the six enormous
characters carved on the rock and representing the
sacred ideographs of *Namu Amida Butsu*—Hail to
Amida the Buddha.

He remembered the days when the keeping of fancy
birds became a great craze in Japan and when canar-
ies and Java sparrows were imported in such quanti-
tities that although the supply quickly overtook the
demand, the voracious appetites of the birds did not
diminish and the dealers had to release the less costly
varieties in order to save themselves from bank-
ruptcy. He remembered how he and his school
friends had then caught many Java sparrows with
birdlime in the trees around Futatabi, only however
to release them again as they and their progency also
ate themselves out of home.

He drifted off into sleep and dreamed that he was
again camping on the sandy waste at Aden. The
chill of morning woke him and he thought he saw
the dawn breaking behind the ranges of mountains
to the east of Kobe. Then with a shudder he realized
that it was the first glimmer of morning light which
silhouetted the ledge of the window high up in his
prison cell. A short while later he was executed and
his memory was no more.

* * * * * * * *

It was 1940. The Battle of Britain had opened.
The days when "so many owed so much to so few"
had dawned. The conquering Germans held all the
coast line facing England, and Churchill offered the

people nothing but "blood, toil, tears and sweat."
The whole country was alerted to repel invasion.

On 2nd September, 1940, four men including young
van Kieboom were put on board a fishing cutter which
made along the coast towards Boulogne. Later they
pushed off in two dinghies and headed for the English
coast. Van Kieboom and one other landed early on
the morning of 3rd September on the edge of Romney
Marsh. They had a suitcase of clothing, provisions
and a radio set all of which they hid in deep grass
and then separated. Van Kieboom was carrying an
ingenious secret code made of linen. Their object
was to settle down in England posing as refugees
from Holland, and then to transmit back to the Germans by radio all the information they could obtain.

An hour or so later at about 5 a.m. van Kieboom
was challenged by a sentry and being unable to give
satisfactory replies was taken before the officer of
the guard. On being searched he was found to be
in possession of a loaded revolver. The suitcase of
clothing, the provisions and the radio set were soon
discovered, but he succeeded in disposing of the linen
code in a lavatory. His assistant, and the two occupants of the other dinghy, were also soon picked up.

The most extraordinary feature of the case was
that a Eurasian such as Charlie van Kieboom should
have been selected for a mission of this nature. His
English was poor and his appearance was such that
wherever he went he was certain to attract attention.
His only qualification appears to have been his skill
with radio sets, which had been his hobby as far
back as his school days in Kobe.

A Traitor Was Executed

Van Kieboom owed much to the friends and fellow-countrymen of his father. It was they who, in part at least, had arranged for his journey to Holland where he completed his schooling and grew to manhood. He owed more to the country of his father, whose nationality he possessed, than to any other. Why therefore he should have gone over to the enemy when his country was invaded may never be known. At his trial Van Kieboom alleged that the Germans had threatened to expose and punish him for smuggling currencies and for trafficking in German paper marks, but at no point did his defence fit the facts nor explain his anxiety to destroy the secret code.

After a secret trial at Old Bailey he and two of his companions were sentenced to death under the Treachery Act, and the fourth was given a long prison term.

THEY CAME
TO
OSAKA

*We arrived at Osaca: heere we
found the people very rude.*
Capt. SARIS' Diary, 1613

Three hundred and fifty-three years ago, at the
same time that Shakespeare was writing and acting
his plays in far-off England, the first Englishman
arrived in Osaka and was promptly imprisoned.

On 19th April, 1600, the Dutch ship "de Liefde"
(Charity) wallowed into Beppu bay in Kyushu—the
one vessel remaining out of a fleet of five that had set
out from Holland about twenty-three months earlier.
She had crossed the Atlantic, sailed down the coast
of South America, through the Straits of Magellan
and across the Pacific. And what a journey of pro-
digious dangers, of death and disaster!

Most of the crew had died of starvation or disease.
Of the original 120 only twenty-four remained and
of those only the English pilot, William Adams, and
six others could stand on their feet. Three died the
day after arrival in Japan and three more shortly
afterwards. The captain was too ill to move.

News of the arrival of the vessel was rushed by
couriers to Shogun Ieyasu Tokugawa then in residence at Osaka Castle. Orders were hurriedly carried
back ordering the captain to be brought to Osaka,
but as he was far too ill to travel, the English pilot,
as next in line, accompanied by one of the crew as

a servant, went instead. They travelled by junk through the Inland Sea and up the Yodogawa to Osaka. In those days, long before the vast reclamation scheme at Chikko, it was customary for the Inland Sea craft to travel well up the river and canals into the city of Osaka and for travellers to land not far from Osaka Castle.

Will Adams in his quaint style described the visit:

> *I was carried in one of the King's gallies to the court at Ozaca....we found Ozaca to be a very great towne as great as London within the walls ....Some faire houses we found there, but not many....*

In this manner the first Englishman came to Osaka. He was not however the first European to see that great city, great even then and great for many centuries earlier since the time the district was first named Naniwa. The Portuguese and Spaniards had probably been there off and on over the previous fifty years, and Portuguese priests had been making converts there for some years.

On the strength of false evidence given against the Dutch vessel by the Portuguese, who were fearful of the entry of competitors into their territory of trade, Will Adams and his servant were imprisoned on suspicion of piracy. After forty-one days imprisonment, during which time Adams was on several occasions questioned by *Shogun* Ieyasu, the peaceful intentions of the Dutch ship were recognised and he and his servant were released.

In the meantime the "de Liefde" had been ordered to Osaka, where she lay anchored off Sakai.

They Came to Osaka

In this manner the first Dutch ship came to Osaka.

There were no Customs in those days, as we know the term, but even had there been, the examination of the new arrivals would have presented no difficulties, because the ship had been well stripped, the crew robbed of their possessions and Adams of his navigational instruments. When those happenings came to the knowledge of Ieyasu, some restitution was subsequently made.

Thereafter in course of time Will Adams became the protégé of the *Shogun* and a person of some importance in the land. He used his influence to obtain a permit for his Dutch employers to trade in Japan. During the next 250 years the foreign merchant houses were restricted at first to Hirado and later to Nagasaki. In the early stages Dutch merchants from Hirado and English merchants from the English East India Company's house, also at Hirado, were frequent visitors to Osaka to transact business with their agents.

The English East India Company withdrew after a stay of ten years of unprofitable trading. Then for about 240 years the Dutch merchants were the only foreign merchants in the field, but were confined under humiliating conditions to the small island of Deshima in Nagasaki harbour. Once every four years a Dutch Embassy set out from Deshima and passed through Osaka en route to Tokyo, or Yedo as it was then known, on a compulsory visit to pay respects and tribute in the form of presents to the *Shogun* and his Court.

This state of affairs came to an end about one

hundred years ago, and in 1859 Yokohama was opened to trade, but it was not until 1868 that European traders were permitted to establish themselves in Osaka.

Preparatory to the opening of Osaka and Hyogo to foreign trade, which was fixed for 1st January 1868, Sir Harry Parkes, the British Minister to Japan, landed at Osaka from H.M.S. "Adventure" on 23rd December, 1867. On the following day a detachment of British soldiers of the 9th Regiment landed as an escort. Sir Harry Parkes found accommodation in a *yashiki*—a superior Japanese residence —near the Osaka Castle and there established the British Legation. Preparations for the opening of the port were well under way.

The locality chosen for the Osaka Foreign Settlement, or the Concession as it was generally known, was an area called Kawaguchi, outside of what was then the city of Osaka. It was almost an island in that it was bounded by water on three sides, by the Tosabori-gawa, the Aji-kawa and the Kizu-gawa. Like the Settlement at Kobe it was originally a waste land that had to be raised and drained to make it fit for occupation. A British Vice-Consulate was established nearby on Christmas Day in readiness for the formal opening and arrival of merchants on New Year's Day, 1868. At both Osaka and Kobe, the Japanese Government had arranged for a number of houses and land lots to be ready for occupation. At Kobe there were insufficient houses to meet the number of applicants, but at Osaka for thirty-nine houses there were only twelve applicants. It is evident that from the beginning foreigners showed little desire to live in Osaka.

The sea approach to Osaka being treacherous, it was decided that the foreign men-of-war and the several vessels bringing the merchants to Osaka and Hyogo should anchor off the port of Hyogo, where the merchants for both Kobe and Osaka disembarked on New Year's morning, the historic occasion being marked by no ceremony other than the firing of a salute from the foreign men-of-war.

From Kobe the merchants who were bound for Osaka made their way either overland or by sea in small sailing craft as opportunity arose. In this manner the first foreign merchants set up business in Osaka. Their stay was short but exciting.

The opposition to the Shogunate Government for having opened Hyogo and Osaka to foreign trade, had been growing in strength and violence. Fighting was taking place in Kyoto and elsewhere. The *Shogun* had resigned, but before quitting the Castle at Osaka he had notified the foreign ministers that he could no longer protect the foreigners. On 30th January, only thirty days after the opening of the port, Osaka Castle was pillaged and set on fire by the Imperialists and thus Osaka lost a fine old castle.

(In 1931 a replica, but in re-inforced concrete, was built on the original foundations, and so in the 1945 air-raids when the Osaka Arsenal, which stood in the immediate rear of the Castle, was showered with bombs the Arsenal was obliterated but the re-inforced concrete and fire-proof replica of the feudal castle fortunately withstood the raids. It thus continues to be the finest show place in Osaka to-day.)

The state of disorder that prevailed in Osaka following the sacking of the old castle was deemed to be so serious that a few days later, after about one month's stay, all the foreign legations, the military escorts, and the merchants withdrew to Kobe. Most of the merchants never returned to Osaka. They preferred to remain in the more attractive Kobe Concession.

Two weeks later a party representing the various legations re-visited Osaka to ascertain conditions. The Imperialists were of course in control. All was quiet, but the British and French Legations were found to have been burnt and all the other legations looted.

Some few of the merchants later returned to Osaka, but those violent happenings coupled with the dangerous sea approach to Osaka harbour caused the British Minister and some others to abandon the idea of establishing a legation at Osaka. Kobe thus became the foreign diplomatic headquarters in the Kansai area and the centre for overseas trade, a position of importance that it would most probably have continued to hold but for the advent of air mail. But first let us trace out the history of the Osaka Foreign Concession.

On 13th April of the same year, Emperor Meiji demonstrated his intention to govern the country as well as to reign, by leaving Kyoto and making an official visit to Osaka, formerly the stronghold of the Tokugawa Shogunate. He entered the city on 15th April, and as the castle had been destroyed, he stayed at the Nishi-Honganji Temple. Three days later he passed in his Imperial barge in front of the Foreign Concession on the way to Temposan to review the Imperial Navy which then comprised six vessels: the flagship "Tenriyo Maru," "Cosmopolite" belonging to the Daimyo of Higo, the "Chusan" (originally a P. & O. vessel) the "Otentosama" of Choshiu, the "Gerard" of Satsuma, and the "Coquette" of Kurume. These vessels had all been purchased from foreign owners and some, it will be noted, retained their original names.

In September, 1868, a young American merchant named Watts, who had established himself in the Osaka Concession, loaded his merchandise on a boat and journeyed up the Yodogawa for the imperial and forbidden city of Kyoto. There he quickly sold his entire stock to the Kyoto merchants, but before delivery could be taken and payment made he was arrested by Japanese soldiers and returned to his consul in Osaka together with his merchandise. The record does not mention what punishment was imposed by the consul.

In this manner the first American salesman set out from Osaka to sell his wares in Kyoto.

A few years later when it was possible for foreigners to obtain a permit to visit Kyoto, the journey there was generally made from Osaka by jinrikisha, the return trip being by boat down the Yodogawa.

The journey from Osaka to Kobe was made overland by jinrikisha in six hours or by sea in two hours, weather permitting.

Even in pre-war days, it was still possible, for

those who cared to allow their imagination to wander, to sense the spirit of the early days in some of the side alleyways of old Kawaguchi. One could picture Mlle. Reymond's genteel Boarding & Day School of eighty years ago—the address was No. 2 Concession —and the lots further down where several of the local grog shops did business. The Osaka Hotel was at No. 6 Concession and presumably was then owned by the father of the school ma'am because the local directory of that time gives his name as Baptiste Reymond.

Another colourful personality was a German named Friebe who undertook the delivery of mail within the Concession. Mounted on a horse he rode from house to house announcing his coming by blowing a bugle.

A visitor to Osaka in 1873 described the Foreign Concession

as appearing to consist chiefly of new roads and vacant lots. The houses that were then in existence showing all their back premises in front and no fronts anywhere.

Except for those houses built on the Bund, most foreign houses both in the Kobe and Osaka Settlements were built with their front verandahs facing the inside of the compounds, presumably so that the occupants would not be disturbed by the curious gaze of those in the streets outside. Many such old buildings were still to be seen in Kobe Settlement before the wartime air raids wiped them out.

1875 was a bad year for trade in Japan, and almost all the mercantile offices and branches that had opened in Osaka were closed. Trade fell to such a low figure that the Kobe Foreign Chamber of Commerce Circular that had hitherto reported the volume of trade in the sister port ceased to mention the business done in Osaka. By 1878 there were only about five or six foreign firms nominally represented in Osaka. Business continued to decline and finally drifted away to nothing. Kawaguchi became more of a missionary colony than a business community.

In 1880 E. H. Hunter of Hunter & Co., realising the great advantages likely to accrue from setting up a foundry and ship-repairing yard at Osaka, as compared with Kobe where all such work had hitherto been done, acquired an excellent site for a ship-building yard on a tongue of land between Ajikawa and Nakatsugawa, there being a water frontage on both sides. A small village occupied the site and the houses had to be transferred elsewhere. This enterprise became the Osaka Iron Works, later to grow into the immense Hitachi Dockyard.

(Elsewhere an engineer named Kirby started the Onohama Dockyard which was later bought by the Japanese Government and incorporated into the Kure Naval Station.)

On 17th July, 1899, when extra-territoriality came to an end, the Osaka Concession at Kawaguchi and the Kobe Concession were handed over to the Japanese authorities and were thereafter administered by the Japanese city authorities.

Today practically nothing but a few old bricks remain in Kawaguchi to remind one that it was once the abode of foreigners.

After the first World War the number of foreign firms in Osaka steadily increased, mainly import houses, and one foreign bank. The export firms, the old *hongs*, the banks and the shipping companies remained in Kobe.

Possibly not many people in postwar Japan have calculated the loss in property values and in other directions that Kobe has suffered and that Osaka has correspondingly gained as the indirect result of air mail. In the export trade it is of course essential that shipping documents arrive at destination not later than the merchandise, which generally meant that they had to go by the vessel carrying the merchandise. The prewar procedure covering the export of goods was streamlined to make that possible, MITI regulations did not exist in those days. Had they existed Japan's export trade would have been strangled and would have withered away. It was thus possible, and necessary, in those days to complete the entire procedure of an export shipment within the space of a day or so, and in fact to do then in about twenty-four hours what now requires up to several weeks. As most overseas vessels departed from Kobe, not Osaka, Kobe developed as the logical and most convenient centre for the export trade. The banks, the shipping companies, the merchants, the suppliers, and all facilities necessary to the conduct of the export trade, including the foreign residences and institutions, were thus centered in Kobe.

Following the cessation of hostilities and the birth of MITI with the multitudinous and complex regulations governing the conduct of trade, a new method of doing business developed and it became more convenient for the foreign merchants, and exporters in particular to be located in Osaka. Air mail had made it possible to despatch shipping documents a week or more after a steamer's departure and yet still arrive at destination before the goods. Air mail had opened up a new method of handling the export trade. Air mail was responsible for the exodus of a large section of the mercantile community of Kobe to Osaka.

In this manner the export merchants, the foreign banks, the shipping and insurance companies came to Osaka.

BEYOND
THE
REEF

O look with pity on the scene
Of sadness and of dread....
And let the plague be stayed.
Hymns Ancient and Modern

When Japan was opened to foreign trade the first
to enter were the genuine merchants, soon followed
by the carpet-baggers, the adventurers, and some
of the dregs of the Eastern ports. Then came the
beachcombers and some years later the tourists.

The beachcomers had long been a plague throughout the Pacific. As each group of islands was discovered, those spots were soon the prey of human
derelicts who at one time or another had deserted
their ships, or had escaped from the convict settlements of Australia and other places. The wrongs
which those creatures did to the simple natives on
the Pacific islands cannot be measured in any known
terms.

In 1789 the American whaler "Hunter" discovered
a small coral island, about three and a half miles long
and two and a half miles wide, situated only twenty-
five miles from the Equator. It was similar in general appearance to many other coral islands of the
Pacific, with a lagoon, a reef, and *beyond the reef* the
wide Pacific Ocean. So favourable was the impression which this small island and the natives made

288

upon the men of the whaler that it was called Pleasant Island. It is thought by some to be the island described by Tennyson—

Rich, but the loneliest in a lonely sea

and where Enoch Arden

Set in this Eden of all plenteousness

Dwelt with eternal summer, ill content.

Soon, however, it became plagued by the lowest dregs of humanity, the human driftwood then cast about the Pacific. The beachcombers on that remote island were beyond the law but fortunately murder and violence among themselves generally kept them to less than ten. Severe outbreaks of dysentery further reduced their numbers, and the inconvenience of occasional droughts which robbed them of even enough water to dilute their liquor, caused some of them to leave in search of other isles.

In 1881 the HMS "Bacchante" made the island and found that an escaped convict had assumed the position of king, and that he and a coterie of equally undesirable characters were preying upon the natives and were almost constantly drunk from drinking a liquor which they distilled from fermented palm juice. For food they lived mainly on pigs and coconuts. The island offered nothing else in the way of fruits or vegetables, and even water was short. It seemed to lack riches, but underneath the soil, and indeed protruding through the soil was untold wealth, the nature of which was not then known. It was not until 1899 when a chemist in Sydney decided to analyse a piece of rock, which for nearly three years had served as a door-stopper in his laboratory, was the wealth of the island discovered. It was found to be phosphate rock of the highest quality.

In 1881 the island had become German territory and the name had then been changed from Pleasant Island to Nauru, which was the native name. The British Company which desired to work those newly discovered phosphate deposits, therefore, had to enter into an arrangement with the German interests controlling the island. An immense tonnage of phosphate rock was shifted in the ensuing years. Then in November, 1914, following the outbreak of the First World War, the British flag was hoisted over Nauru, and in 1919 the entire interests of the British company, known as the Pacific Phosphate Company, were taken over jointly by the United Kingdom, Australian, and New Zealand Governments. The enterprise was thereafter operated under the name of the British Phosphate Commissioners.

Much wealth was taken out of Nauru, but much money, effort, and care was expended to improve the lot of the natives. In 1920 leprosy was found to be spreading among the natives, whereupon the latest treatment and techniques were introduced. A segregation village was created and the disease thereafter was confined to a mild though obstinate form.

For two decades until December, 1941, shortly after the outbreak of war in the Pacific, the natives passed through a period of progress and enlightenment. They forgot the wrongs that had been done them by white men of the past. Then suddenly a Japanese naval landing party occupied the island, and once again murder and violence were law on that pleasant island.

Beyond the Reef

The object of this article is not to recount the discreditable deeds and atrocities perpetrated by that Japanese naval landing party both against the British resident civilian officials and against the natives, but rather to tell the story of a party of simple natives who passed *beyond the reef*, farewelled by their friends singing Christian hymns.

* * * * * * *

Leprosy has had a home in Japan for many centuries. During the war years, in most of the important prisoner-of-war centres abroad, where large numbers of Japanese prisoners-of-war were being held in Allied hands, there were generally one or two cases of leprosy that manifested themselves among the Japanese prisoners.

In truth it must be said that in prewar days the attitude of the Japanese Government and of the public towards those unfortunates who suffered from leprosy was not enlightened. Often a family cast out any members unfortunate enough to contract the disease and thenceforth they wandered about the country as waifs, neglected and avoided by all. The attitude of individuals was guided by fear, and if such is any defence for a terrible atrocity we give it here as the only one that can be said in defence of a vice-admiral condoning the slaughter of over sixty lepers.

* * * * * * *

Upon arrival in Nauru the Japanese naval landing party learned with fear that on this small island, there were over sixty lepers segregated in one corner. Soon afterwards the Japanese told the islanders that arrangements had been completed to transfer the lepers to Truk where they would be hospitalised and receive the latest medical treatment. And so the lepers were gathered on the beach, under the coconut trees, whilst their families and friends sat on the opposite side of the road under guard of Japanese sentries to farewell them. Fear and doubt were in their hearts, but they attempted to buoy up the spirits of those about to leave by the singing of Christian hymns.

Whilst the lepers were being embarked on two large sampans, smoke was rising over the coconut palms from their huts, which had been fired. Their last link with their native isle was already being destroyed.

The sampans were taken in tow by a naval launch. The singing swelled and travelled across the lagoon to those passing *beyond the reef*. Some knelt in prayer. The lepers in the sampans took up the hymns which travelled back across the lagoon to the Japanese sentries on the shore and to the friends and relatives still singing under the coconut palms. The hymns continued well after the sampans had passed beyond the reach of sight and sound—*beyond the reef*.

In the days and months which followed the simple islanders on Nauru continued to hope and pray, although with misgiving in their hearts, for the safety and welfare of their loved ones *beyond the reef*.

Of an evening they sang their plaintive native songs, counterparts of which are to be found in all Pacific isles; songs of their beloved who had gone *be-*

yond the reef where all is rough and cold; singing that although their dreams may grow old they would shed no tears of regret, but would send a thousand flowers of remembrance on the waves when the trade winds began to blow.

* * * * * * *

In truth when the sampans had been towed twenty miles out to sea, and well out of sight of land, the Japanese in the launch cut the towing ropes, set the sampans adrift and then circled them, pouring machine-gun fire into them until they sank with all on board. The natives on Nauru knew nothing of this happening. They continued to sing their plaintive songs of hope.

The atrocity came to light in Tokyo some four years later.

ANTICS
IN
THE NUDE

> *I pray you pardon me for writing such fopperies, which I doe to the intent to have you laugh a little.*
> RICHARD COCKS' Diary, 1620

In course of time some student may gain a degree by writing a thesis on "strip," as it is known today, and not unlikely he will give credit for the introduction into Japan of that spectacle, to some of the carpet-baggers who came into this country after the war as camp-followers of the Occupation Forces. Certainly to them must go credit for inspiring such extravaganza and nonsense as *The Lady was a Stallion* and other similar "strip" classics, so widely advertised in the press. Then there were the advertising stunts of four or five years ago, now fortunately a thing of the past, where young ladies dressed in butterflies, bangles, and high-heeled shoes rode down the Ginza in decorated motor vehicles.

Of course the female form unclothed was known in Japan prior to the Occupation, but entrepreneurs had not presented it quite in the form of "strip." Neither the people nor the government would have tolerated anything quite so vulgar as that. Instead they created restricted quarters where the hostesses were clothed in about as many undergarments as our Victorian great grandmothers, had their teeth blackened and their heads protected with an array of

294

protruding bamboo hairpins much like the armour of a porcupine. Instead of scarlet letters on their sleeves to indicate the corps to which they belonged, they had their *obi* or sashes tied in front.

From the point of view of art there was something to be said for these arrangements, because there came a time when aspiring young artists, who were seeking a new mode of expression, discovered in it an agreeable method whereby they could pursue their artistic studies in places that appealed to them most. Within the limitations of their pockets many of the artists of the eighteenth and nineteenth centuries set up their ateliers, as it were, within the boudoirs of the ladies of the *Yoshiwara,* and thus were born many of the famous *ukiyoe*—or pictures of the fleeting world of transient pleasures—which now are the prized possessions of the British Museum, London, the Metropolitan Museum of Art in New York, and other famous museums. There the public may view the young ladies without any idea as to what they are or where they resided.

This unusual circumstance whereby the artist lived not upon commissions to paint the portraits of the great, but rather upon the favours of his lady friends of the demi-monde, has created one of the many curious differences between the art of the west and that of Japan. Whilst the picture galleries of Europe and America are cluttered up with portraits of men and women once great, or just opulent, but now largely forgotten, the artists in Japan at that time were so busily engaged in recording in discreet detail the love life and chores of the ladies of the *Yoshiwara,* that there was little time or desire to do much in the way of recording for posterity the features of many of the great of that period. Few people will dispute the success of those unconventional artists or deny that the world is greatly richer for their wood block prints.

Although the strip dance (which now seems to be as well-known to tourists as cloisonne ware used to be) was introduced into Japan as late as the chewing gum era, nevertheless Nagasaki had its *Chonkina* dance, a description of which can be found in John Paris' *Kimono*. A crude imitation of the *Chonkina* could be seen in the back rooms of some of the cheap dives of Kobe and other port cities, but in all probability *Chonkina* was not a Japanese invention. More likely it was inspired by sailors and other visitors from overseas in the early days of some three centuries ago when Nagasaki was the *"Gay Paree"* of the Far East.

A modification of the dance was described by Dr. Thunberg, the Swedish physician and scientific investigator who was attached to the Dutch East India post of Deshima, in Nagasaki harbour, in 1775:

The girls are provided with a number of very fine and light gowns, made of silk, which they slip off one after another, during the dance, from the upper part of their body, so as frequently to leave them to the number of a dozen together suspended from the girdle which envelops their loins.

Whilst the nude does not figure prominently in early Japanese art, except in the so-called "spring" books and "pillow" books, in which pictorial presentations the artists permitted their imaginations to run riot, nevertheless the modern Japanese artist is devoting much attention to the subject. That the Japanese artist is struggling with the female form is evident from the ladies with blotched skins and deformed limbs who so frequently grace the walls of modern exhibitions of art in this country; that a fair section of the public who frequent bookstores to do their magazine reading, is interested in the same subject is evident from the fact that the art magazines are generally kept under glass to preserve them from dog-ears and limp covers.

The responsibility, if it is a responsibility, for introducing to Japan the first picture of a western nude most probably goes to an Englishman, Capt. John Saris, commander of the "Clove," the first ship of the English East India Company to visit Japan. That was in 1613 during the reign of James I of England. The Daimyo or Lord Governor of Hirado paid a visit to the "Clove" accompanied by some ladies of his court. Capt. Saris records in his diary:

I gave leave to divers women of the better sort to come to my Cabbin, where the picture of Venus did hang very lasciviously set out in a large frame. They, thinking it to be our Ladie (the Virgin Mery), fell downe and worshipped it, with shewes of great devotion telling me in a whispering manner (that some of their own companions, which were not so, might not heare) that they were Christianos, whereby we perceived them to be Christians converted by the Portugall Jesuits.

Saris seems to have had quite a penchant for the

form of art, miniatures of which geisha used once to carry around in their purses for good luck, because the following appears in the Court Minutes of the East India Company:

December 16, 1614. Some imputations and assertions being cast upon Captain Saris for certain lascivious books and pictures brought home by him and divulged which is held to be a great scandal unto this Company and unbeseeming their gravity to permit, Mr. Governor assured them of his dislike thereof....and therefore purposed to get them out of his (Saris's) hands if possibly he could, to be burnt....

Under date of 10th January, 1615, there appears a further entry:

Mr. Governor acquainted them that great speeches having been made of certain books brought home by Captain Saris....he hath procured them from Capt. Saris and shut them up ever since, and now hath brought them forth that such as have heard derogatory speeches used upon the Exchange and elsewhere should now likewise be eye-witness of the consuming them in the fire which he hoped would give satisfaction to any honestly affected ....And thereupon in open presence put them into the fire where they continued till they were burnt and turned into smoke.

Thus ended the first Japanese "spring" books to be brought into England.

As witches, among other things, were also occasionally burnt in those days, historians have been somewhat uncertain as to just how bad, or how good,

Capt. Saris' pictures were. Possibly they would cause less excitement to-day on the Exchange than they did three hundred and fifty years ago. Standards change over the years, and in Japan no less than elsewhere. There was a time less than thirty years ago when Rodin's scuptural masterpiece "The Kiss" was exhibited in Japan behind drawn curtains, which were only pulled aside for artists, who like doctors were thought to be able to look upon the geography of nude forms without experiencing too much shock. Possibly Rodin's masterpiece could be exhibited to-day in the window of any department store without stopping the traffic or raising more than a snicker.

One of the earliest of antics in the nude in which foreigners were involved, was in Capt. Saris' time in Japan. During the late summer months in those days of sail there were always several ships laid up in the port of Hirado. They came in on the southerly monsoon at the beginning of summer and after discharging their rich cargoes of lead, tin, iron, steel, leather, glassware, cannon, ammunition, and gunpowder, and also spices from the Indies, they had to wait until autumn before loading their outward cargoes of rice, brimstone, porcelains, art-pieces, silver, and gold, and be ready to sail south again with the winter northerly behind them. At the peak of trade there were over six or seven hundred seamen ashore, bent upon entertainment in the many dubious houses that were seeking their trade. When the men had spent their money, the keepers of those houses gladly extended them credit against the security of their clothing, whereupon the sailors later had to make their way back to their ships, drunk and in a semi-naked condition, among the ribald gibes of the populace. Richard Cocks, head of the English House, writing home to the East India Company in 1621, complained:

And as soon as our men goe along the street the Japons kindly call them in and geve them wines and whores till they be drunk and then stripp them of all they have (some of them stark naked) and soe turne them out of dores.

But Cocks admitted the fault was not always with the Japanese, *"for som of our men are bad enough,"* and later he wrote:

I know I need not to adviz of the unrulynesse of many our marreners, and som of them not of the meanest sort, whoe daylie lie ashore att tipling howses, wasting their goodes and geving bad example to others.

And again:

And that which maketh me more afeard then all the rest is the unreasonablenesse and unrulynesse of our owne people which I know not how it will be amended.

* * * * * * *

When in 1860 the first Japanese embassy visited the United States, the New York newspapers of that time described how upon the arrival of the Japanese party at the grand ball given in their honour at the Metropolitan Hotel in New York, the band struck up the tuneful melody *Kathleen Mavourneen*, that being the best that the bandmaster (probably an Irishman) could think of in the absence of a Japanese national anthem. The Japanese guests then:

sat down in quiet amazement at the rapid evolutions made by the lady dancers, who twirled around in the giddy waltz with a rapidity that would have done credit to an artificial fire-wheel.

What the New York reporters did not know was the confused speculation that was passing through the minds of the guests as to why European women should so completely clothe their form in the daytime with skirts so low that they dragged in the dust rather than show an ankle, and with blouses with neck-pieces supported on whale bone so high that they even hid their Adam's apples, whereas at night on formal occasions they displayed their shoulderblades and protruded their chests rendered the more massive by the corsetry of those days.

It is obvious that the last-mentioned feature of foreign women of a century ago must have made a big impression on the Japanese people, because I have before me an illustrated A.B.C. book and dictionary published in Tokyo in the year 1873 for the use of students of English. A is for "air," B is for "breath" (both wonderfully enough are illustrated with sketches), whilst P is for "parapet" and here the artist seems to have gone wrong because he has illustrated it with the well developed upper anterior portion of the torso of a woman. There seems also to be some error in the illustration against N for "naval," where the artist has drawn the front view of the abdomen of a *sumo* wrestler!

Workmen and porters in Japan (or coolies as the foreign press and literature of those days preferred to call them) wore during the summer months a single garment known by the musical name of a G-string, which ancient outfit although exactly one garment less than a modern Bikini swim-suit did in fact represent about a yard more of material! Those sights so offended the foreigners of those days that the Japanese authorities in Yokohama posted notices in Japanese reading in part as follows:

Those who come from divers places to Yokohama and make their living as porters, carters, labourers, coolies and boatmen are in the habit, especially in the summer, of plying their calling in a state bordering on nudity. This is very reprehensible and in future no one who does not wear a shirt or tunic properly closed by a girdle will be allowed to remain in Yokohama....

An Imperial Rescript was later issued on the subject of dress, and police regulations provided that the police should remonstrate with those who exposed their bodies unnecessarily.

That those regulations did result in some change, slight though it may have been, is evident from the following description of a rickshaw-man's clothing as seen by the wife of a British Ambassador when she arrived in Japan some years later

His clothes were of the impressionist kind, some rather slight good intentions carried out in cool blue cotton, the rest being brown man and straw sandals.

Arising out of the police regulations governing dress there was what came to be known as the Jonas Case—one of those antics which threw the foreign community into such fits of indignation that the

Kobe Chronicle devoted three learned and lengthy leading articles to the subject. The days of extra-territoriality had just come to an end and foreigners had become subject to Japanese law. It was a hot summer day and Mrs. Jonas was passing down Shin-saibashi-suji in Osaka in a rickshaw with her seven-year-old daughter who was wearing a light sleeveless summer dress, whereupon a policeman put them under temporary restraint and then ordered the child home to dress properly!

The Governor of Osaka made a form of apology and the policeman was reprimanded, but at this late date we extend a word of sympathy to that confused man. If he had ever seen in those days a foreign woman bathing at the seaside clad in tunic and bloomers, not the modern brief variety but flounced and gathered in below the knee and firmly anchored with buttons and bows, with cotton stockings (and black ones at that), sandshoes and hat, he must surely have believed that foreign women considered it a mortal sin to show any flesh. He could hardly have been expected to know that it is fashion not logic which dictates what portions of the human frame may be displayed.

When the Japanese commenced to adopt Western dress, the etiquette associated with that portion of male clothing known as trousers proved to be the most puzzling, particularly in the finer points that the buttons must never be released from the button-holes in public, and must be replaced in the button-holes in private. That a button out of position could so scandalise our great-grandmothers when young as to throw them into a swoon, but can if necessary be suffered in fortitude by women of today without calling for smelling salts and other restoratives, is a fact which indicates that our ideas change. However, the change was not sufficiently great as to render unnecessary the quaintly worded notices in English that appear in the gentlemen's wash rooms of some European hotels where the management strive in a few words to explain the involved etiquette of the trouser-buttons to their Japanese guests.

And here one of the antics of the Occupation—a contribution to the "Now it can be told" secrets—an unofficial "Top Secret." When the female personnel of the Occupation came into Tokyo in 1946, at first the New Kaijo Building, and later other immense blocks of office buildings were converted into quarters for them, a fact that quickly became known to the male personnel occupying quarters in neighbouring buildings, and more particularly to those whose rooms commanded a view, even although a very distant one, of the windows of the female blocks. It was then that the Japanese vendors of binoculars suddenly noticed a considerable increase in sales. So excellent and high-powered were the Japanese binoculars, that even those Occupationaires living at a distance of nearly a mile from the New Kaijo Building were not discouraged in the pursuit of their optical studies.

When a man fell out of a window in his excitement, it was suggested by his pals, at the court of inquiry into the accident, that a few of the girls in the New Kaijo were possibly seeking to carve out a new career for themselves after their return to the States, because they seemed to be practicing in their rooms, to a vast and unseen audience, the art of strip!

There are antics also in the trade notices. The advertising poster in near English that recently appeared drawing attention to the exciting features of a local circus, including "Lady tamer with wild breasts," recalls the advertisement, issued by the cultured pearl producers of Miye Prefecture, which might appeal to some Oriental potentate seeking suitable garb for his dancing girls, but to ladies and gentlemen (if they be gentlemen) about to make a purchase of pearls, the wording must surely prove inept:

....That's the Pearl....the apple of the eye to all the fair sex of the world....How the graceful arc of the necklaces rest on your breasts enhance your charm....how the tiny pearls are growing up.... and looking forward to the happy days when they can adorn your graceful figure....

The chapter will now be brought to a timely end with a quotation from a letter which we received from a Japanese student:

Early summer has come. Trees and Grasses have put on beautiful green clothes. Contrary to nature we have took off our clothes.

MESDAMES CHRYSANTHEMUM AND BUTTERFLY

> *To gild refined gold, to paint the lily,*
> *To throw a perfume on the violet,*
> *Is wasteful and ridiculous excess.*
>
> Shakespeare—*King John*

When French naval officer Julien Viaud, alias Pierre Loti, came ashore at Nagasaki in 1885 and propositioned a tea-house girl through the medium of one of the local inhabitants, he had no idea that he was providing the background for one of the world's most popular operas. Of course Loti had not done anything original, but he was the first to record his experiences in a book that gained world fame.

More than half a century later the G.I's did everything that Lóti had done, but by coining the word "shacking-up," they attempted to express in one word all that Pierre Loti had put into a whole book. At any rate *Madame Chrysantheme* set some minds in the West stirring and the tourist traffic to Japan perceptibly moved upwards. A new cast of characters—and somewhat more respectable ones—a few additions, several dramatic twists and the story then the libretto of *Madame Butterfly* were born. It then required the musical genius of Puccini to produce an opera that could always be sat through with closed eyes, but with keen enjoyment, if the stage setting proved too disturbing or if poor Cho-Cho San were too monstrous in bulk to look upon. Of course only Japanese or foreigners familiar with Japan ever writhed in their seats and reacted that way. The audiences in the West lapped up the music as they sat enraptured at the pseudo-Japanese scenes that unfolded themselves.

With the Occupation and the advent of air travel, Japanese scenery and customs became so much more widely known to the world abroad that during the postwar years greater attention had to be given to the stage-settings and the production of this opera for Western eyes than in prewar days. Closer attention has also been given to geography—there were occasions when the producers made Cho-Cho San sing that lovely aria *Some day he'll come* whilst gazing across Nagasaki Harbour at Fuji San in the distance!

Casting Cho-Cho San was always a problem abroad. Not infrequently she was tall, and half as tall as she was wide. For awhile Tamaki Miura proved a solution, but she gained such a liking for Continental cooking that she also became quite a rotund Butterfly.

The recent Italian movie production of *Madame Butterfly* with Italians playing the American parts, with Japanese in all the Japanese roles, with Takarazuka revue girls in the parts of the geisha girl bridesmaids, and with Japanese technicians and consultants to provide stage settings that will appeal to both Western and Oriental audiences, without inviting too devastating criticism from either, has set "a new high." It is indeed a spectacular production. The settings were in fact so distractingly beautiful that we were frequently compelled to shut our eyes and seek escape, until we became sufficiently composed to concede to the producers the poetic and operatic licence to which they are entitled.

For those who delight in criticising, there is a little scope. The gardening experts may have been outraged at the sight of cherry-blossoms bursting from a tree with bark suspiciously like that of a pine. Electricians may have been astonished at the brilliant illumination that a few old-fashioned *andon*—vegetable oil lanterns—were able to provide, and the U.S. Navy paymasters in the audience, if there were any, must have wondered how a lieutenant had come by the cash to maintain a love-nest that even a reckless rear-admiral would have hesitated to embark upon. Experts in eugenics might quibble with the casting of a fair-haired blue-eyed child as Cho-Cho's son, but biologists could explain him as one chance in a million. Personally we would have liked to see Cho-Cho San handle the telescope with greater skill, more as her naval lover would have done, and less like a drunken sailor. That is all.

The sartorial experts, however, must have been puzzled at the incongruous dress of U.S. Consul Sharpless. Why he should have been given trousers of a 1954 cut, instead of the fashionable stove-pipe type of more than half a century ago, is not clear. Certainly he was provided with elastic-sided shoes in order to be able the more readily to slip them off when entering the Japanese mansion, and so avoid a diplomatic incident by walking on the *tatami* with shoes on. Not, however, Pinkerton, when on their wedding night he carried Cho-Cho San across the threshold, or rather the *engawa*. Certainly a stir spread through the audience, both Japanese and foreigners alike, as they spotted his loutish behaviour. But Cho-Cho San was evidently enjoying the experience so much that we personally think he would have been a cad had he dropped her to take off his shoes.

In striding across Japanese tatami with shoes on, he may have remembered that better men than he had done the same. It all started in 1856 with U.S. Consul-General Townsend Harris who did not believe that the dignity of a great nation could be upheld by an envoy shuffling about in stocking feet. Later the Bishop of London apparently felt the same about the dignity of the Church, and still later George Bernard Shaw definitely felt the same about the dignity of George Bernard Shaw. On one occasion in Tokyo, when he entered a Japanese mansion, a female servant padded behind him with a small carpet on which she hoped he might be persuaded to stand, but Shaw, with his characteristic perverseness, maintained a stride that always kept him about three feet ahead of the carpet.

However, let us return to the Italian film.

This superb production did at least make one thing abundantly clear. It left no doubt as to why Pinkerton propositioned Cho-Cho—a fact that was never clear to us before as we used to watch the fatty tissue of some double-chinned European soprano vibrating as she lingered on the top notes. Furthermore it was possibly one of the few occasions on which Pinkerton was physically capable of carrying Cho-Cho about in his arms, so lithe and exquisite was she.

Incidentally neither Cho-Cho San nor her beautiful bridesmaids had their necks (or their faces) plastered with white powder as the make-up of that period would have required. The modern style make-up rendered them immeasurably more beautiful. Certainly it confirmed a theory we have long held, radical though it is to Japanese, namely the most delectable part of a geisha is *not* her neck!

Again we repeat this Italiano-Japanese production is a most beautiful presentation of a famous opera. But let it stop at this. Let it not in the future be reproduced on any grander or more beautiful scale. Let the millionaire mansion be not increased in size to that of an imperial palace surrounded by a moat. Let not all the flowers in the Japanese floral calendar be scrambled and all bloom at once, or the number of Cho-Cho's bridesmaids be increased from twenty to a hundred.

If the opera reaches any greater heights of beauty or exaggeration the surrealists will surely take revenge, as they have always done, and will produce something brutally realistic and more in line with stark facts.

Instead of Lieut. Pinkerton, U.S. Navy, we would then most likely have a deserter from some old tramp, one of the bums and beachcombers of Nagasaki days. His confidant not a U.S. Consul, but one of the many foreigners who in those days drifted, generally drunk, on the edge of the fringe of the mercantile community. The marriage broker would be one of the usual rikishaw pimps, and the marriage-nest not a millionaire's mansion, but a disorderly four-and-a-half mat room above the rikishaw stand near Dockside.

The time about 8 a.m. A blowsy girl would be gazing vacantly across a coal dump at the rear of the rikishaw-stand. Her father, a rikishaw-man, would be sipping tea from a chipped teacup. Instead of singing, "Some day he'll come" she would be heard to mutter in Japanese, not in Italian, "That guy'll never come back!"

* * * * * * *

Pierre Loti and his Chrysanthemum, also G.I. and his gal are, or were, real personages. Pinkerton and his Butterfly are fictional characters. Nevertheless the people of Nagasaki have discovered what the people of Spaarndam in Holland also discovered, namely that the demands of tourists must be met. The Dutch built a statue of Hans Brinker, the famous but mythical boy who is credited with having saved the land by plugging the leaking dyke with his finger. The Japanese of Nagasaki have recently discovered the house where the fictional characters Pinkerton and Butterfly lived together. Now American tourists, and some others also, make pilgrimages to this mecca every day, and sigh and wonder, and sigh again, as they gaze at this newfound love-nest of poor Butterfly.

This article appeared in *The Mainichi* on 8th July, 1955, as a review of the spectacular film *Madame Butterfly*—produced by the Japanese film company, Toho, in conjunction with the Italian companies Rizzoli Films and Gallone Productions.

LET'S CLIMB FUJI

> *The Countrey of Japan is . . . . moun-*
> *tainous and craggie, full of rockes*
> *and stonie places.*
> Rev. Arthur Hatch, 1623

"He who has never climbed Fuji is a fool. He who climbs it twice is a greater fool." There is an odd mixture of truth and fallacy in this whimsical proverb.

Few people are fortunate enough to make the ascent and descent of Fuji-san in perfect weather. Even if fortunate with the weather, climbers see only two routes at the most, and so one ascent may whet the appetite for another.

Not unlikely the conditions under which Fuji had to be climbed in the feudal days of a hundred years or so ago were so arduous that nobody but a fool would have thought of climbing it twice.

Mount Fujiyama, meaning Mount Fuji Mountain, was the redundant manner in which the less well informed foreigners of the early days, and for several decades thereafter, referred to the peerless mountain of Japan.

The first ascent of Fuji by a foreigner was made

This article appeared in *The Mainichi* on Aug. 16, 1955.

312

in 1860, when Sir Rutherford Alcock, first British Minister to Japan, exercised his right of travel in the interior by visiting that mountain. The party which set out from Yedo comprised in addition to the British Minister, seven other Britishers, one of whom was a botanist. Also there were a large number of Japanese, including one of the vice-governors of Yedo and several minor officials, an interpreter, palanquin bearers, grooms, porters, servants, and followers, and a troop of pack horses. Of course most of the members of this lengthy procession waited at the base of the mountain. The climbers on arriving at the top of Fuji *"having sufficiently recovered breath, we proceeded to climb to the highest point of the crater, where Mr. Alcock's standard bearer unfurled the British flag, while we fired a royal salute from our revolvers in its honour and concluded the ceremony by drinking the health of Her Gracious Majesty in champagne iced in the snows of Fusijama."* So wrote one of the party.

The English botanist appears to have been particularly busy, because on returning he listed the botanical names of seventy-six different plants seen on the mountain.

The next ascent by foreigners was six years later in 1866, when a party of Europeans slept one night on the mountain and were absent from Yokohama just eight days, as compared with about twice that time taken by the Alcock party.

In October (which is dangerously late for climbing), 1867, Sir Harry Parkes, who had succeeded Sir Rutherford Alcock as Minister, climbed Fuji accompanied by his wife and a large party of friends. All routes up the mountain are divided into ten sections known as stations, and as it was a holy mountain, women were not then permitted to climb higher than the eighth station. Lady Parkes was certainly the first foreign woman, and possibly the first of her sex, to reach the summit.

In the decades that followed, the climb became increasingly common among foreigners but trips then required more organization than at present. Among the most essential items to be taken along was a bag of charcoal and a can of Keatings Flea Powder. The early guidebooks and descriptions of the climb devoted much space to the famous Fuji fleas, but DDT has now robbed Fuji of its greatest terror.

In 1906 a Japanese won a wager by riding to the summit on horseback and since then there have been many other stunt ascents.

In July, 1917, the Tokyo *Jiji* newspaper sponsored a race from Tarobo, above Gotemba to the summit and offered prizes of ¥200, ¥70 and ¥30 to the winners. Of the 700 applicants, all Japanese, twenty competitors were selected after careful physical examination. The winning time was two hours thirty one and one half minutes, a record to that date.

Despite the introduction of the much publicised bus services and other so-called conveniences and marks of progress, the conditions that prevail today are in some respects so much worse than those of one hundred years ago that it is not surprising it is still said that only a fool would climb Fuji twice.

However in the days when those inveterate travellers Yajirobei and Kitahachi of *Hizakurige* fame were touring around Japan, they could at least approach the mountain over soft leaf-strewn paths, view the gorgeous scenery and breathe the cool air, fragrant with the perfume of wild flowers. How different is travelling today when the initial stages are covered in a criminally overloaded bus, jammed so tight with suffering humanity that all pious thoughts are obliterated from one's mind and the only view is that of the back of somebody's neck. Amid the noise of tortured gears and the stench of overheated bearings, one now approaches this sacred mountain cramped in a bus that pitches and tosses along a road as primitive as those of the middle ages.

From Kawaguchi-ko railway station, one of several approaches to Fuji, the bus ride is for over two hours through superb scenery—ever changing vistas, successive belts of vegetation, shady forests, a riot of wild flowers and great rhododendrons—and yet little of this can be seen by those inside the buses, so jammed are they with standing passengers. Although a spare bus may be held in reserve, the operators will not permit it to depart until all standing room in the previous bus is crammed tight. In callous disregard of public safety and the repeated warnings of tragic accidents elsewhere, the operators risk the lives of many that they may gain some additional profit. Possibly a time will come when the long-suffering Japanese public may no longer suffer greedy or ignorant transportation operators to insult and torture their bodies and minds by herding them into public conveyances like so many cattle into a stockyard.

Let's Climb Fuji

There are many foreigners who have climbed Fuji twice or thrice—I know of one who has climbed it five times—and if the trip with all its inconveniences should so appeal to foreigners, how much more must it appeal to Japanese whose culture and art are so closely associated with that great mountain. But the vast majority of Japanese who climb Fuji are either students or persons in their 'teens or early twenties. If the average Japanese has not been able to climb Fuji in his student days, he is generally content—and not without reason—to remain a fool and view it from a distance. Of course there are exceptions. Aged people can be seen making the ascent, and even blind people climb Fuji with the assistance of friends.

All prices on the mountain are fixed by the local tourist association and perhaps one should not begrudge the keepers of the mountain huts their livelihood under difficult conditions, nor forget that the season is a short one of little more than two months and that they do at times have unexpected losses in the way of storm damage during the winter. Nevertheless the charge of ¥350 for little more than a square yard or so of floor space and the use of a *futon* during a few hours of rest, although well within the reach of most foreigners climbing the mountain, seemingly was beyond the pocket of most of the Japanese climbers, many of whom slumbered outside the huts in the cold awaiting the dawn. That ¥350 was an excessive charge may also have been evidenced by the energy with which some of the touts sought customers.

The charge in 1941, according to the Japan Tourist Bureau's *Official Guide* for that year, was ¥3 to ¥4 "including supper and breakfast." In 1880 accommodation on Fuji was 20 sen per person per night including rice.

That touts have long been a nuisance along Japan's highways and particularly at the most important scenic centres is recorded by Hiroshige and other famous woodcut artists of the past, but it is something new to meet touts whose livelihood is so lucrative that they can afford to be tipsy while at work, and yet that seemed to be the condition of many who annoyed me whilst waiting for the first bus on the first stage of the ascent and whilst resting at several of the huts on the way up during night-time. The following morning on the way down I saw the same men sober, but at another hut I observed with some astonishment that the hut-keeper and his wife were drinking a large bottle of beer (retailed there at ¥270) with their lunch and had opened a small bottle of lemonade (retailed there at ¥50) for their child. That they should drink high-priced stock, which had been brought up the mountain at such cost and effort, seemed to betoken a degree of prosperity not usually enjoyed by such folk.

That the U.S. Forces have long been in these parts was evident from the aggressive and prosperous touts who pressed their unwelcome attentions and their crude English on me.

"Hey, Bud, you sleep my house!"

Such was the greeting that was spluttered in an alcoholic spray into my face at close range at "Lucky

Seven" Rest House on the Seventh Station. Such English as spoken by low type touts was not a feature of climbing Fuji in prewar days but such annoyances, unfortunately, are now the experience all too frequently of foreign travellers in Japan.

Yet it is possible that even such crudities in English may serve as a convenience to those foreigners who, knowing no Japanese whatever, would otherwise feel a sense of helplessness, and are content to suffer such familiarities, and the humiliation (unintentional though the rudeness may be) of having their wives and daughters addressed by such touts in English that might well be reserved for *pom-pom* girls.

It is interesting to recall that the narrator, attached to Sir Rutherford Alcock's party when they climbed nearly a hundred years ago, wrote:

We did not meet with a single instance of rudeness or incivility on the part of the people, nor did we, during the whole course of our journey to the top of Fuji and back again to Yedo meet a drunken man.

That names such as "Lucky Seven," better bestowed on saloons of the port cities, and that other crudities of western culture should have found their way along the pilgrim path to Fuji-san was to me distressing, but I thanked the native gods that not all the traditions of the past have been lost. There are still many pilgrims pious enough to dress in the traditional white clothing; there are some who recite a prayer at every few steps. "May our six senses be clean and undefiled," and some wisely add the supplication "May the weather continue fine." Climbing

Let's Climb Fuji

Fuji during bad weather can be dangerous, and being marooned for a couple of days in one of the huts during a typhoon would, at the current prices prevailing on the mountain, be ruinous for the pockets of many climbers.

Fortunately the traditions of the past are not forgotten even by the great majority of climbers who, like the writer, set out in a spirit of pleasure rather than on a religious pilgrimage. Almost everybody who climbs Fuji carries a pilgrim's staff, sold at the fixed price of ¥80, from which dangle on a rayon ribbon two tinkling bells, in lieu of the pilgrim's brass bell of old, and which cost a trifling ¥20 extra. The majority of climbers cannot afford to purchase food or refreshments at the prices that rightly advance as one climbs skyward, but nevertheless few climbers set out without budgeting themselves for the fee of ¥10 at each station for a stamp to be branded with hot irons on the staff. A flag, which can be purchased on the summit for ¥50 is attached to the staff for the descent. This is a modern touch that commercialism has introduced into the pilgrimage, but I must confess from experience that the self-satisfaction that one derives on the descent from the display of the flag in proof of achievement to those climbing upward is well worth ¥50.

Long ago an overweight foreign tourist, infuriated at having been persuaded to attempt the ascent of Fuji, dubbed it "that colossal heap of humbug and ashes," but if for humbug we substitute garbage, there could be no quarrelling with the truth of the epigram. The trash and garbage that litters this great pilgrim-way offends the sight at every step and yearly it grows worse.

When Hokusai painted his famous *Hundred views of Fuji* over a century ago, there may have been some litter of wooden *bento* boxes and such like trash, but it would soon have disintegrated and would have been washed away by the next melting snows. Under present conditions of modern food packing the unsightly mess of empty food cans and bottles is a steadily accumulating mess and constitutes a hazard for those who move off the regular paths.

The dawn of day and the rising sun as seen from the summit of Fuji is one of the sights of the world. As the first rays of sunlight touch the peak and then illuminate the whole mountain the entire eastern side sparkles with the glitter of myriads of diamonds, but personally I would prefer Fuji in her pristine glory. Being unable as I am to admire the beauty of garbage, I was mentally disturbed at the hazards to public safety represented by those scintillating empty food cans and the glittering fragments of broken beer and cider bottles.

Fuji-san and the National Park area of which it is the centre, stands as a challenge to some of the best brains of this country. Let us hope that this place of beauty, possibly the most precious thing that Japan possesses, this sacred mountain about which has been woven that delicate web of Japanese culture, thought, and art will be perpetuated for posterity in the most fitting manner. The task is so immense that it calls for some of the best brains of the nation. The heritage at stake is too great to leave to fifth-rate, albeit conscientious, officials lacking the breadth of knowledge for such a task. Even the present sanitary arrangements, so resembling those of a hoboes' camp, and the present neglect of Fuji and all its approaches would be preferable rather than that some Coney Island type of architecture should find its way to this peerless mountain.

It is to be hoped that when this great task is undertaken there will be planners big enough to seek information on the methods employed by other countries with similar problems. America has examples to offer of the best and worst in planning. Australia, in a great experiment of planning a capital city on a virgin site set in an open countryside, is displaying at Canberra a breadth of vision that might well be looked into. Every detail must pass the city planners. Even the wording, the colour, the shape and design of shop signs in Canberra must be approved. Under similar regulations there would be no opportunity for uneducated Japanese who have learnt the little they know of English whilst employed as menials in some American army organization to imprint their ideas and their "Lucky Seven" culture on this holy mountain.

Such visions as I have may require the spending of much money, but some sacrifice is called for if Japan's great Fuji-san is to be presented in a worthy form.

Having climbed Fuji twice—what a fool I must be—and at an interval of twenty years between each visit, I was disappointed to find how little had been done to make this thing of beauty accessible to the people of Japan and how much is being done to cheapen and defile it. The impression gained is that this national asset is being exploited by bus companies and many other local monopolists.

Japan possesses in Fuji-san a tourist attraction that cannot be measured in terms of money and yet it is so surrounded by obstructions that few sensible foreign tourists ever attempt to look upon it from closer range than about ten miles.

At present it stands as a confession of neglect on the part of those whose duty it should be to safeguard the national assets. It is a bad advertisement for Japan who strives so hard to sell her natural attractions to the tourists of the world. For the present at least, by all means keep the tourists at a distance of ten miles, so that they may not be able to see this venerated mountain at close range—this colossal heap of garbage and ashes.

WE BURIED
OUR DEAD
HERE

> *We went and measured a buriall*
> *place and had 13 tattamies square*
> *allowed us.*
>
> RICHARD COCK'S Diary, 1620

In the early days of sail, when trading vessels from the West began to put into Japanese harbours, the stay in port, whilst waiting for the favourable winds on which to sail south, often extended to several months. Deaths among the crews from violence and disease were more frequent then than now, and the problem of a burial place for the dead soon arose.

Capt. John Saris, in command of the "Clove," arrived in Hirado on 12th June, 1613, to set up a trading post for the English East India Company. The first mention of death was in September when Saris relates in his diary that the steward of the "Clove" died as the result of a fight with another crew member. It had previously been arranged that, when the "Clove" should leave Hirado on her return voyage, some Japanese sailors would be engaged to ship as crew to make up deficiencies caused by desertions and other losses en route. Fearing that those Japanese would be unwilling to serve if they knew the steward had died on board, Saris ordered that the quartermaster should.

bury him on an Iland as secretly as might be, in
respect we were about to get some Japans to goe

323

*along in our ship, which it might be hearing of
the death of any one, would make them the more
unwilling.*

When the "Clove" sailed, Richard Cocks was left
in charge of the English House at Hirado, and in
the years that followed he makes mention in his
diary of a number of deaths at the English House.
The first seems to have been *"a Masters mate, having
been sicke of consumption."* Cocks thereupon requested of the Japanese authorities *"a buriall place
for him among the Christians, which he granted me.
So we put the dead corps into a winding sheet and
coffind it up."* A difficulty then arose because the
Japanese priests at the nearby temple would not permit the coffin to be conveyed along the street in front
of the temple. Cocks decided to transport the coffin
to the other side of the town by sea, but there were
further difficulties:

*We had much adoe to get any one of these countrey
people to make the grave, that a Christian was to
be buried in. Neither would they suffer the dead
corps to be conveyed by water in any of their
boats.*

All obstacles were finally overcome *"and after the
corps was enterred we returned all to the English
House and there made collation."*

Thereafter that cemetery is often referred to by
Cocks as the *"ordenary buriall place."* It was on the
hill side behind the town and open to all foreigners.
The site is still marked by a stone to the unknown
dead.

Later Cocks relates that Davis, the English car-

penter *"died this morning at break of day of the small
pox, he being choked with them."* Eight days later
his mate Heath *"dyed of a lingaring disease which
began with a bloody flux."* On coming to bury Heath
they found that the grave of Davis, who had been
buried a week earlier, had been desecrated:

> ....*som villanous people had diged up the coffin
> and stolne the winding sheet and his shert and left
> the carcasse naked upon the grown—a villanous
> act. So they soonk the other coffin into the sea.*

Cocks refers in his diary to other deaths also.
There was one *"whome was coffind and carid to the
Christian buriall place with a hearse of blak bayes
carid over him,"* and another *"having byn sick of a
consumption a long time departed out of this world
this night past and was buried this day in our ordenary buriall place....many other accompanied the
corps to grave....the preacher made a speech out of
the Capter read in the buriall."*

Apparently the "ordenary buriall place" was soon
full, for in later years there is reference to another
cemetery; but when the Christian persecutions were
at their height all those Christian cemeteries were
swept away:

> *Now by order of the Emperour all the Churches
> and Monasteries are pulled down, and all Graves
> and Sepulterres opened, and dead mens bones taken
> out.*

There is a record that in September, 1619, Will
Adams the English pilot was *"sickly and minded to
take physic."* In May of the following year he died.
Cocks wrote in his diary *"I cannot but be soroful for*

the loss of such a man as Capt. William Adams," but because of a gap of nearly one year in Cocks' diary, history does not record where Adams died. An early English resident of Yokohama discovered on the summit of one of the hills at Hemimura, near Yokosuka, two monuments purporting to mark the graves of Will Adams and his wife. Historians are, however, satisfied that Adams died at Hirado in Kyushu, and was buried there, despite the monuments near Yokosuka and the other memorials erected during recent years that would indicate otherwise. Not unlikely his grave at Hirado was one of those that was destroyed when the Christian persecutions broke out a year or so later, and his bones were among those *"scatterred to the winds."* It is considered unlikely that an English Protestant, such as Will Adams, would have been cremated in those days, or that his Protestant friend, Richard Cocks, would have permitted cremation. As the Japanese did not practice embalming, the body could hardly have been conveyed over the long journey from Kyushu to Yokohama. More than likely a lock of hair or some other relic was carried to his widow and was subsequently buried beside her, under the monument which may still be seen there.

In the early days of the Dutch settlement at Nagasaki the Japanese would not permit a Christian to be buried on land; the bodies had to be taken out to sea. Later, a burial plot was given to the Dutch.

Christopher Fryke, an Englishman, who made a voyage to Japan in some unexplained way in 1683, wrote

We Buried Our Dead Here

In this Port dyed three of our Men and a Carpenters Boy. Some Japanese carried them out of the Harbour in a small boat, into open Sea, where they threw them over: for they are so far from suffering any Foreigners to be Buried among them, that they will not permit them to be thrown so much as in in the water that is near them.

In 1795, H. M. Sloop "Providence" under the command of Capt. Broughton was on a voyage of exploration in the Kuriles and along the coasts of Sakhalin and Hokkaido. A landing was made in Muroran Bay to bury a sailor who had died. Thus it was that H.M.S. "Providence" became, it is said, the first British warship to visit Japan. Japanese officers were sent to look after the visitors, and to restrict as far as possible their movements and their contacts with the populace. The British were treated with all civility, which is understandable considering that they had a warship behind them, but they were speeded on their way as fast as the Japanese could arrange. An account of the happening survives, but not the grave. It disappeared, as did so many others. Only the record now remains.

With the development of the whaling industry in which a great deal of American capital was invested, whalers were sailing into all the oceans, but all who died at sea near Japan were buried at sea, for Japan would not permit any to land on her shores. Even the Loochoo islanders were more hospitable. A number of graves of seamen are to be found on the Loochoo Islands—Ryukyu or Okinawa as they are known today. The whalers were forbidden to land

327

in Japan, to bury their dead or to pick up supplies of fresh water and vegetables, because of the Japanese interdicts against the people having any intercourse with the world outside. It could be argued that in some measure it was fortunate for Japan that such prohibitions existed. Certainly it is a fact that some whalers were manned by crews so lawless, and so devoid of all the finer instincts, that, had they been permitted unrestricted entry, the disgrace which the few could have brought upon the Western world might have proved a hindrance to the subsequent development of good relations with Japan. Those good relations began to grow once Perry had pointed his guns and forced Japan to open her doors to trade.

When Commodore Perry came to Japan to negotiate a treaty with the Japanese the problem of a place for the burial of the dead again arose. Perry offered to purchase a piece of ground from the Japanese for the burial of a marine then lying dead and for other Americans who might die, but the Japanese demurred and wished to arrange for the body to be conveyed to far-off Nagasaki for burial there in the place reserved for foreigners. Finally they agreed to the body being buried near Yokohama. Later a site at Shimoda was selected. It was the knowledge of the desecration of earlier Christian graves that caused Perry to insert a clause into the agreement with the Japanese that *"near the temple of Yokushen at Kakizaki a burial ground is to be set apart for Americans where the graves and tombs shall not be molested."*

There are four graves in that little graveyard, including an assistant surgeon, a sailor and a marine, in addition to the one who was first buried in Yokohama. All are marked with tombstones in Japanese form. Little did those Americans who are buried there know, as they lay on board their ships desperately ill, and possibly looking with regret at their fate ahead, of dying in a far away part of the globe, and of being buried in a strange and little known land, that immortality was ahead for them. They will be remembered probably for centuries, and certainly long after many great men have been forgotten. Their graves have always been well cared for and have since become a place where the international bonds of friendship are cemented more firmly, because that little cemetery at Shimoda is one of the places where an international ceremony takes place each year on the occasion of the anniversary of the arrival at Shimoda of Commodore Perry and his black ships.

In 1855 the Russian frigate "Diana" was anchored in Shimoda when that port was wrecked by an earthquake and a following tidal wave. The sea bed in Shimoda port offers little grip for ships' anchors. The "Diana" dragged her anchor and was driven ashore and wrecked. Three Russian seamen who were drowned are buried in the same temple ground as the Americans, but on the opposite side.

About a year later Townsend Harris, the first American consul-general to Japan, shortly after arrival at Shimoda wrote in his diary:

Visited the village of Kakizaki (Oyster Point) opposite Shimoda. The temple of this place, is set apart for the accommodation of Americans. The rooms are spacious and very neat and clean and a person might stay here for a few weeks in tolerable comfort. Near the temple is the American cemetery which contains four neat tombs prettily fenced in. It is very small only about 15×10 feet.

Later there is the entry:

27th April, 1857: The Rhododendron Althea is now in beautiful flower-colours chiefly pink. I have planted some of them in the cemetery where the four Americans are buried.

Decoration Day, which Harris thus inaugurated in Japan during his lonely stay at Shimoda, later came to be regularly observed with formal and grander ceremonies.

With the opening of the Treaty Ports a space was set aside in each port for a foreign cemetery. In Yokohama the cemetery was located on that high ground overlooking the port—the high ground which in course of time came to be known as the Bluff. Therein are to be found the graves of many of the foreigners who fell victims to the swords of the assassins around 90 years ago, some of which cases are described elsewhere in this book. In the great earthquake of 1st September, 1923, a part of the cemetery slipped down the hillside and many of the old graves were destroyed. The effects of that and other earthquakes in Yokohama are to be seen in the many cracked and broken tombstones in that old cemetery.

In Kobe the need of a cemetery was found, even before the port was opened, to receive the bodies of two naval officers, one a lieutenant on the British flagship H.M.S. "Rodney," who had died of heart disease, and the other an Asst. Surgeon in the U.S. Navy who had died of consumption on board the U.S.S. "Hartford." Both vessels were anchored at the time off Hyogo, awaiting the opening of the port to take place on New Year's Day, 1868.

A wind-swept sandy plot of ground at Ono-hama near the mouth of the Ikuta River, and outside the area which was to be the Foreign Settlement, was hastily set aside as a burial ground. There it was that on Christmas Day, 1867, the dead preceded the living in the opening of the port of Kobe to foreigners. Within a few months that cemetery also was to become the resting place of victims of assassins.

The selection of the site at Ono-hama was an unfortunate choice and in the early days was a matter of constant anxiety to the foreign community, because at times of heavy rain it was in danger of being washed out to sea, should the Ikuta River overflow its banks. In addition it was then so close to the sea that water was to be found within a few feet of the surface. That necessitated the digging of shallow graves. Frequently the foxes used to come down from the hills, scrape the earth away from the graves and gnaw at the newly buried coffins.

Japan was not troubled by body-snatchers seeking cadavers for the dissection tables of medical students —the resurrection men who so disgraced society in England and elsewhere around the early part of the last century. But there were ghouls in Japan also. So close were the coffins to the surface in Ono cemetery, that on one occasion somebody exhumed the body apparently searching for jewelry and treasure which the Japanese then thought were buried with foreigners. No such loot being found, the graves were not further molested by such marauders. But there were a few occasions in those early days when coffins were opened and an attempt made to cut the liver out of newly buried corpses.

The superstition existed among some people in Japan that the liver and certain other viscera of a bear were unusually effective in the treatment of leprosy and certain other diseases. From there it was a short step for such people to imagine that the liver of a foreigner would be so much more efficacious.

* * * * * * *

Similar beliefs sprang up again among some of Japan's troops during the undeclared war with China from 1937 to 1941, and several cases occurred of such viscera being smuggled into Japan by returning troops. Considering the faith in weird medicines that exists even today, and not only in Japan, it is not surprising that human livers should have been so sought after. Even in these more enlightened days great value is attached by some Japanese to the blood and flesh of freshly killed snakes. A thriving business is done in all the important cities by well-known snake establishments, where desiccated centipedes, charred skulls of monkeys, and live snakes are their regular stock in trade.

During the Pacific War there were a number of recorded Japanese atrocities committed against Allied dead with the purpose of removing the livers. The most notable perhaps was that which occurred on Kairiru Island, off the northern coast of New Guinea.

We Buried Our Dead Here

That small island was occupied in the early stages of the wan and became the headquarters of Japanese naval forces in the area. When the Allied offensive got under way in the form of island hopping, the island was by-passed. The Japanese remained in occupation, but were cut off from their home bases and under constant fear of attack. So much did their morale suffer in the months and years that followed, that few Japanese naval units had so many atrocities chalked up against their senior officers, as did those Kairiru headquarters.

Amongst those atrocities was that of the beheading of an Australian airman who floated ashore after his plane had crashed in the sea. He was executed with a samurai sword at nighttime, by the light of blazing fires, in a ceremony conducted with a view to bolstering the declining spirits of the men. Afterwards, and in secret, his brains were removed from the skull and part of the flesh of his buttocks cut away by the senior officers' batman, for use by some of the officers in experimental cannabalism. Before the body was buried a warrant officer removed the liver, and then hung it up to dry on a nail in the kitchen. One morning some months later the desiccated liver was missing. Although the warrant officer stormed and threatened his men, nobody would admit to the theft. The next time it turned up was after the war, on the Japanese repatriation ship by which those remaining on Kairiru Island were being repatriated to Japan. It changed hands several times en route in trade deals among the men, and was subsequently smuggled into Japan at the port of entry where the unit was disembarked. All further trace of it was then lost, but no doubt it was disposed of at a profit to those who attach medicinal value to such ghastly relics.

* * * * * * * *

In 1952, the Ono cemetery, the earliest foreign cemetery in Kobe, was removed to a new site deep in the glorious Kobe hills behind Futatabi Mountain. The mortal remains of those who now rest behind Futatabi were first buried three-quarters of a century and more ago, as has already been mentioned, among the pines of Ono-hama, on the sandy waste near the mouth of the old Ikuta River. In the course of time the river was moved further east to make room for the expanding city of Kobe. Harbour reclamation schemes followed which transformed the old cemetery from a wind-swept site near the river mouth to an inland position. In course of time the sea breezes were blocked by ugly red godowns. The noise of the city penetrated its quietness and between rain showers the old pine trees and tombstones were thickly covered with dust stirred up by traffic on the roads just beyond its walls.

The remains of that early band of foreigners are now laid amid more peaceful and beautiful surroundings in the new foreign cemetery behind Futatabi, but the pattern of their lives, and those of the foreign community in the early days, can be traced in broad outline from the brief inscriptions on the original gravestones.

Not many seem to have lived to old age. There are the young mothers who failed to survive the risks then of childbirth; the children who all too frequently fell victims of diphtheria and enteric fever that raged in those hazardous days; the men of high hopes who came East but died young at their own hands, or as a result of their own excesses; the tragic and untimely deaths; the seafarers who died lonely in a foreign port; and finally that little band of men whose fate is written in the pages of history of eighty-five years ago.

An American admiral, a lieutenant and ten sailors of the U.S. Navy were accidentally drowned when crossing the bar at Osaka. But more tragic still the eleven French sailors who were massacred at Sakai, near Osaka, as has been related elsewhere in this book.

It was to avoid incidents such as this that were taking place all over Japan where foreigners happened to be gathered, that a trail, which came to be known as the Tokugawa Road, was cut through the hills behind Futatabi.

Daimyo processions on their way to and from Osaka were thus able to by-pass Hyogo, and so avoid the possibility of a fracas with the foreigners, who had been allotted as a place of residence and business a sandy waste, which was eventually developed into the picturesque foreign settlement of Kobe—a little municipality complete with its own foreign police force, fire brigade, foreign tradesmen and shops. A model settlement with red bricked pavements and streets lined with willow trees.

Actually with the Imperial edict banning the wearing of swords by the samurai, the dangers of disorders and violence that the Tokugawa Road behind Futatabi had sought to avoid quickly disappeared. The road therefore was not much used.

The forest encroached upon it, but nevertheless as late as thirty years ago it was still possible, although with considerable difficulty, to trace it out through most of its length.

I recently endeavored once again to follow out the road, but found that development and the passing of time had completely obliterated most of it. Being weary from following many false trails, I rested upon a log, reflecting on the curious circumstance that whereas the Tokugawa Road had been built so that the *daimyo* processions would not pass near to the abode of foreigners, yet the final resting place of the foreigners of those early days is now in the new cemetery adjacent to that old Tokugawa Road.

While thinking of the past and perhaps drowsing lightly, a very old charcoal-burner came along and broke upon my reveries. It was near sunset. He bowed and sat down on the log beside me. I remarked on the solitude of the place.

"Yes. But after dark the foxes and badgers are about. And on moonlight nights there are others also moving along this path," he replied.

"What others," I asked.

"There are *daimyo* processions, palanquins with drawn blinds, standard bearers, two-sworded samurai and porters carrying large black lacquered chests containing the clothes of the lords and ladies. They can often be seen resting among the shadows in the clearings."

We Buried Our Dead Here

"Have you seen them?" I inquired.

"No. But it is common knowledge. It is also said that they sometimes meet the French sailors, the ones who were killed long ago across the bay near Sakai. But there is no violence now. When they meet, they greet each other respectfully, then gravely pass on their way. All this is well known. But when I come along here at sunrise" concluded the charcoal-burner "there is nothing to be seen!"

....now I believe there is such a place as Japan
which has been confirmed to me several hundred ways.
Bernard Mandeville—*Fable of the Bees* (1705)

ABOUT THE AUTHOR

H. S. Williams was born in Melbourne, Australia, in 1898. He was headed for a scientific career; at first as a junior analyst in the Commonwealth Laboratory of Australia, then as a medical student at the Melbourne University. He was already seriously interested in the Japanese language and history as a hobby, and at the end of his third year in medicine he came to Japan on a holiday.

On arrival in Japan, an advertisement in the former *Japan Advertiser* caught his attention, and by replying to it he hoped to have the opportunity of seeing inside one of the *hongs* in Japan of which he had read so much. He later went for an interview, confident in the belief that he would not be engaged. To his great dismay he found that he was hired as an assistant in the old Scottish *hong* of Findlay Richardson & Co. Ltd. He thereupon temporarily postponed his return to Australia, but eventually decided to give up his career and make his future in Japan.

Later Williams became managing director of the silk firm of Cooper Findlay & Co. Ltd.

In 1941 he left Japan and enlisted in the Australian Army. He attained the rank of major and saw service in Africa, the Pacific, and Burma. He arrived back in Japan a few weeks after the surrender as a member of the Occupation Forces, and remained in the Australian Army in Japan until 1949 when he resumed his business career.

H. S. Williams is now Managing Director of A. Cameron & Co. Ltd. and sole Trustee of the famous James Estate at Shioya, near Kobe.

In 1953 he commenced writing historical articles for various publications abroad, and for the *Mainichi* in a series entitled "Shades of the Past," out of which writings this book was born.

339

CHRONOLOGICAL TABLE
INCIDENTAL TO ARTICLES
IN THIS BOOK

About	550	Buddhism trickled into Japan from India via Korea.
"	747	*Daibutsu* at Nara was cast.
	1271	Marco Polo travelled to Asia.
	1542	Portuguese arrived in Japan.
	1600	Will Adams arrived in Japan as pilot on Dutch ship " de Liefde."
	1604	Englishmen fought with Japanese off Malaya.
	1609	Dutch commenced to trade with Japan.
	1613	Capt. John Saris arrived in Japan on " Clove " and opened English East India Trading post at Hirado.
	1614	Proclamation issued suppressing Christianity.
	1622	Great martyrdom of Christians at Nagasaki.
	1623	Richard Cocks closed the English trading post and left Japan.
	1636	Japanese forbidden to go abroad.
	1637	Shogun Iyemitsu decided to close Japan to the Western World.
	1638	Shimabara rebellion and massacre of Christians.
	1638	Seclusion policy proclaimed in Japan.
	1641	Dutch trading post confined to Deshima.
	1690	Dr. Kaempfer arrived at Deshima.
	1825	Expulsion decree re-issued, forbidding foreign ships to enter Japanese waters.
	1830	Brig " Cyprus " fired on by Japanese shore batteries.
July	1853	Commodore Perry's ships arrived in Yedo Bay
Feb/Mar	1854	Commodore Perry returned and signed a treaty of peace and amity with Japan.
Oct.	1854	British signed similar treaties.

Chronological Table Incidental to Articles

Aug. 1856	Townsend Harris, first U. S. Consul-General, landed at Shimoda.
Nov. 1857	Townsend Harris arived in Yedo and had audience with Shogun.
July 1858	Townsend Harris signed treaty of amity and commerce with Japan.
July 1858	Lord Elgin arrived in Japan.
Aug. 1858	Anglo-Japanese treaty of commerce and friendship signed.
June 1859	Rutherford Alcock arrived as Britain's first Minister to Japan.
1 July 1859	Yokohama, Nagasaki and Hakodate opened to foreign trade.
1860	First recorded ascent of Fuji by a foreigner.
1860	Japanese Mission to U. S. A.
1861	British Legation in Yedo attacked.
1862	The Richardson murder.
1864	Major Baldwin and Lieut. Bird murdered.
25 Dec. 1867	First burials in Ono Foreign Cemetery, Kobe.
1 Jan. 1868	Hyogo and Osaka opened.
Jan. 1868	Admiral Bell and 11 men drowned at Osaka.
Jan. 1868	Osaka Castle burnt.
4 Feb. 1868	Bizen soldiers fired on Kobe Foreign Settlement.
3 Mar. 1868	Taki Zenzaburo committed harakiri.
8 Mar. 1868	Eleven French naval men massacred at Sakai.
16 Mar. 1868	Eleven Japanese executed at Sakai.
Nov. 1868	The Emperor left Kyoto and entered Yedo which thereafter became known as Tokyo—the eastern capital.
1868	Restoration of the Emperor and overthrow of Shogunate.
1 Jan. 1869	Tokio opened to foreign trade.
24 Jan. 1870	U. S. S. " Oneida " in collision and lost.
24 Aug. 1872	*S. S.* " America " on fire in Yokohama harbour.
1881	The *Kimigayo*—National Anthem—played for first time.
1885	Pierre Loti came to Nagasaki.
1890	Attempted assassination of the Czarevitch at Otsu.
1896	The Carew Poisoning Case at Yokohama.
1899	Extra-territoriality ceased.
1906	The Garter Mission arrived in Japan.
1931	Osaka Castle reconstructed in reinforced concrete.
Dec. 1941	Japanese naval landing party occupies Nauru Island.

342

Chronological Table Incidental to Articles

Aug. 1945   Occupation troops entered Japan.

1952   Transfer of earliest foreign cemetery in Kobe, from Ono to Shuhogahara behind Futatabi.

1955   Italian-Japanese film of *Madame Butterfly* released in Japan.

GLOSSARY
AND
BIOGRAPHICAL NOTES

A

Adams, Will English navigator. Arrived in Japan in 1600. Was later known as *Anjin Sama* (pilot).
Married a Japanese lady. Died in Japan in 1620 at age of about 56 years.

Alcock, Sir Rutherford (1809-1897) Arrived in Japan as first British Consul-General. Appointed Minister in 1859.
In 1865 was transferred to Pekin and succeeded by Sir Harry Parkes.

Amida An important Buddhist diety.

B

Banzai Literally " ten thousand years. " An expression of great emotion by the Japanese, equivalent to " Hurrah, " or in " Dai Nippon Banzai " to " Long Live Great Japan. "

Bento A lunch. When sold is packed in a light chip-wood box.

Bizen Name of a province and clan in Okayama prefecture.

Bluff That section of Yokohama, overlooking the town and harbour, where most foreigners built their homes, when they ceased residing within the Concession.

Bon See *O-bon*.

Boy-san An office boy, a bartender, or a waiter in a restaurant. Stewards on board Japanese vessels resent being called *boy-san*.

Brinkley, Capt. F. Came to Japan as an instructor in gunnery to Japanese Naval Department. Later became editor of *The Japan Mail*. Author of various books on Japanese subjects. Died in 1912.

Bu A silver coin in circulation when Japan was opened to foreign trade in 1859, later equivalent to about ¼ yen. Called by foreigners *boo*.

Bund The road along the water front in an Oriental port.

Bunsei The era of Bunsei (1818-1830).

Glossary

C

Chamberlain, Basil Hall (1850-1935) Arrived in Japan in 1873 and became a teacher at the Imperial Naval School. Later became professor of Japanese philology at Tokyo Imperial University. Wrote many important books on Japanese subjects, the best known of which is *Things Japanese*.
Left Japan in 1905 owing to ill health and retired to Geneva.

Cocks, Richard Chief of factory of English East India Company at Hirado from 1613 until it closed in 1621.

Concession See Settlement.

D

Daibutsu Large statue of Buddha or Amida.

Daimyo Literally " great name." A term applied to territorial nobles, the annual income from whose lands was assessed at not less than ten thousand *koku* of rice (about 50,000 bushels.)

E

Engawa Verandah of a Japanese house.

F

Foreigner The meaning of the word in Japan is a non-Japanese, but it is often used in English conversation in the sense of a Westerner.

Fryke, Christopher An Englishman who published a book in London in 1700, describing a voyage which he made to Japan in 1683.

G

Geisha Literally a " person of talents. " A professional Japanese female entertainer called upon at parties and banquets to entertain the guests. They undergo rigorous training and are accomplished dancers and singers. Most of them have patrons. Lower class geisha are often little different from prostitutes.

Godown A warehouse.

H

Hachiman Shinto deity of war.

Hara-kiri Suicide by disembowelment. There were two forms, one voluntary, the other compulsory, the latter being imposed as a penalty for certain offences. The Japanese rarely use this word, preferring the more genteel Chinese form of the word—*seppuku.*

346

Glossary

Harris, Townsend (1804–1875) Arrived at Shimoda 21 Aug., 1856, as first U. S. Consul-General in Japan. Appointed minister in 1859. Resigned in 1861.

Hatch, Rev. Arthur A chaplain in the service of the English East India Company, who visited Japan in 1621 and then wrote a description of the country.

Hatoba Wharf or quay.

Hearn, Lafcadio (1850–1904) Arrived in Japan in 1890. Had various teaching appointments. Married a Japanese lady in 1891 and became a Japanese subject—Koizumi Yakumo—in 1895.

Hepburn, Dr. J. C. American physician and missionary in Japan 1859–92. Compiler of English–Japanese Dictionary, Dictionary of Bible (in Japanese) etc.

Hiogo Previously the commonly accepted Romanised form of spelling for Hyogo.

Hirado An island near the northwest coast of Kyushu where the Dutch and English trading posts were established in the 17th century.

Hizakurige A well-known Japanese guide-book written about 1814 in comic and narrative form by Ikku Jippensha.

Hizen Name of a province and clan in Kyushu, near Nagasaki.

Hong Foreign trading firm, a word rarely used nowadays in Japan.

I

Ichibu Silver coin in circulation before the introduction of the Yen. The value varied from 10d to about 1s8d according to the exchange.

Ippuku Literally " one puff. " Travellers on the highways in Japan are greeted and invited to enter the roadside tea-houses for a rest and to smoke a pipe.

Iyemitsu (1603-1651) The third Tokugawa *Shogun*. He closed the country, forbade the building of ships for oversea voyages and attempted to stamp out Christianity. He was buried at Nikko.

Iyeyasu (1542-1616) Founder of the line of Tokugawa rulers. He became *Shogun* in 1603. He was buried at Nikko.

J

Jinrikisha Literally *man-power-vehicle*, contracted to rikisha, and later Anglicised to ricksha, rikishaw or rickshaw.

K

Kabuki Japanese drama, generally classical or historical, where

Glossary

the female parts are taken by male actors.

Kaempfer, Engelbert (1651–1716) German traveller and physician. Arrived in Japan Sept., 1690. Left in 1693. His *History of Japan* was published after his death.

Kago A basket slung on a pole and carried by two men, in which the commonalty travelled; in the early days, foreigners preferred *kago* to palanquins, because they were more airy. They went out of fashion, except on mountain paths, when rikisha were introduced.

Kami A Shinto deity.

Kansai (or Kwansai) Literally " west of the barrier." General term applied before Restoration in 1868 to country west of the guard-house or barrier on the Hakone pass.

Kanto (or Kwanto) Literally " east of the barrier." General term applied before Restoration in 1868 to country east of the guard-house or barrier on the Hakone pass.

Kencho Prefectural office.

Kitano-cho That high section of Kobe which became the residential quarter for the elite of the *taipans*, when they ceased residing within the Concession.

Koban Large flat oval-shaped gold coins issued by various *daimyo* and other authorities in feudal days.

Kobo Daishi See Kukai.

Koku A measure of rice equal to about 5 bushels.

Kukai (774–835) Buddhist priest and scholar. In 816 he retired to Mt. Koya where he founded the famous monastery. So much in the way of paintings, carvings, writings, etc., are attributed to him, that it is doubtful he could have accomplished them all, even had he lived a thousand years.

Kwannon Buddhist deity of mercy.

L

Loti, Pierre (1850–1923) Pen name of L. M. Julien Viaud. French author. Wrote *Madame Chrysantheme* and others.

M

Mason, W. B. Came to Japan in 1875 and for over 25 years was in the service of the Japanese Government in Departments of Communications and Education. Collaborated with B. H. Chamberlain in producing *Murray's Handbook for Japan*. Killed in earthquake 1st Sept., 1923.

Meiji Era The era of the reign of Emperor Meiji (1868–1912).

Mexican Dollar Japan had no currency of a well determined value when trade was opened in 1859, and so the foreign traders

Glossary

brought in Mexican $ which passed as currency in the Foreign Settlements. A reputable silver yen also referred to as a $, of 416 grains and 900 fineness was minted in 1879.

Mikado Term once used in foreign circles to designate the sovereign of Japan. In prewar years the Japanese normally used the expression *Tenno Heika* (Divine Emperor) when referring to their Emperor. Nowadays *Tenno* often suffices.

Mitford, A. B. (later Lord Redesdale) 1837–1916. Attaché in Japan 1866–70.

Mon A Japanese farthing of former days. A copper coin with a square hole in the centre.

N

Namu Amida Butsu Buddhist ritual prayer or chant—Hail to Amida the Buddha.

Nippon Same as Nihon, meaning Japan.

Norimono See palanquin.

O

Obasan An old woman, a grandmother.

Obi Ornamental sash with bow at back. Worn by women. When the bow was tied in the front it was the mark of a professional prostitute in the old days.

O-bon Buddhist festival in July when the ancestral souls or spirits of the dead are said to return to earth for three days.

Oiran In feudal days a high class prostitute, generally depicted with many large bamboo hairpins in her hair.

P

Palanquin A curtained box-like conveyance, suspended on a pole and carried by four men, in which a person rode in a sitting or semi-recumbent position. Used by higher classes. In Japanese—*norimono*.

Parkes, Sir Harry (1828–1885) Appointed British minister to Japan in 1865, which post he held for 18 years.

Pom-pom girls Name coined by G. I.'s in the early stages of the Occupation for streetwalkers.

R

Rickshaw)
Rikisha) See jinrikisha.

Glossary

Ronin Literally "wave-man," a term applied to samurai who were not attached to any clan one who had given up or had been dismissed from the service of his feudal master, and for the time being was his own master.

S

Sake An alcoholic beverage obtained by fermenting rice. Generally served after warming to about 43 degrees centigrade.

Samurai A member of the military class, entitled to wear two swords, a longer and shorter one, the latter like an over-grown dirk.

Saris, John English merchant and sea captain who made first voyage to Japan (1612) on behalf of English East India Company and obtained permission for English to settle in and to trade in Japan.

Satow E. M. (1843–1929) Attaché and later (1895) British Minister to Japan.

Satsuma Name of a clan whose territories comprised a portion of Kyushu island.

Settlement That section of land, generally waste land outside the Japanese town, that was originally set aside as the place of trade and residence for foreigners.

Shinto "The Way of the Gods," the name given to the mythology and vague ancestor and nature worship which preceded the introduction of Buddhism into Japan. Latter developed to include State Shinto, Sect Shinto and popular Shinto.

Shogun Literally "the general commanding an island."
Term applied to the administrative or de facto rulers of Japan in feudal days, as distinguished from the sovereigns who were kept in seclusion in Kyoto. Also known as Taikun (Tycoon).

Shogunate The government of the Shogun.

Shoji Sliding doors fitted with paper, or paper and glass, to enable light to penetrate a Japanese room from the outside.

Shroff Originally men employed by banks and merchants in the East to examine coin and see whether it was genuine. Now often a cashier or clerk in accounts department.

Siebold, Dr. Philipp Franz von (1796–1866) Arrived in Nagasaki in 1823 as physician attached to Dutch East India Company. Banished from Japan in 1830 for making a map of Japan. Returned in 1860 on a semi-official mission.

T

Taikun (also Tycoon). Literally "great lord," and the term

Glossary

employed by the Japanese in earlier treaties, and in their official correspondence with foreigners, to designate the Shogun.

Taipan A word borrowed from early trading days in China, meaning the manager or " big boss, " as distinct from assistants, in foreign firms.

Tatami Straw floor mats, $3' \times 6'$, found in houses, temples and other Japanese style buildings. Two such mats represent the unit of area known as a *tsubo*.

Teahouse The word is used to denote the modest little resthouses which are situated alongside country roads, and also the elaborate Japanese style restaurants in the cities, which also serve as places of entertainment, to which geisha may be called.

Thunberg, Charles Peter (1743-1828) Swedish physician, naturalist and traveller appointed physician to Dutch East India Company at Deshima.

Tokaido The great highway of Eastern Japan from Yedo (Tokyo) to Kyoto.

Tokio Previously the commonly accepted Romanised form of spelling for Tokyo.

Tokugawa The family and line of Shoguns founded by Tokugawa Iyeyasu in 1603 which controlled Japan for a period of about 250 years.

Torii Gateway to a Shinto shrine.

Tosa The name of a province and clan on the island of Shikoku.

Townsend Harris See Harris.

Trade Dollar In 1875 the Japanese Government commenced minting a silver coin stamped " Trade Dollar 420 grains 900 fine " which it was intended should take the place of the Mexican Dollar. In 1879 it was substituted by a new Silver Yen of 416 grains and 900 fineness.

Tsubo Unit of area, about 36 sq. feet, equivalent in area to two *tatami* (Japanese mats).

Tycoon See Taikun.

U

Ukiyoe A wood-block colour-print of popular school, depicting the life of feudal Japan.

V

Viaud, Julien See Loti.

Y

Yedo Old name for Tokyo; capital of Tokugawa Government.

Glossary

Yen Japanese monetary unit. Originally equivalent to 50 U. S. cents at par. In pre-war 1941 the official rate of exchange was about 22 ¢, but the unofficial and open market rate was much lower. In 1958 the value of the yen is a little more than ¼ ¢, or 360 yen to US $.

Yoshiwara Licensed quarter in Tokyo, but applied loosely by foreigners to any licensed quarter. Abolished by law April 1957.

INDEX

Adams, Will, 99; arrives in Japan, 277; death of, 325; flies Cross of St. George, 31; visits Osaka, 277

Airmail in Japan, effects of, 286

Alcock, Sir Rutherford, 22; arrives in Japan, 178; climbs Fuji, 313; "scum of the earth" episode, 214, 250

"America," wooden steamer, burning of, 147

Assassinations in Yokohama, 179

Attack on British Legation in Yedo, 179

"Auckland," American brig, 163

Australian convicts and bushrangers, 75

Baedeker, Karl, 236

Baldwin, Major G.W., 20th. Foot Regt., 94

Beachcombers, 288

Bell, Admiral, 335

Biddle, Commodore, 146

Birds, craze as pets, 274

Bird, Lieut. R.N., 20th. Foot Regt., 94

Bishop of Hongkong, (Dr. George Smith) 60, 215

Bizen, Daimyo of Okayama, 106

Black-Eyed Susan, 92

"Bombay," P.&O. Steamer, 132

Brinker, Hans, 311

Brinkley, Capt. F., 211

British Grenadiers (march), 268

British Consulate at Nagasaki, 19; at Osaka, 280

British Legation at Yedo, attack upon, 26, 65, 179

British Phosphate Commissioners, 290

Brotherhood of the New Life, 68

Broughton, Capt., 327

Buddhist pilgrims, 241

Buddhist temples, 136, 241; offered as accommodation, 178

Burials, 159

Carew poisoning case, 184

Cesarevitch (see Czarevitch),

Chamberlain, Basil Hall, 221, 262

"Charity," Dutch ship (see "de Liefde"), 277

Chinese, 81; coffins, 150; gambling, 151; indentured labour 141; returning to China, 148

Chonkina dance, 233, 296

Chosen Corporation, 254

Christianity—banned, 99; edict against, 78; persecution of, 33

Christmas Days in Japan, 99

Clark, E. Warren, missionary, 160

"Clove," English ship, 236; arrives in Hirado, 297, 323

Cocks, Richard, 300, 324; celebrates Christmas, 101

353

Index

Convict Settlements in Australia, 288

Currency manipulations, 251

"Cyprus," brig, 76

Czarevitch, attempted assassination of, 168, 170

Daibutsu at Kamakura, 94

Daimyo's denial of slander, 213

Daimyo processions, 107, 125, 336

d'Anethan, Baroness, 199

de Becker, Dr. J.E. 188, 193

Decoration Day, 330

"de Liefde," Dutch ship, 277

Deshima, 102, 279; description of, 39

"Diana," Russian frigate, 329

"Dupleix," French cruiser, 115

Dutch at Shogun's Court at Yedo, 43

Dutch East India Company 296; periodical visits to Yedo, 37

Eckert, Franz, 266

Eifukuji (temple) Hyogo, 110

Elgin and Kincardine, Earl of, arrives in Nagasaki, 52; arrives in Shimoda, 177

Embassy, British, at Tokyo, 181

"Emperor," yacht, 51, 60

Emperor Meiji, 172, 282

English East India Company, 297; at Hirado, 30, 100, 279

English regiments in Yokohama, 94

"Euryalus," H.M.S., 252

Execution of eleven Tosa men, 119

"Experiment," English ship, 34

Fenton, Bandmaster William, 268

Fire Brigades, foreign volunteers, 17

Fitch, London merchant, 248

Flag of Hachiman, 29; St. George's Cross, 28; Stars & Stripes, 53

Fleas, 230, 314

Foreign cemetery at Ono, Kobe, 331, 334; at Shuhogahara (Futatabi) Kobe 334; at Yokohama, 330

French sailors massacred at Sakai, 115, 335

Fryke, Christopher, 326

Fuji, Mount, 312

"Furious," British war-vessel, 51

Garter Mission to Japan, 35

Geisha, 310

Geisha, The (light opera), 232

George, Prince of Greece, 170, 175

Gilbert & Sullivan, 25, 232

Goble, Jonathan, 165

Gold—coins, 249; exported from Japan, 249; parity in Japan, 249

Graves of British seamen at Muroran, 327 ; of U.S. personnel at Shimoda, 328; of Russian seamen at Shimoda, 329

Griffis, Dr. W.E., 217

Guide books 229

Harakiri, 106, 113

Harris, Thomas Lake, 62

Harris, Townsend, 20, 54, 56, 79, 178, 309; extracts from diary, 38, 82, 214 ; journey to Yedo, 85; celebrates Christmas, 103; at Shimoda, 80 ; describes his accommodation at Shimoda, 329

Hearn, Lafcadio, 221, 262

Hepburn's system of spelling (Japanese words), 232

Heusken, Henry C.J., 54, 81; murdered in Yedo, 178

Hideyoshi's Kitano tea-party, 248

Hirado, 30 ; burials at, 324

Hitachi Dockyard, 285

Hojuji (temple), graves of Tosa men, 122

Index

Holly for Christmas, 100
Hyogo, 100 ; opened to foreign trade, 280
Hunter, E.H., 285

Ichibu, exchange, 249
Ichinotani, foreign residents at, 260
Iemitsu, Shogun, closes Japan, 78
Ieyasu, Tokugawa Shogun, 277

James Estate, Shioya, 260
Japan closed to Western world, 78
Japanese—banquets, 56; Embassy to Europe, 66 ; Emperor in Kyoto, 60, 84; first Embassy to U.S.A., 267, 300; national anthem, 266; naval vessels in 1868, 283; regulations re dress, 302; servants, 32; atrocities, 290, 332;
Japan Herald; obituary notice of, 211
Japan Mail, 193, 197, 211
Japan Times & Overland Mail, 114
Japan Tourist Bureau's Official Guide, 231
Jardine Matheson & Co., 18, 264
Jinrikisha (see Rickshaw)
Jonas case in Osaka, 302

Kaempfer, Dr. Engelbert, 38, 80, 267
Kawaguchi Foreign Concession (Osaka), 280
Kimigayo, 266
Kimono, novel by John Paris, 233, 296
Kobayashi Beika (see de Becker)
Kobe Foreign Concession attacked, 107
Kobe Hills, 272
Kobe Women's Club, 223
Kobo Daishi, 104
Korean national anthem, 270

Kukai (see Kobo Daishi)
Kwannon, Buddhist Goddess of Mercy, 238

Leprosy, 290, 332
Licenced quarters, 143, 225
Livers, human, superstition re, 332
Loti, Pierre, 229, 306

Madame Butterfly, 232, 306
Madame Chrysanthemum, 229, 306
Mamiya Hajime, ronin assassin, 94
Marco Polo's account of Japan, 247
"*Maria Luz*," Peruvian barque, 140
Mavourneen, Kathleen, 268, 300
Meiji, Emperor, 172, 282
Meriken Hatoba, Kobe, 223
Mexican dollars, exchange value, 249
Meylan, G.F., 49
Mikado, The, (light opera), 232
Mikado's decree against assassination of foreigners, 109
Mitford, A.B., (description of harakiri), 111
Miura, Tamaki, 233, 307
Morrison, Consul Geo. S., 19
Murray's Handbook for Japan, 223, 230
Myokokuji (temple), 118

Nagasaki, 306
Nanten berries, 100
Nauru Island, 290
Nicholas II, Emperor of Russia, 169
Nio, guardian gods at temple gates, 245
"Number Nine," Yokohama, 233

Oliphant, Laurence, 64
"Oneida," U.S.S., sinking of, 129
Ono Foreign Cemetery, burial of French sailors, 116
Order of Merit, conferred on

Index

Japanese, 36

Osaka, 277; description of, 42; opened to foreign trade, 280

Osaka Castle, 277, 281; burnt and sacked, 127

Osaka Foreign Concession at Kawaguchi, 280

Osaka Station, gift shops, 241

Otsu, attempted assassination at, 170

Pacific Mail Steamship Co., 146

Pacific Phosphate Company, 290

Page, Asst. Surgeon, C.H. 103

Paris, John, author, 233, 296

Parkes, Sir Harry, 181, 280; attacks Bizen troops, 108; climbs Fuji, 314; valedictory notices in Japanese Press, 219

Patch, Sam, 163

Penal settlements in Australia, 74

Pentonville Prison, 272

Perry, Commodore, 54, 146, 328

Phallic worship, 261

Photographs, 258

Pilgrimages to temples and shrines, 238

"Pillow" books, 296

Pleasant Island, 290

Prostitutes as artist's models, 225, 295

"Providence," H.M. Sloop, 327

"Retribution," British warship, 51

"Return," English ship, 34

Richardson, Charles Lenox, murder of, 91

Rickshaw, 165, 283

Rickshaw-men, 170

Rodin's "The Kiss," 299

Rubinstein, Serge, 253

Sailing ships, foreign, in Japanese harbours, 323

Sakai, massacre of French sailors, 115

Saris, Capt. John, 31, 236 ,323; collection of Japanese curios burnt, 297

Satow, Sir Ernest, 120, 195

Sentaro (see also Patch), 164

Shaw, George Bernard, 309

Shimazu, Daimyo of Satsuma, 90

Shimidzu, Seiichi, ronin assassin, 94

Shita-ni-iro, 90, 107

Shioya 101; James Estate at, 260

Shoes, removing, before entering Japanese house, 309

Shogun's Court, Yedo, Dutch at, 43

Shuhogahara (Futatabi) Foreign Cemetery, 120, 334

Silver, 249

Smith, Dr. George (Bishop of Hong Kong), 60, 215

"Spring" books, 296

St. George's Cross, 28

Strip tease, 294

Superstitions re human livers, 332

"Susquehanna," U.S.S., 164

Taki, Zenzaburo, 107, 113

Tamaki, Miura, 233, 307

Temples for accommodation of foreigners, 53, 178

Terry, T. Philip, Guide to Japanese Empire, 44, 230

Thirty-three Holy Places of Kwannon, 238

Thunberg, Dr. 48, 296

"Tiger," English ship, 29

"Tiger's Whelp," English ship, 29

Tokaido, description of, 86, 89

Tokio Times, 213, 219

Tokudo Shonin, Buddhist abbot, 238

Tokugawa road near Kobe, 107,

Index

125, 336
Tourist traffic in Japan, 229
Treaties with Japan, 58, 80
Trust & Loan Agency Co., 263
Tsuda, Sanzo, 170
Turnor, Lieut. A.H. 103

Ukiyoe, 224, 295

von Siebold, 48
van Kieboom executed, 275
Viaud, Julien (see Loti)

Whaling ships, 145, 327
Wheeler, Dr. E., 187
Woodcut prints, 224

Yacht "Emperor," present from
    Queen Victoria, 51, 60
"Yedo-Mail" four-horse coach, 92
Yen minting commenced, 253
Yokohama Foreign Cemetery, 97,
    200
Yokohama United Club, 184
Yoshiwara licenced quarters, 223,
    295

Other TUT BOOKS available:

BACHELOR'S HAWAII by Boye de Mente

BACHELOR'S JAPAN by Boye de Mente

BACHELOR'S MEXICO by Boye de Mente

A BOOK OF NEW ENGLAND LEGENDS AND FOLK LORE by Samuel Adams Drake

THE BUDDHA TREE by Fumio Niwa; translated by Kenneth Strong

CALABASHES AND KINGS: An Introduction to Hawaii by Stanley D. Porteus

CHINA COLLECTING IN AMERICA by Alice Morse Earle

CHINESE COOKING MADE EASY by Rosy Tseng

CHOI OI!: The Lighter Side of Vietnam by Tony Zidek

CONFUCIUS SAY by Leo Shaw

THE COUNTERFEITER and Other Stories by Yasushi Inoue; translated by Leon Picon

CURIOUS PUNISHMENTS OF BYGONE DAYS by Alice Morse Earle

CUSTOMS AND FASHIONS IN OLD NEW ENGLAND by Alice Morse Earle

DINING IN SPAIN by Gerrie Beene and Lourdes Miranda King

EXOTICS AND RETROSPECTIVES *by Lafcadio Hearn*

FIRST YOU TAKE A LEEK: A Guide to Elegant Eating Spiced with Culinary Capers *by Maxine J. Saltonstall*

FIVE WOMEN WHO LOVED LOVE *by Saikaku Ihara; translated by William Theodore de Bary*

A FLOWER DOES NOT TALK: Zen Essays *by Abbot Zenkei Shibayama of the Nanzenji*

FOLK LEGENDS OF JAPAN *by Richard M. Dorson*

GLEANINGS IN BUDDHA-FIELDS: Studies of Hand and Soul in the Far East *by Lafcadio Hearn*

GOING NATIVE IN HAWAII: A Poor Man's Guide to Paradise *by Timothy Head*

HAIKU IN ENGLISH *by Harold G. Henderson*

HARP OF BURMA *by Michio Takeyama; translated by Howard Hibbett*

HAWAII: End of the Rainbow *by Kazuo Miyamoto*

THE HAWAIIAN GUIDE BOOK for Travelers *by Henry M. Whitney*

HAWAIIAN PHRASE BOOK

HISTORIC MANSIONS AND HIGHWAYS AROUND BOSTON *by Samuel Adams Drake*

HISTORICAL AND GEOGRAPHICAL DICTIONARY OF JAPAN *by E. Papinot*

A HISTORY OF JAPANESE LITERATURE *by W. G. Aston*

HOMEMADE ICE CREAM AND SHERBERT *by Sheila MacNiven Cameron*

HOW TO READ CHARACTER: A New Illustrated Handbook of Phrenology and Physiognomy, for Students and Examiners by *Samuel R. Wells*

IN GHOSTLY JAPAN by *Lafcadio Hearn*

INDIAN RIBALDRY by *Randor Guy*

JAPAN: An Attempt at Interpretation by *Lafcadio Hearn*

THE JAPANESE ABACUS by *Takashi Kojima*

THE JAPANESE ARE LIKE THAT by *Ichiro Kawasaki*

JAPANESE ETIQUETTE: An Introduction by *the World Fellowship Committee of the Tokyo Y.W.C.A.*

THE JAPANESE FAIRY BOOK compiled by *Yei Theodora Ozaki*

JAPANESE FOLK-PLAYS: The Ink-Smeared Lady and Other Kyogen translated by *Shio Sakanishi*

JAPANESE FOOD AND COOKING by *Stuart Griffin*

JAPANESE HOMES AND THIER SURROUNDINGS by *Edward S. Morse*

A JAPANESE MISCELLANY by *Lafcadio Hearn*

JAPANESE RECIPES by *Tatsuji Tada*

JAPANESE TALES OF MYSTERY & IMAGINATION by *Edogawa Rampo; translated by James B. Harris*

JAPANESE THINGS: Being Notes on Various Subjects Connected with Japan by *Basil Hall Chamberlain*

THE JOKE'S ON JUDO by *Donn Draeger and Ken Tremayne*

THE KABUKI HANDBOOK *by Aubrey S. Halford and Giovanna M. Halford*

KAPPA *by Ryūnosuke Akutagawa; translated by Geoffrey Bownas*

KOKORO: Hints and Echoes of Japanese Inner Life *by Lafcadio Hearn*

KOREAN FOLK TALES *by Im Bang and Yi Ryuk; translated by James S. Gale*

KOTTŌ: Being Japanese Curios, with Sundry Cobwebs *by Lafcadio Hearn*

KWAIDAN: Stories and Studies of Strange Things *by Lafcadio Hearn*

LET'S STUDY JAPANESE *by Jun Maeda*

THE LIFE OF BUDDHA *by A. Ferdinand Herold*

MODERN JAPANESE PRINTS: A Contemporary Selection *edited by Yuji Abe*

MORE ZILCH: The Marine Corps' Most Guarded Secret *by Roy Delgado*

NIHONGI: Chronicles of Japan from the Earliest Times to A.D. 697 *by W. G. Aston*

OLD LANDMARKS AND HISTORIC PERSONAGES OF BOSTON *by Samuel Adams Drake*

ORIENTAL FORTUNE TELLING *by Jimmei Shimano; translated by Togo Taguchi*

PHYSICAL FITNESS: A Practical Program *by Clark Hatch*

POO POO MAKE PRANT GLOW *by Harvey Ward*

PROFILES OF MODERN AMERICAN AUTHORS *by Bernard Dekle*

READ JAPANESE TODAY *by Len Walsh*

SALMAGUNDI VIETNAM *by Don Pratt and Lee Blair*

SELF DEFENSE SIMPLIFIED IN PICTURES *by Don Hepler*

SHADOWINGS *by Lafcadio Hearn*

A SHORT SYNOPSIS OF THE MOST ESSENTIAL POINTS IN HAWAIIAN GRAMMAR *by W. D. Alexander*

THE STORY BAG: A Collection of Korean Folk Tales *by Kim So-un; translated by Setsu Higashi*

SUMI-E: An Introduction to Ink Painting *by Nanae Momiyama*

SUN-DIALS AND ROSES OF YESTERDAY *by Alice Morse Earle*

THE TEN FOOT SQUARE HUT AND TALES OF THE HEIKE: Being Two Thirteenth-century Japanese classics, the "Hojoki" and selections from the "Heike Monogatari" *translated by A. L. Sadler*

THIS SCORCHING EARTH *by Donald Richie*

TIMES-SQUARE SAMURAI or the Improbable Japanese Occupation of New York *by Robert B. Johnson and Billie Niles Chadbourne*

TO LIVE IN JAPAN *by Mary Lee O'Neal and Virginia Woodruff*

THE TOURIST AND THE REAL JAPAN *by Boye de Mente*

TOURS OF OKINAWA: A Souvenir Guide to Places of Interest *compiled by Gasei Higa, Isamu Fuchaku, and Zenkichi Toyama*

TWO CENTURIES OF COSTUME IN AMERICA *by Alice Morse Earle*

TYPHOON! TYPHOON! An Illustrated Haiku Sequence *by Lucile M. Bogue*

UNBEATEN TRACKS IN JAPAN: An Account of Travels in the Interior Including Visits to the Aborigines of Yezo and the Shrine of Nikko *by Isabella L. Bird*

ZILCH! The Marine Corps' Most Guarded Secret *by Roy Delgado*

Please order from your bookstore or write directly to:

CHARLES E. TUTTLE CO., INC.
Suido 1-chome, 2-6, Bunkyo-ku, Tokyo 112

or:

CHARLES E. TUTTLE CO., INC.
Rutland, Vermont 05701 U.S.A.